"Readers will find Julie Bell's ~~A Place of Abundance~~ he heartfelt, encouraging, and exciting. Through the authentic struggles that Alicia and the other characters face throughout the story, Julie helps us to look past all of our failings in our walk with the Lord or in our journey to finding salvation, and reminds us of God's unfailing and unconditional love for his children."

—Staci Bailey, Teacher

"An interesting plot that captures and holds your attention to the very end. One of the best fiction novels I have ever read."

——Kathleen Cates

"A compelling story of God's everlasting love for us as well as the love between his people. I was captivated the entire time!"

—Salena McKay, Teacher

"*A Place of Abundance* is full of adventure and heart-pounding excitement. It is filled with all types of emotion from tears to joy to compassion to love."

—Marilee Meadows, Teacher

"A perfect example of how God brings hope in even the most hopeless situation."

—Amanda Schrader

A PLACE OF
ABUNDANCE

A PLACE OF ABUNDANCE

A NOVEL

JULIE BELL

Tate Publishing & Enterprises

Published by Tate Publishing & Enterprises, LLC
127 E. Trade Center Terrace | Mustang, Oklahoma 73064 USA
1.888.361.9473 | www.tatepublishing.com

Tate Publishing is committed to excellence in the publishing industry. The company reflects the philosophy established by the founders, based on Psalm 68:11,
"The Lord gave the word and great was the company of those who published it."

Book design copyright © 2010 by Tate Publishing, LLC. All rights reserved.
Cover design by Kellie Southerland
Interior design by Chris Webb

Published in the United States of America

ISBN: 978-1-61663-625-8
1. Fiction / Christian / Romance
2. Fiction / Christian / Western
10.06.21

For my parents, Chris and Linda. Thank you for always providing me with unconditional love and support. I love you both very much.

Prologue

Texas 1867

Richard Barnes sat back in his seat, exhausted and ready to be home. The train had just pulled out of the station, and he was relieved to feel the steady roll of the train underneath him as he laid his head back and settled in for the journey home.

"Excuse me." A male voice broke his reverie. "May we sit here?" The man gestured to the two seats across from Richard.

"Go ahead," Richard responded. He watched as a man in his late thirties helped his wife to her seat and then proceeded to sit down himself. Richard sat up a bit and leaned forward, extending his hand. "Richard Barnes."

"I'm Wayne Carter, and this is my wife, Elyse," Wayne responded as the men shook hands. Elyse gave a warm smile in his direction.

"It's good to be going home," Elyse said. The men both heartily agreed.

"We own a horse ranch in Darby, Kentucky, and were out here looking at some horses. We brought some for trade too. There were some mighty fine animals this year. We found a couple of nice yearlings to bring home with us," Wayne told Richard.

Richard responded with a smile and decided he was very glad this couple joined him. They carried on in light conversation for a while longer before they all settled back to enjoy the scenery and think of the home that was waiting for them. After only a few minutes, the three weary travelers drifted off to sleep.

The sudden jerk of the train threw Richard off his seat and onto the floor. He hit his head on the seat in front of him and felt Wayne helping him up. Still dazed from his fall, he looked around to see panic on the faces of the people around him. Women who had children on the train were clutching them close to protect them from the severe jerks of the train as it came to a rapid halt.

"What's going on?" Richard asked.

Wayne was struggling to look out the window to see what the problem was. "I don't know. I can't see anything. But we shouldn't be stopping right now, that's for sure." His wife clung to him, and he saw the fear in her eyes.

"Now don't worry, dear. It's probably nothing." He wrapped her in his arms. Richard stood from his seat and looked around the train. So far no one seemed to know what was going on.

"Look!" a voice rang out. Richard and Wayne both looked out the window to see five horses riding alongside the train. The faces of the men on the horses were hidden by bandanas. Richard strained to get a good look and watched in fear as four of the men leapt off their horses. Other passengers witnessed it too, and some of the women began to scream, causing the children's tears to flow. Richard noticed that one very small man remained on his horse and watched the other horses. The thought flitted through Richard's mind that he didn't look like he could be more than a boy.

Suddenly the door to the passenger car of the train slammed open, and the men walked calmly inside, wielding guns. The passengers stared in stunned silence. *Oh God*, Richard inwardly cried. *What are we going to do?* One of the men bellowed for everyone to throw their money in the aisle. People quickly moved to do as he bid. Coins landed along the aisle as another man swiftly collected them. As he picked up the money, the conductor came into the rear of the train car, startling the robbers. Richard heard the sound of guns fired and slid his eyes shut. His last thought was of home.

CHAPTER 1

Darby, Kentucky, 1870

The morning broke fresh as Caleb walked outside toward the barn. The horse ranch that he owned and operated was always alive in the mornings. The ranch hands were already setting about completing their morning tasks as Caleb walked up to the foreman.

"Mornin,' boss," John drawled.

"Mornin,' John. Any news on the filly yet?" Caleb was anxious about one of his prize horses who was expected to deliver her first foal any day now.

"Yep. She had a fine colt early this mornin' just before daybreak. They're in the south pasture down yonder," he answered as he motioned with his head in that direction. John made sure that he was current on all of the happenings at the Blue Star Ranch. He liked to make sure that he was in charge of everything that went on.

"Excellent. I'll go see to them after breakfast." Caleb strode back to the house, where his sister, Claire, would be waiting with breakfast. He and his sister had lived together and ran the horse ranch since their parents died three years back. He smelled bacon sizzling on the pan before he opened the door.

"Hold it right there, Caleb Carter!" Claire was quick to stop him in his tracks. "You just go back out there and clean those muddy boots off before you track dirt all over my clean kitchen." Caleb smiled to himself as he stepped down on the back doorstep and began to stomp off his boots. If there was anything Claire would not stand for, it was a dirty house. Caleb finished cleaning his boots and entered again. The two sat down at the table and prepared to say grace.

"Thank you, Father," Caleb began, "for blessing us with another to day to live for you and to serve you. Help us to be mindful of you throughout this day. Bless this food and the hands that have prepared it. In Jesus's name, amen."

Caleb and Claire began to fill their plates with the delicious bacon, eggs, and pancakes. Claire was quite a good cook, and Caleb felt fortunate for that. Most single men were living on whatever food they could muster up themselves. Indeed, he was blessed to still have his sister.

"The new colt was born last night. Figured I'd go out and take a look at him after breakfast. Should be a fine breeding horse." Caleb began to recount to his sister his conversation with the foreman. "You know, John's mentioned this a couple of times now, and I've been thinking myself that we need another hand or two out here. The ranch is growing, and the men already have too much to do. I think I should put up an ad or something for another hand. What do you think?"

Claire loved the way that her brother always included her in the decisions for the ranch. She knew that it was all ultimately his decision, but to be asked always filled her with a sense of belonging and purpose.

"I think that's a good idea. We do need more help, and pretty soon we'll be getting more horses than we can handle." Claire smiled as she passed some more bacon to her brother, who always seemed to have an insatiable appetite.

"All right, I'll go into town right after I check on the colt."

"Sounds good. The ladies from the church are coming by here for our weekly Bible study later this morning. I've already packed a lunch for you." Claire was always looking out for her older brother. Caleb sometimes felt as though she thought he was as helpless as a newborn pup, but he enjoyed the attention nonetheless.

"Thanks. Well, I'd better scoot. See you later, sis." He grabbed his lunch and ran back out the side door from the kitchen. Claire got up and began to clean up and prepare for the ladies' arrival in a few hours.

Alicia woke up in a daze. The events of the past week reeled through her mind as she tried to make sense of all that had happened. Just five days earlier, she and her mother were brushing down their horses in the barn. It all happened so suddenly. Alicia shuddered at the thought of what happened and tried desperately to push it from her mind. *What's next?*

She wondered with all of her might how she was supposed to put the pieces of her broken life back together again. After her father died three years ago, Alicia and her mother did their best to survive. Her mother worked as a waitress and cook at the small town's only restaurant, while Alicia finished school and got odd jobs here and there. Her mother and she had been doing fine—until five days ago, when her mother was taken from her forever.

Now Alicia was alone.

Alicia slowly rose from her bed. Her head was pounding so hard that she practically stumbled as she walked down the hallway into the kitchen. Outside the sky was clear and blue, and she could hear the birds chirping. She put some coffee on and made her way back to her room to dress for the day.

Walking outside with her cup of coffee, she sat on the porch and forced herself only to think about how to move on. She knew that if she dwelt too long on the reality of her life right now, she would just fall apart. She was not a quitter and knew that she had to muster up strength to continue.

As she sat deep in thought, she heard the jingle of a buggy coming toward the house. She looked up to find Cathy Brown steering the horses in her direction. Alicia inwardly groaned as she thought about how she now had to make conversation and probably talk about God doing this with her good in mind. It was too much for Alicia to handle.

"Good morning, Alicia dear," Cathy said as she slowed her horses. "I came by to check on you and to bring you some meals that the other ladies and myself prepared for you." She came down easily enough from the buggy and walked toward Alicia.

"I know this must be so hard for you, honey. How can I help?"

Alicia shrugged. She was in no mood to talk.

"I've been praying for you. The whole church family has," Cathy gently told her.

Alicia and her family had gone to church all of Alicia's life, and her parents were very strong in their faith for the Lord. But the death of Alicia's father had hit her hard, and she wasn't so ready to believe in a God that would take her wonderful father away. And now her mother was gone too. No, Alicia was not ready to believe in or trust the God that her parents so readily put their trust in. Look where that had gotten them. Cathy could see the pained look in her eyes and began to pray for her. She knew how difficult it had been for Alicia these last three years.

Father, I know that you're working for Alicia's good and that through all of the pain you'll bring her through. Please help her to realize that she needs you in her life and to stop pushing you away.

Alicia cleared her throat. "Thank you, Cathy. I think I'm going to go for a walk." She got up and started walking down the path that led toward the small creek behind the Barneses' home. Cathy watched as sadness washed over her for the poor, heartbroken girl. She would have prayed even more fervently if she had known what course Alicia would decide to take.

A course that would change her life forever.

Chapter 2

"Bill, I need to post an advertisement for the ranch," Caleb addressed the man behind the counter.

"Sure thing. What do you want it to say?"

Caleb began to dictate his ad while Bill wrote.

"Wanted: Extra hand needed to help on the Blue Star Ranch in Darby. Immediate. Contact Caleb Carter."

"I didn't know you was needin' another hand down there." Bill helped with the post office and the newspaper for as long as Caleb could remember. He was a good man who was once a cattle driver in Texas. His leathery face and arms could attest to that.

"Yep. And pretty fast too. The ranch is growing every day. Just this morning one of our prize fillies gave birth to a fine new colt. He'll be quite the breeder." Caleb began to think about how much the ranch had grown since he was a child and how much he loved the horses. He leaned against the counter as Bill began again.

"You know, the school's needin' another teacher. That's another ad to put in the paper. It's not just your ranch that's growin,' Caleb." Bill scratched his head as he began to think of what words he should use for the next ad.

"What happened to Mrs. Keene?"

"She up and moved back to Georgia to live with her sister. She was gettin' awful lonely."

Caleb understood why the old schoolmarm felt so lonely. She came alone to the town to teach, and while she was here, she spent all of her time alone in her little two-room home next to the schoolhouse. The schoolhouse also served as the church, which she never attended. Many of the ladies from the church family tried to reach out to her, but she was stubborn and set in her ways. She wanted to be alone, and alone she truly was. Caleb frowned slightly at the thought.

"Well, I'd better be going, Bill. Thanks for your help." Caleb turned and walked out the door. He put his hat back on and swung easily into the saddle of his stallion, Midnight. As he slowly rode out of town, his mind began to wonder about what the future would hold for his growing town.

Alicia continued to walk slowly as she tried to think of how to continue with her life. She walked past the creek where her father took her fishing; she walked through the meadow where she and her mother picked wildflowers for the kitchen; she walked through the open spaces where she ran and played as a young child. Her heart ached, and nausea swept over her several times as the pain threatened to engulf her. Her mind was flooded with thoughts of how unfair it all was. She was only eighteen and now all alone with no name or money to her credit. She did not want to end up a penniless spinster, but she began to think the worst.

My life is over. Why don't I just kill myself? Then we'd all be together again. No, Alicia, you can't do that. You have to make your parents proud. They raised you to be capable and independent. You can't let them down.

Alicia crumpled to the ground as the tears began to flow freely. She sobbed over how much she missed them; she sobbed over how to move on; she sobbed over all of her surroundings and everything she saw. Everything reminded her of her parents. Her father would take her on walks all over the little town. She knew every path and trail, every creek and lake that was in the area. Her mother would take her to town every Saturday, and they would sell eggs and shop for new material for dresses. Every piece of the town and the area around it was a painful reminder that her parents were gone and that she was alone.

Why, God? Why? Why did you let this happen to my family? My parents loved you and served you. What am I supposed to do now? You've left me all alone, and I'm scared. Anger began to course through Alicia as she continued to think. *You don't love me or my family, and I want nothing to do with you!*

Alicia stood up in a fury. She was so hurt and confused and felt a surging ache from deep within her. The pain was greater than she could imagine, and she felt too weak to fight it. She took small, deliberate steps because that was all she could manage. As she began to walk home, she knew that the ache was for her parents, but she was aware that it may be for something more as well. She resolutely walked toward her home with a plan forming in her mind.

The next day Alicia arrived to town with a strong determination to move forward with her life. She did not have the luxury of time on her side to wait for something to come her way. She knew that she could not go on with life in the home that her parents raised her in. It was too full of painful memories. Alicia could see her parents everywhere. She could still smell her mother's perfume in the house and hear her father's whistle as he would come inside after plowing the fields. The only solution that came to Alicia was to leave. Part of her knew that she was running away, but she didn't care. What other choice did she have? Pain and grief threatened to swallow her whole, and she felt trapped. She had to leave Groves. She simply had to.

Fear engulfed her petite frame and drove her forward with plans to put everything behind her and run from all her pain. Her auburn hair was blowing freely, and her green eyes held a set resolve to be strong. She had cried until every emotion flowing through her was spent. She determined not to allow life's cruelties to beat her, and she marched straight to the newspaper office.

"Good morning, Mrs. Harris," she said briskly.

"Why, Alicia. Good morning, dear. I didn't expect to see you in today. How are you?" Mrs. Harris could tell just by a mere glance that Alicia was not well. Her normally bright green eyes carried a shadow over them, and her entire being seemed to sag with grief. Mrs. Harris was a kindly woman who had tried on many occasions to reach out to Alicia.

"I'm fine, thank you," Alicia responded. She wasted no time in getting to the point. "I've decided to leave Groves. There are just too many memories, and I need to start fresh somewhere else. I'd like to see some papers from the nearest counties to get some ideas and see if there are job offerings anywhere."

Mrs. Harris's mouth dropped. "Alicia, honey, don't you think you are being a bit rash?" Mrs. Harris's mind reeled to find the right words. "There are places here to work. You can sew or cook. Everyone here loves you. You would be taken care of."

Her words were spoken with such empathy and depth of feeling that Alicia almost let the tears that were threatening spill over. She firmly told herself not to cry and stood her ground.

"Thank you, Mrs. Harris, but I'm afraid that I must leave. The farm is not even ours, remember? Mr. Johnson bought it and has been running it since Father died. He was just kind enough to let us stay on."

"Yes, and he'll continue to let you stay on. Please reconsider this, Alicia." Mrs. Harris's eyes were pleading, and it was almost more than Alicia could take.

"No," she said sharply. "Thank you, but I'm leaving tomorrow and would like to see some papers, please." Alicia instantly felt regret at being so sharp. Mrs. Harris had always loved and taken care of her family. Mrs. Harris turned and looked through a stack of papers.

"These are the latest." She handed Alicia four papers. Then she turned to continue with her own work.

Just stick to your plan. She moved to a bench by the window and began to read. What she didn't know was that Mrs. Harris was praying the entire time, asking God's guidance and blessing on her life.

After an hour of searching, Alicia found an ad that interested her very much. It was in a town about fifteen miles west called Darby, and there was an advertisement for an extra hand on a horse ranch. Alicia smiled to herself. *That's ideal. There's nothing I know more than horses, and to work with them every day on a ranch would be perfect.* Alicia's spirits lifted, and she felt the first glimmer of hope. She walked up to Mrs. Harris, who still had her back to her as she continued with her article.

"Mrs. Harris," Alicia began. Mrs. Harris turned around and looked at her with soft, motherly eyes. Alicia could feel tears beginning to form, and she swallowed hard to keep them from falling. "Thank you, Mrs. Harris. I think I found just the thing. I'd like to buy this paper from you if you don't mind."

Mrs. Harris told her to keep the paper and to make sure and write to let them know how she was doing.

"I will," Alicia promised. "I'm sorry that I was sharp earlier, Mrs. Harris. I didn't mean to be so rude with you."

With that, Alicia turned and walked out of the office. She was headed home to pack the few things that she had. She knew that come daybreak, she would set out for Darby and would not rest until the job was hers.

Chapter 3

Caleb propped his feet up on the coffee table in the living room as he thought about what Pastor Tyler had said in church that morning. He was reading out of 1 Corinthians, and Caleb tried to replay the service in his mind.

"Turn in your Bibles to the book of First Corinthians, chapter thirteen, verses four through eight and then verse thirteen." Pastor Tyler waited while the sound of pages shuffling was heard. Once they quieted, he began to read.

"'Charity suffereth long, and is kind; charity envieth not; charity vaunteth not itself, it is not puffed up. Doth not behave itself unseemly, seeketh not her own, is not easily provoked, thinketh no evil; rejoiceth not in iniquity, but rejoiceth in the truth; beareth all things, believeth all things, hopeth all things, endureth all things.

"'Charity never faileth; but whether there be prophecies, they shall fail; whether there be tongues, they shall cease; whether there be knowledge, it shall vanish away.'" Pastor Tyler paused for a moment. "And now verse thirteen, 'And now abideth faith, hope, charity, these three; but the greatest of these is charity.'"

Pastor Tyler took a breath and waited while the truth of the scripture began to sink in with the church members.

"I grew up on these verses, yet I never tire of reading them again. They talk about love. Do you ever notice how often we read scripture but yet it does not seem to stick with us? How many times have we read these verses, and many others, but have never set about applying them to our lives?

"Paul is writing to the Corinthians to encourage and teach them. In chapter twelve, he emphasizes how every child of God has a spiritual gift that they can use to serve him. Everyone has different gifts, but they are all equally wonderful and blessed in God's eyes. After all, he was the one who formed you and gave you your special gift. You must use whatever it is to serve him, for his glory.

"Paul goes on to emphasize the importance of love. He tells the Corinthians that even the greatest of spiritual gifts, if they are not motivated by love, are as nothing. Love is one of the most important things that Christ tried to teach us. And look at how all-encompassing love is. Look back at verse four: 'Charity suffereth long, and is kind; charity envieth not; charity vaunteth not itself, it is not puffed up.' The verses are clear in the all-encompassing power of love. How are you showing your love to others? Are you applying these verses to your life? Are you showing the love of God to those you come in contact with? Remember that this week and meditate on these verses. Challenge yourself to apply them to your life."

The service was over shortly after that. Caleb and Claire visited with members of the church family for a while before heading back to the ranch. Caleb was now comfortably settled in the living room, going back over the sermon and wondering just how good of a job he was doing showing the love of Christ to those he met. He thought he was good and fair to all of his ranch hands. He determined to be more observant in the coming week and pick out areas of weakness.

"Hi," Claire said as she walked in. "Am I disturbing you?"

"Not at all." Caleb smiled at his sister. "I was just thinking about the sermon this morning."

"I know. I have too. I always learn something from his teaching. That was a particularly tough sermon for me this morning. It made me realize how much I don't show Christ's love to everyone. Twice last week I snapped at Mrs. Thorne at the general store. She was just so nosy and rude that I could not hold back my temper any longer. She really knows how to get under my skin. I will apologize the next time I see her." Caleb was proud of how seriously his sister took her faith in the Lord. Their conversation soon ended, and Caleb picked up the paper while Claire began to embroider an apron. They were both startled by a knock at the door.

"I wonder who that is," said Caleb as he got up. They had not heard a buggy approach.

Caleb opened the door and stared at what he saw. Claire, coming up from behind, stopped short as well and stared quizzically at the small frame in the doorway.

"Good afternoon. Are you Mr. Caleb Carter?"

"I am," Caleb said.

"My name is Alicia Barnes." Caleb stared at the young girl whose appearance was hidden by manly clothes. She wore baggy pants and a button-up long-sleeved shirt, complete with boots and a hat large enough to practically engulf her entire head. She looked bone-weary, and Caleb wondered how far she had traveled. He looked past her to see a brown mare tied to a hitching post in front of the ranch house. Caleb was sure that she could not be more than seventeen or eighteen. He was completely mystified as to what this young girl could want.

"Please come in, Miss Barnes." Caleb held the door as she walked in. If she was nervous, she hid it very well from the Carters. She raised her chin and stood to her full five feet two inches and entered the house. They were equally surprised by her confidence. Claire led the way into the living room, and Alicia and Caleb followed close behind.

"Please sit down, Alicia. My name is Claire." Claire made herself comfortable and invited Alicia to do the same. Caleb and Claire exchanged a look as they wondered what could have brought her to their door. She looked tired and underfed. Compassion washed over Claire as she realized that she was probably her own age. Claire was barely nineteen, and her brother was approaching twenty-three.

"Well, Miss Barnes, what can we do for you?" Caleb tried to sit back and relax, but his body began to feel tense.

"Mr. Carter, my name is Alicia Barnes…" Alicia began to spill everything as fast she could for fear that she would lose her nerve. Caleb and Claire had to listen hard to keep up. "I'm from Groves, and I read your ad in the paper, and I've come to answer it. There's nothing I know better than horses, and I'm a hard worker. Both of my parents are dead, and I need work. I have to move on, and I want to start fresh in a new town. Mine was too full of memories." Alicia looked off for a moment and then waved a hand. "Anyway, I hope you'll take me on. You will find that I know just as much as any man out there."

Alicia finished her spiel and watched them wide-eyed. Caleb and Claire both heard the desperation in her voice and saw the pain in her eyes. They were filled with compassion, but it was a while before either could speak.

Did she really just ask what I think she did? Caleb wondered to himself. *Does she realize how much work is involved in running a ranch? I cannot have her doing those types of chores.* Caleb felt torn. He wanted to help poor Alicia Barnes, who had left everything to move on, but he knew that he could not possibly hire her on.

The gentleman in Caleb took over. Women were not supposed to be subjected to that kind of rigorous work. Caleb looked over at Alicia and saw a helpless young girl who reminded him of his sister. He immediately felt drawn to help and protect this young woman, who had so bravely stepped into their lives.

"Miss Barnes," Caleb began, "it was very courageous of you to come all this way to start over." Alicia's heart began to sink as she heard the hesitation in his voice. Alicia's shoulders dropped, and she lowered her head. Caleb tried to proceed as gently as he could.

"You must understand, Miss Barnes, that running a horse ranch is extremely difficult, and I cannot subject women to that kind of work. Even my sister is not allowed to help with most of the duties." Caleb watched as tears began to form in Alicia's eyes. It was almost more than Caleb's tender heart could bear. Alicia fought the tears away, furious at herself for even having them, and squared her shoulders.

"Please stay with us until you decide what to do, Miss Barnes. We have plenty of room, and we would love to help you in any way that we can. I'm sure there's work to be had in town somewhere, and in the meantime you can stay with us." Caleb hoped with all of his heart that she would stay with them for a while.

"Oh yes, please do," Claire put in. "I'd love to have some company, and we really do have plenty of room." Claire smiled at her, and Alicia began to feel more at ease. She could have kicked herself for nearly crying earlier. However, she did not want to be an imposition. After all, she had burst in on their home uninvited. What must they think of her? But then, what were her options? She was determined not to go back to her hometown.

She pulled her hat off and wavy, auburn hair tumbled down around her shoulders. She did not look as young without the hat, and Caleb felt something strange turn in his stomach. He pushed the thought and feeling away, convincing himself that it was something he ate. Alicia sat back and looked Caleb squarely in the eye.

"Mr. Carter, I don't think you understand. I need a job. I'm strong and I'm not afraid of hard work. All I'm asking is for you to give me a chance."

Caleb looked over to Claire and raked a hand through his hair. This Alicia Barnes was making this harder on him than it already was. He looked back over to her and shook his head.

"I'm sorry, miss, but I've made my decision. Like I said, I'm sure there's work in town that you can find. We'd be glad to escort you there first thing in the morning to look." Caleb's tone left no room for argument.

"But if you would just—" Caleb raised a hand and cut her off.

"I'm sorry, Miss Barnes." Alicia sighed.

"Very well. I must apologize for bursting into your home uninvited. I do not wish to intrude. I think I'll just head to town myself and see what I can find. Thank you, though." Alicia began to push herself off the couch, but Caleb and Claire would not be so easily swayed.

"No, you won't," Claire said emphatically. "It's Sunday afternoon. You'll never find a job today. Believe us, you are not intruding. It would be wonderful to have some company, and we would not think of letting you just go off into town and hope to find work and a place to stay. We want you to stay with us, and tomorrow we'll all go to town together. Besides, you need a hot bath and meal."

Alicia felt relieved. The thought of going into town with no idea as to what to expect was frightening. She really didn't like the clothes that she was wearing either but thought that she might have a better chance at getting a job on a ranch with clothing that looked suitable for the position. If she was to go into town, she would need to change. And the thought of a hot bath sounded very good after the long ride.

"You must stay," Caleb added. "It is already late in the afternoon. You would not get far before dark. Like Claire said, tomorrow we will take you into town to see about a job, but as far as my sister and I are concerned, you can stay right here."

Alicia could not stop the tears this time. They began to trickle down her face, and she turned to compose herself. Their hospitality and kindness was more than she had hoped for.

Alicia ate dinner with the Carters and found that she was growing quite comfortable with them already. She felt refreshed after her bath, and the warm food in her stomach was doing wonders to help her mood. Caleb and Claire were respectful, and it was obvious how much the brother and sister adored each other. Alicia remained uncertain about whether or not her decision to leave was too rash. Was it a decision made out of haste and an overflow of emotions? She pushed these tormenting questions away, and forced herself not to look back. Deep down she knew she had to leave Groves for her own sanity.

After dinner, Caleb took Alicia on a brief tour of the ranch. It was expansive and covered many acres of land, but Caleb wanted Alicia to at least be familiar with all of the stables, corrals, and horses. He had already seen to her horse, but he wanted her to be assured that the horse was safe and taken care of.

"Here are the main stables, Miss Barnes. Your horse will remain here. She'll be well taken care of. There's my horse, Midnight, and in the stall next to it is Claire's horse, Ginger." Caleb was walking through and pointing out various horses and other things that he thought might be of interest to her. He showed her where they kept all of the supplies and food for the horses as well. She was beaming as she walked through the stables and past all of the horses. She reached out to several and lovingly stroked them. Caleb could see that she was indeed quite familiar with and comfortable around horses.

She stopped by the stalls that held Caleb and Claire's horses. She reached out and began to softly talk to Midnight. Caleb stood back and watched in awe. His stallion was not known as a friendly horse, and most of the townsfolk steered clear of him. They kept their horses away from Midnight too. Alicia continued to coo at the animal and stood close to his nose to allow him to acclimate himself to her scent. She then moved to his left side and stroked his mane, all the while continuing to speak soothingly to him.

"Well, I would not have believed it if I hadn't seen it with my own eyes!" Caleb declared. Alicia looked up at him and smiled.

"I have to admit, Miss Barnes, that I did not necessarily believe you really knew your way with horses. I can see now that I was quite wrong."

Alicia looked up at him satisfactorily and for the first time realized how handsome this man was. *Nonsense*, she thought as she quickly looked away.

"Midnight does not like many people. Only me and John, for that matter. Claire is scared to death to be near the animal. She calls him the black beast of the ranch." Caleb chuckled.

"Who is John?"

"John Carpenter. He's the foreman."

"Oh. And what about Claire's horse?" Alicia moved to the next stall and began to stroke Ginger.

"Ginger is the tamest horse we have here. She is sweet and easy to ride. Claire loves her."

Alicia could see why Claire loved the animal so much. She had a peace about her that was relaxing. Even though Alicia knew what she was doing where Midnight was concerned, she knew she had to keep her guard up—a guard that she could let down around Ginger.

Soon afterwards they went inside and each parted to prepare for bed. Alicia went into the spacious guest room that the Carters offered her and sighed. Never had she expected this. Things were going better than she dreamed they possibly could. Could she really be taking the first steps of moving on? Caleb and Claire were so gracious. They seemed to love everyone and everything. Alicia had never seen a love like theirs before. Granted, her family always loved each other dearly, but outside of the family there was not much expression of love and compassion.

Her family would never have taken a strange woman in indefinitely with the intent of finding her a job in town and getting her settled. Thoughts of her family brought another wave of tortuous sadness and despair spiraling through her body. The pain and grief were still so fresh that it sometimes took her breath away. She climbed into bed and stifled her sobs in her pillow. When she finally regained control of her emotions, she fell asleep with the hope that tomorrow would bring something new and exciting her way.

Chapter 4

Caleb, Claire, and Alicia set out for town early the next morning. The wagon moved smoothly along the dirt road, but Alicia's stomach was doing such wild flips that she had to close her eyes and breathe deeply several times to try and regain some calm. She had not been this nervous when she set out for Darby. Why was she so nervous now? Alicia continued to try and force the butterflies away.

They rode into town, and the first place they stopped was at the news office. The latest goings-on of the town were sure to be known here. Caleb helped Claire and Alicia out of the wagon and headed inside.

"Good morning, Bill," Caleb addressed the newsman. "How are you today?"

"Well, Caleb, I ain't been feelin' so good lately. Doc says I have a bone spur in my heel." Bill looked so put out over his news that Caleb had to work hard to stifle his amusement.

"I'm sorry to hear that, Bill," Claire put in from behind. She gave old Bill one of her smiles that was known for melting anyone's heart. It worked, and he temporarily forgot to feel sorry for himself.

"Bill, this is Alicia Barnes. She's new to town, and we are hoping to find a job for her," Caleb introduced. Alicia stepped up with more confidence than she felt. Bill looked down at her and squinted his eyes, trying to get a better look.

"Hmmm," he grumbled. "How old are you?"

"Eighteen."

"Well, you don't look older than fifteen. Not sure one so young can find much here."

Alicia raised her chin in indignation.

"I have been working to help my family for more years than I can count, and I can do almost anything. Cooking, cleaning, sewing, waiting tables." Alicia tried to keep the confidence in her voice as old Bill stared down at her. "And I can break in any horse in Kentucky." She added as she glanced at Caleb. Caleb raised an eyebrow in surprise and then rushed to her aid.

"She's right, Bill. Even Midnight is taken with her. I saw it with my own eyes. Now what's available?" Caleb's voice took on a tone of authority, and Bill turned away to gather some news clippings.

Bill rifled through some of the papers, then suddenly stopped and looked up.

"I got it! The perfect job for a young lass. Mrs. Keene quit teachin,' and it's only September. We got to get us a new teacher in there. What about that?" Bill looked pleased with himself for coming up with such a promising job opportunity.

"That would be ideal, Alicia," Claire said. "And the children are such angels. You will love them." Alicia could see that everyone was taken with idea, but she was not so sure. She had never taught anyone before. She was smart as a whip herself, but could she teach other children? Although, it would seem truly ideal. A secure job in a new town where she has already made friends. What more could she ask for? These thoughts were whirling through her mind as Caleb addressed her.

"What do you think, Miss Barnes? We could go talk to the board right now." Alicia looked up and saw Caleb smiling down at her. She was not aware of just how much he wanted her to find a job and stay in Darby. Alicia's chin rose again. She was up for a new challenge and adventure. She never tried to teach before. Why not at least try? And after all, wasn't this why she left home in the first place?

"That's a good idea." The three of them thanked Bill and made their way out to find the members of the board.

Later that afternoon Alicia found herself in the schoolhouse along with Caleb and Claire and the seven members of the education board. Alicia's heart was pounding as they began to ask her questions. She couldn't believe it—everything was happening so fast. The questioning did not last long. They asked her if she had ever taught before and how far she had gotten in her own education. While she had to admit that she had never taught before, the board was impressed with her level of intelligence and with her ability to be capable and talented at so many things.

The demand for finding a schoolteacher before much more of the school year was over was bearing down heavily upon the board. They asked Alicia and the Carters to leave while they took a vote. A few minutes later they brought the three of them back in to announce that they would use Alicia Barnes as the schoolteacher for the year. But there was one condition. This year was temporary—Alicia had this year to prove herself as a teacher before they would consider her as the permanent town teacher.

Am I really here? she thought on the ride home. *Am I really going to teach school? I know nothing about teaching children. And they will all be at different levels. How did my teacher do it?* She tried hard to remember how her own teacher had handled all of the different grades in the same room. *I can do it.* She tried to convince herself. *I can teach these children. And if I fail, then I will have just tried something new and had another new adventure.*

Alicia's thoughts were interrupted by Claire. "I'm so excited for you. It will be so much fun to teach the children. You will just love them. And the little house by the school will be perfect for you. I'll help you get it ready. Of course, you do not have to move in right away. You should get settled and get a routine down first, but when you do, I will help you. And of course your horse can stay at the ranch. Oh, and the church also meets in the school building on Sundays. How perfect it will all be."

Claire continued on in an excited tone. She smiled and chattered all the way to the ranch. Alicia looked over at her new friend and felt very fortunate to have her. But that raised a new issue in her mind. The school building was also used for the church. Alicia knew that meant that she was expected to attend. She wondered about how to deal with that. *Maybe I'll just go and fulfill my social obligation while I am here. I will be expected to be there. And a house next to the school! That is perfect, along with the ranch to keep Cocoa. This may all work out after all.* She tried to still her thoughts long enough to concentrate on Claire and respond.

Caleb was having thoughts of his own. He had forgotten about the little house next to the school and was suddenly very grateful that it was there for Alicia. He sensed her need for independence. It was as if she was out to prove that she could survive on her own. However, he couldn't deny that he would miss her. He couldn't quite put his finger on what he felt when she was near, and he knew he wanted to learn more about this brave young girl. Indeed, he was relieved that she would have a suitable place to live and that he could explore with caution these new feelings.

Father, he silently prayed, *please bless Alicia in the days ahead as the new schoolteacher. Please guide her and give her strength. I know that you brought her here for a reason. Please guide me in your will.*

The following week was filled with preparations for Alicia's new job. She remained in awe over the way that Caleb and Claire threw themselves into helping her build a new life. Alicia was scheduled to start teaching the following Monday, which only gave her six days to prepare. She and Claire had already made numerous trips to town and ordered things from the general store that may be of use.

A great deal of the supplies was left in the little room that was to become Alicia's home after Mrs. Keene left. Claire and Alicia spent hours scouring the little home and the schoolhouse for necessary items and found all of the books that Alicia would be teaching from. There was also a map that needed to be hung in the schoolhouse, and she found a globe. There was a chalkboard and a bit of chalk left. The children supplied their own slates and pencils.

Alicia was not sure what else would be needed, so she ordered a calendar, some extra pencils, paper, and slates, and she ordered a few extra books that she thought the children might enjoy. The town was relatively small and had no library of any sort to read about other things and places in the world. She ordered a book on England's history, a geography book, books about the Middle East and Africa, and a book of elementary French. She believed that exposure to other cultures and languages would be good for the children.

Claire was delighted with all of Alicia's ideas for the school and wondered why Alicia had never thought of teaching before.

When preparations for school were not being made, Alicia helped around the ranch. She spent most of the time indoors helping Claire with the cooking and the cleaning. One late afternoon the two of them had been taking the laundry off the clothesline when Claire spotted a harmless garter snake approaching them. She screamed for all she was worth. Alicia was amused at the way Claire's nose crinkled up and her face turned red from screaming. Alicia was used to dealing with creatures herself and had no fear of nonvenomous snakes.

She walked toward the snake and quickly snatched it up. It began to wriggle in her hand in a furious attempt to be released. Alicia held her grasp on it and held it up for Claire to see. Alicia's eyes danced with merriment while Claire screamed again and ran for the house. Alicia burst into laughter, and she put the harmless reptile down and shooed him toward the field.

Caleb ran up when he first heard the scream and was standing by the back door watching the whole scene. He let out a hearty laugh when Claire ran for the protection of the house. He watched Alicia and was once again amazed at her ability to handle herself. She seemed so confident. She herself was laughing as Caleb made his way toward her.

"I believe you might have scared my baby sister." He grinned down at her.

"I believe you may be right. It was awfully funny, though." Alicia was not able to suppress the giggles that were coming forth. "Do you think she will be upset with me?" Her giggles began to abate, and now she thought about how cruel she must have seemed.

"I don't think so. Claire is very good-natured and is used to that sort of thing from me." Caleb chuckled.

"Even still, I had better go in and apologize. Excuse me." Alicia smiled as she left and knew that Caleb was right. Claire was much too good-natured to hold this incident against her.

Despite all of the planning and preparing and settling into a new routine with the Carters, Alicia found time every day to go down to the stables to see the horses. This was also Alicia's time to let her guard down and release the pain that she had bottled inside her and tried to hide from her two new friends. She often found herself clinging to her horse and crying for her parents and for days gone by when life was easier and she had family.

She quickly grew acquainted with all of the horses and loved them dearly—especially the spirited horses. At her parent's farm she used to love to ride the spirited horses because they were uninhibited and moved so swiftly. Alicia loved her own Cocoa very much, but Cocoa was calm and gentle, which is why Alicia's father gave her to Alicia in the first place. But Alicia often found herself wishing that Cocoa were more wild and reckless—sort of like Midnight.

Caleb often found Alicia out with the horses toward sundown after all of the hands had finished work for the day. It was at these times that he felt the most puzzled about her. They really did not know her at all after having spent only a few days with her, and so far she had been very quiet about her past and her life. Caleb and Claire both sensed the grieving that was still going on within her for her parents, so they did not pressure her with questions. It was an unspoken decision between the two of them to give Alicia time and space and let her come to them when she was ready.

As Caleb watched her that night, he noticed that she seemed a bit melancholy. She hid her emotions quite well at the house, but when she was with the horses, she tended to drop her guard. He knew that she had much on her mind and in her heart, and he prayed that she would one day decide to share her feelings with him and his sister.

"Hello," he said softly. Alicia watched as his full frame came into the stables. She judged him to be at least six foot two.

"Hello," she replied, equally soft.

"Have you been out here long?"

"No, only a few minutes." Her face was turned from him, and the temptation to ask what was wrong was so strong within him that he quickly began to search for another subject of discussion.

"Would you like to go on a ride with me tomorrow morning? I'll show you the rest of the ranch." One look at Alicia's beaming smile told Caleb that he had chosen the right topic. Her green eyes sparkled as she turned to face him.

"I would like that very much." She paused and looked thoughtful for a moment.

"What is it, Miss Barnes?" Caleb asked politely.

"Please call me Alicia. I was wondering if perhaps you would consider allowing me to ride one of your horses." She tried not to get her hopes up as she waited for his reply.

"Of course. Which one would you like?"

Alicia instantly knew that she wanted to ride the black stallion, but she refused to ask for that one. Caleb would be riding him.

"I was hoping I could right Knight." She glanced toward the far end of the stables where the only other stallion, a creamy colored one, was tossing his head.

Caleb looked hesitant.

"Are you sure? Why that one?"

"I want to ride a high-spirited horse. They are so much more fun." Alicia knew, however, that her real motive was two-fold. She also wanted to prove to Caleb that she was capable of riding his wilder horses, not just calming them with her soothing touch.

"Tell you what," Caleb began, "how about we save Knight for another ride and take out Sugar tomorrow?" Sugar was calm and gentle. Caleb had no intention of allowing Alicia to ride the stallion without first observing her riding abilities.

Alicia did not look surprised and chastised herself for being so hasty to ride one of her generous host's most-prized horses.

"Of course. I should not be so hasty to ride your horses. I did not mean to take advantage of your generosity." The words were spoken with sincerity and humility. Alicia watched Caleb, whose eyes had remained soft the entire time. She wondered how a man could be so tender and loving and decided that it must be due to his years of working with horses.

"Alicia, you do not need to apologize. Claire and I want you to feel at home here, and you are welcome to ride the horses. I just think it might be best to save Knight for another time."

Caleb smiled down at this unique young woman who, in his mind, was as high-spirited as Knight and Midnight. Alicia thanked him for his kindness and they parted. Alicia walked slowly back to the house, looking forward to the ride in the morning. She had been hoping for an opportunity to see the rest of their beautiful ranch.

Chapter 5

Saturday morning was clear and crisp. It was perfect for riding. Alicia sprang out of bed and quickly slipped into clothing suitable for riding. She hurried downstairs to the kitchen to help Claire make preparations for breakfast.

The three of them made short work of breakfast and soon were on their respective horses, riding toward the far end of the ranch. Claire had decided to join them, and they were both pleased to have the extra company.

They rode leisurely, and Alicia found herself thankful for the slower pace. She turned her head in every direction, trying to take in all of the beautiful scenery. She had never seen such gorgeous land. This particular section of the ranch was not as flat as the rest of the property. They were riding along rolling hills dotted with patches of forest. Everything was so green, and there was a beautiful lake at the bottom of one of the hills. Everywhere she looked was enchanting, and horses could be seen in various directions. Caleb and Claire watched with pride as Alicia tried to drink it all in.

They stopped their horses by the lake, and Caleb and Claire moved to sit under the shade from a nearby tree. Alicia moved much more slowly, still trying to take it all in.

"It's so beautiful," she breathed.

"I know. It is glorious, isn't it? This has always been my favorite part of the ranch," Claire responded. She smiled as she looked toward the lake.

"Papa taught us how to swim in that lake." Claire looked wistful as memories of her parents flooded her mind. Alicia was quiet and stood motionless, and Claire suddenly realized how insensitive she had been. Her remark had no doubt brought forth Alicia's own memories. She stood and moved toward her new friend.

"I am sorry. I did not mean to bring up painful memories for you." Claire's voice was filled with regret. Alicia looked at her and smiled slightly.

"You have every right to talk about your parents. I know you both loved them dearly. Please do not feel that in order to protect my feelings you have to cease discussing your own memories." She really did want to know more about the Carters and the parents who had raised such fine children. She had not yet told them that her own father died three years ago and that her mother had only been gone for two weeks. The Carters assumed that Alicia had just recently lost both.

Alicia sat under the tree with them. She suddenly felt the urge to share some of her story with the Carters. She wanted them to know her better. She was aware they had never questioned her, and she deeply appreciated their regard for her privacy and feelings. They were all sitting enjoying the scenery when Alicia broke the silence.

"My father died three years ago," she began. "He went to Texas to inspect some cattle," she continued. "He rode the train, and on the way back, there was a hold-up. Four men boarded the train. Bandanas covered their faces, and they were all armed. They shot almost all of the passengers and stole everything of value. There were only a few survivors. My father was not one of them." Alicia's eyes were filled with tears. Her voice broke as she continued. "There was a fifth man waiting outside with their horses. They all escaped and have never been caught. My mother and I received a telegram. That was one of the worst days of my life."

Alicia's tears flowed freely now as the pain came rushing back to her. Claire held Alicia as her own tears fell uncontrollably.

Caleb had not expected this. He stood and walked toward the lake. *So that's why you brought her to us, Lord,* Caleb inwardly prayed. He looked over the water for a time and then returned to the girls as their tears began to subside.

Caleb laid a hand on his sister's shoulder.

"Thank you for telling us, Alicia," he said huskily. There was no mistaking the pain she saw in his eyes.

Caleb's hand tightened on Claire's shoulder as he took a deep breath.

"Alicia, Claire and I would like to share with you too," he began. He paused for a moment. Alicia watched as the muscles in Caleb's jaw flexed as he struggled to find words.

"Our parents died three years ago." He watched Alicia as the realization began to dawn on her.

"They spent three weeks in Texas buying, selling, and trading horses. They rode the train home, and their train was attacked by five men too."

Alicia's eyes widened. Claire lowered her head as tears trickled down her face. Caleb's own eyes held tears, but he never let them fall.

"I am so sorry," Alicia whispered.

They sat in silence for a long time. Claire dried her tears and was the first to speak.

"I am so glad that God brought you to us, Alicia." Claire could see what Alicia refused to believe—God's sovereign hand in control of every situation and working for the good of all his children. Alicia smiled, but Claire could see the hesitancy behind it.

"What's the matter?" she gently asked.

"God does not want anything to do with me and quite frankly, I don't want anything to do with him," Alicia stated matter-of-factly. Claire was stunned, and Caleb was rendered completely speechless. After a moment, Claire regained her voice.

"Why do you think that, Alicia?" Her eyes were soft and her tone was tender. She was silently praying for wisdom.

"Because I went to church all of my life, and God took my parents away. They were devout believers who loved and served the Lord. He took them away and left me all alone. I did not have a brother or sister to help me. I was left *alone*. God does not love me or want to take care of me. If he really is such a great God, then why would he let such things happen to those who love him?" The words came gushing out of her as her voice went from anger to fear to desperation.

Claire felt sadness wash over her as she realized how alone and miserable Alicia felt. Until now, neither she nor her brother had any idea of these emotions that Alicia had bottled up inside. Alicia sat with her head hung low and looked very young and vulnerable. Compassion swelled Caleb's heart.

"Alicia, I'm so sorry that you feel this way. But you must know that God does love you and has only the best planned for you. The Bible tells us in Romans 8:28 that God works for the good of those who love him. You must try to hang on to that, Alicia." Caleb searched her face for signs of understanding, but her expression remained emotionless.

"Claire and I were crushed at the news of our parents' deaths, and we were very scared. And I must admit, we did question God. But he has proven his love and faithfulness to us time and again as he helped us move forward. He is a sovereign God who loves us and wants his best for us. We may not always understand why things happen, but we can never lose faith." Caleb stopped then, uncertain as to how to continue. He knew that she had to come to realize and accept this for herself.

Claire finished Caleb's thoughts aloud to Alicia.

"Alicia, just know that you're not alone. Caleb and I are praying for you and are available if you ever want to talk."

Claire gave Alicia a big hug, and the conversation turned to lighter subjects. They continued riding around the ranch and finished by racing back to the house. Caleb's stallion won easily, but they all had a marvelous time. Caleb hid very well the turmoil that had begun in his heart. Alicia did not share his faith in the Lord. His heart sank at this news. He desperately wanted Alicia to feel the peace and joy of knowing God's Son in a personal relationship. He also knew that until she did, he would have to lay aside all romantic feelings toward her. He knew this would be no easy task. He began to pray for Alicia's salvation and strength for himself to be able to show her God's love yet hold his own emotions in check.

He was only vaguely aware of the fact that she still had not shared how her mother died.

Chapter 6

Alicia joined Caleb and Claire for church the next morning. She had known all week that she would attend with them, but after their discussion the day before, the Carters were not sure she would want to. The service went by smoothly, and at the end Alicia's attention was suddenly caught by Pastor Tyler's words. He was introducing her to the congregation as the new schoolteacher. Alicia's heart began to pound as the pastor spoke.

"Friends, I have a special announcement to make this Sunday. The Lord has blessed us with a wonderful new schoolteacher to replace Mrs. Keene. Miss Alicia Barnes." The pastor smiled at her, and Alicia felt Claire nudging her to stand. Alicia slowly rose and felt as if her legs would give way any minute. All eyes turned to face her as color began rising to her cheeks. She smiled courageously and then sat back down.

"Miss Barnes will begin teaching your children tomorrow morning at eight o'clock."

The pastor then went on to wish the church family a blessed week. Alicia was relieved the embarrassing part was over. She suspected that there would be an announcement, but she had not fully prepared herself for it. She was still blushing as they rose to sing the final hymn.

When the service was over, Alicia moved with the intention of quickly exiting and returning to the ranch. But everyone rushed to meet the new young schoolteacher. There was a swarm of people around her, and Alicia knew a moment of panic as she felt trapped in a mob of people. They were all smiling faces anxious to make her feel at home, and Alicia soon relaxed and chatted, mostly answering questions. There were parents around her introducing their children and already extending dinner invitations to her. Many of the ladies from the church were warmly inviting her to join in all of the church activities and Bible studies.

Alicia's fear quickly left her in the midst of all the chaos. She actually felt a bit of relief at having been received so openly. She wondered to herself what made the people of this town so friendly and warm. She spent half an hour after church visiting with families of the children that she would be teaching and failed to notice all of the young men that were standing nearby, waiting for a chance to introduce themselves to the beautiful new schoolteacher.

Caleb noticed, however, and he was a bit worried about how she would handle the mob. One look at her confident smile made him wonder why he even thought she might need a lifeline. Every day she proved how she was accustomed to taking care of herself.

The families began to chat amongst themselves and bid Alicia good-bye, and Caleb watched as several of the young men began to approach. He quickly stepped in and put his hand on Alicia's elbow to lead her outside.

"I want you to meet the pastor," he informed her. Alicia was inwardly relieved at this subtle rescue. She caught a glimpse of the men for the first time and found herself uncomfortable. Caleb's timing was perfect. They walked to the front door, where the pastor and his wife were shaking hands and greeting parishioners. Caleb led her to Pastor Tyler and introduced them.

"Well, Alicia, it's nice to meet you. We are so glad that

you have come to teach our children. We were afraid the children might not get much of an education this year." The elderly pastor had a twinkle in his eye as he talked to the young woman. Alicia was instantly drawn to him and reminded of the ache in her heart. Her parents wouldn't want her to be so set against God and church. She forced those thoughts away as Pastor Tyler turned to introduce Alicia to his wife.

"Alicia, it's a pleasure having you with us," Gloria Tyler said as she took Alicia's hands. "You are an answer to prayers, my dear." Alicia smiled at the kind woman. She was reminded of her parents and a time in her life when she believed God would take care of her. Her whole being filled with grief as she fought to maintain her calm composure.

She raised her chin.

"Thank you. It certainly is a pleasure meeting both of you."

She and Caleb continued on so the Tylers could continue greeting and visiting with other members of the church family. Alicia looked over and saw a handsome young man speaking with Claire. She was a bit surprised. Claire never mentioned having any interest in any of the men in town. Of course, the subject had never come up before. Alicia's curiosity rose as they approached them.

"Mark, how are you?" Caleb shook the man's hand.

"Doing well. Yourself?"

"Can't complain."

Alicia glanced over at Claire, who never took her eyes off Mark. Caleb turned to Alicia and spoke.

"Alicia, this is Mark Brewer. He is the town banker. Mark, this is Alicia Barnes, our new schoolteacher."

Mark was a handsome man. He was only a couple of inches shorter than Caleb, and he was slender and clean-shaven. His blue eyes complemented his wavy blonde hair. He was a contrast to Caleb's own rugged features, dark brown hair, and mahogany eyes. Alicia could see why Claire found him attractive.

"It's a pleasure, Miss Barnes," Mark said as he extended his hand to her. Alicia returned the handshake.

"Likewise," she responded.

"Mark, will you be joining us for supper?" Caleb inquired.

"I thought you'd never ask," Mark replied. Claire was beaming. Alicia could hardly wait until she could talk to Claire about this in private.

Claire was in a flurry as she worked on preparations for the evening meal. Alicia came downstairs to help her and had to work hard to stifle the laughter that was bubbling up within her. She walked into the kitchen to find Claire covered in flour, frantically picking up the vegetables she had spilled all over the floor. The entire kitchen looked like a tornado had been through. There were pots and pans everywhere. It was so unlike Claire and her usually tidy kitchen that Alicia finally succumbed and burst into laughter.

Claire looked up at her in full frustration. Beads of perspiration dotted her forehead.

"Alicia," she cried, "this is not funny. Mark will be here in a few hours." She tossed some carrots in a bowl and sat back on her heels in defeat.

"This is a disaster," she wailed. "I'm not usually this nervous!" Alicia took pity on her poor, lovesick friend. She reached down, took hold of her arms, and helped her into a chair.

"Let me take care of the meal, Claire. You go get

cleaned up and rest a bit." She smiled at Claire. "Don't worry. Everything will be fine."

"I don't understand what has come over me. Every time I see him, my stomach does flips and I can't see straight." Alicia watched as Claire stopped talking and started smiling. Alicia knew that Claire had already forgotten that she was even in the room.

Claire then began to speak, but her voice sounded dreamy and the look in her eyes was distant.

"Mark asked Caleb's permission to begin calling on me the day before you came to us. Caleb likes Mark very much and quickly gave his blessing. We have even spoken of marriage." That last word was spoken so sweetly that Alicia had no doubt that her friend was indeed in love with this man.

Claire suddenly caught herself daydreaming and quickly snapped back to reality. She looked over and noticed that Alicia had a twinkle in her eye.

"Don't look so smug, Alicia Barnes. One day it will be your turn, and then you will turn to mush at the very mention of his name."

"Oh, no. I am not ready for anything like that anytime soon," Alicia quickly responded. Claire had a mischievous look on her face as she eyed Alicia, who merely smiled innocently back.

"I think I'll take your advice and go clean up and rest for a bit. I'll come back down and bake an apple pie for dessert." Her tone was light as she practically floated out of the room. Alicia watched her go and felt joy over her friend's happiness. There was a dull ache inside her heart for someone of her own, but for the moment she was stubbornly set against it. Love involved risk. Loving someone meant you might lose them someday. The thought of losing again was more than Alicia could bear.

All of Claire's worries were put to rest as the night began. Everything went smoothly. The dinner that Alicia prepared was scrumptious and savory. Their dessert of apple pie was excellent too. The Carters had a special recipe for their apple pie that had been in the family for ages and had won countless baking contests. Mark was aware that Claire made the pie so he made a particular fuss over it, causing Claire to blush deeply.

Alicia observed Mark and Claire closely and saw how deeply they cared for each other. She would often catch them exchanging looks filled with love and tenderness. Claire was completely relaxed in his presence. She glowed all evening.

Alicia quickly came to like Mark as well. He was a neat and rather serious man, but he had a heart as big as the ocean. He had a rather dry sense of humor that Alicia found most amusing. Claire's sweetness and sensitivity was a wonderful compliment to Mark's sensibility and seriousness.

She watched Caleb as well. He was always quick to laugh heartily—a trait Alicia found attractive. He was not afraid to laugh, and try as she might, every time that he laughed, she would find herself laughing too. He was encouraging and thoughtful as well. There were many moments where any normal brother would have poked fun at his sister for what was said, but Caleb just sat back and smiled at the couple. Alicia found herself amazed for the hundredth time that week that she could find such wonderful people.

As the evening continued, the four of them had a marvelous time chatting and playing a game of cards after dinner. The evening came to an end much too soon for all of them. Alicia left for the kitchen to begin clean up, and Caleb promptly joined her in an effort to give the couple a few minutes alone. Alicia was grateful for the help and again marveled at Caleb's sensitivity toward others. She stood staring at him for some moments before she caught herself. He was looking right back at her with a slightly puzzled look on his face.

"What's wrong?" he asked.

"You are a really great brother. Claire's very lucky."

Caleb bowed low as if he were an English gentleman asking a lady to dance and ended up with a dishtowel thrown at him. He caught it and let out one of his infectious laughs. Alicia laughed in return.

"Mr. Carter, you may dry the dishes."

"Yes, ma'am," he drawled with a smirk as he moved to do as he was bid.

Mark reached for Claire's hand and gently brushed a kiss against the back of it.

"I had a wonderful time," he said softly, leaning against the railing on the back porch.

"So did I."

"I like Alicia. I think it is wonderful that God has brought you all together."

"Yes, so do I." Concern clouded her voice.

"Is something wrong?"

"I don't think Alicia is a believer," she said with conviction. "I just pray that God will open her eyes and help her to see his grace and love at work in her life. She told us that she grew up in church. I think she has just shut her heart to the truth after the death of her parents. We both want her to become a child of God." Mark nodded in understanding.

"I will pray for her, darling."

He gently ran a finger down her smooth cheek then cupped her face in his hands. He brushed a kiss on her lips and turned to leave.

Chapter 7

Three weeks had passed, and Alicia began to settle into a routine. Her first few days as schoolteacher had been rocky as she soon discovered how difficult it was to manage so many grade levels at one time. However, it had not taken her long to fall in love with the children. With the exception of only a couple, they were all excellent students who had good manners and respect for authority.

They, in turn, adored their new schoolteacher. She was like a breath of fresh air compared to their former one, who was old and never had any interaction with them except for disciplining. Alicia quickly taught herself how to manage and deal with the daily pressures of teaching the children. She even took them out once a week on nature walks as part of their science lesson. The children had all been thrilled as they trooped through the woods near the schoolyard, and Alicia pointed out various plants and insects.

Outside of school, Alicia spent many evenings supping with the children's families. Most of the parents had all been quick to extend a dinner invitation to the new teacher. Alicia herself was most anxious to oblige. She wanted to learn all she could about her new students and their families. The only homes she was not invited to were the ones that were a considerable distance from town.

The families that Alicia spent time with were all warm

and welcoming. Alicia was pleased that the children had such good atmospheres to return to when the school day was complete.

She spent the rest of her time organizing and arranging. The little house by the school had needed some repairs, so Alicia wasn't able to move in until a week ago, and there were still things to be cleaned and put away. Alicia found the house rather cramped. There were only two rooms. The larger room contained a small table with two chairs, some cupboards, and a stove. The smaller room was meant as a bedroom. It had a small bed, a chest of drawers, and a small washbasin. All in all, it was a little cozier than Alicia would have liked, but she was not going to complain. It was more than she dreamed of when she first set out for Darby. She continued to spend a great deal of time at the Carters' ranch. She kept her own horse there because the ranch was only a few miles out and within walking distance of the town. The Carters were very dear to her, and she loved to be around all of the horses.

This particular day was a Friday afternoon. The children had only been gone for a short time, and Alicia was taking advantage of some time to herself. The schoolhouse was clean, so she began walking through town toward the fields. She decided a walk in the open would be wonderful. She took off at a brisk pace with her hair flying freely. The wind had blown her bonnet off, and she now let it swing from her arm as she carried it.

She had not gone far when a deep voice came up from behind her.

"Good afternoon, Miss Barnes."

She turned with a start.

"I'm sorry. I didn't mean to startle you." She looked up to find a pair of blue eyes looking down at her.

"Hi, Paul," she responded casually. Paul Vickery

was the deputy in town, and she had only made his acquaintance once. He seemed to attract the eye of all the local girls at church, but at the moment she could not remember if he had ever approached any of them. Personally, Alicia couldn't see what the other girls saw in Paul Vickery. While he was a kind man, he had a large nose and was balding slightly.

"Where are you going?" he asked.

"Oh, just for a walk."

"Mind if I come along?"

Alicia shook her head. In truth, she really wanted to be alone. She did not want to be seen walking unaccompanied with the town deputy. It would cause the tongues of all the town gossips to wag. But what could she do? Tell him that no, she really preferred to be alone? She knew that would have been insultingly rude. She then made a spur-of-the-moment decision.

"My walk is taking me to the Carter ranch," she casually began. She cast a sidelong glance at him to see his brief frown. "I want to take Cocoa for a ride before it gets too dark."

She smiled sweetly at him. She suspected that if he knew she was going to the ranch he might let her be. She soon discovered that was not to be the case.

"All right," he said as he continued walking by her side. "I think that's an excellent idea. You take extremely good care of your horse. It's a very admirable trait." Alicia turned slightly to see if he was joking, but he was sincere. He continued. "You know, there are many men that I know who could not care less for their horses, yet those horses provide their very livelihood. I think it's such a shame."

"Yes, you're right," she agreed. Perhaps she had been too quick to judge Paul. She only hoped Caleb would understand that their meeting was innocent.

Wait a minute, she thought. *Why am I worried about what Caleb thinks? Why do I care if he sees me walking with Paul?* The thought troubled her and preoccupied her thoughts for the rest of the walk. Paul did not seem to notice her pensiveness and continued to make small talk.

They walked onto the ranch, and Alicia noticed Claire hanging some clothes on the line to dry. She spotted them and waved.

"Hi," she called.

"Hi." Alicia waved back and started walking toward Claire. Much to her surprise, so did Paul. Alicia caught the raised eyebrows that Claire sported, but only for a moment before she greeted them both naturally.

"It's good to see you." The two ladies shared a brief hug, and Claire turned to Paul.

"Hello, Paul. How are you today?"

"I'm doing well, Claire. And yourself?"

"Great." She turned to her basketful of wet clothes. "Just hanging some laundry."

"Oh, let me help you with that," Alicia quickly suggested, needing an escape.

"Thanks, but there's no need. I can get it done in no time."

"That's all right. I'll help anyway." Alicia moved to reach some clothespins and then remembered Paul. She turned to face him. His heart soared at one look at her auburn hair blowing in the wind and an angelic smile on her face. She seemed completely unaware of his thoughts toward her, but Claire did not miss his look. She continued hanging clothes as Alicia began to address Paul.

"Thanks for walking me over here. I'm going to help Claire then go for a ride. I'll see you around." It was all said very politely. Alicia had no intention of encouraging him, but she also had no desire to be rude.

"It is I who thank you, Miss Barnes." He tipped his hat to the ladies and bid them a good day. He was barely out of earshot when Claire turned to her with a wide grin and a smug look in her eyes.

"What was that all about?"

"Oh, I don't know," Alicia shrugged and tried to sound as nonchalant as possible. "I was going for a walk. I was originally headed to the meadow just to walk and be alone for a while, then all of sudden he was there. I could not just tell him to go away. So I decided to come here." She looked at Claire rather pitifully, which made Claire laugh.

"I don't see what's so funny."

"Alicia, can't you see he's taken with you?" Claire said between giggles.

"I was afraid of that," Alicia responded. Claire turned to fully face her.

"You mean you don't want him to be attracted to you?" She found it hard to believe that Alicia was not flattered by Paul's attention. She could name at least a dozen girls in the county who wanted to catch his eye. But then, she would also be relieved because she knew the special feelings Caleb had for her.

"Well, no," she slowly answered. "He's a nice man, but I don't want to give him any false ideas. I have no intention of being romantically involved with anyone. I like my life the way it is." Alicia turned back to the clothesline and finished hanging the last shirt.

"I need to go check on Cocoa now. I think I'll take her for a ride." Claire watched her go but wasn't about to believe that Alicia had no intention of being romantically involved with anyone. It was true that Alicia was hurting right now, and that with love comes risks, but Claire knew that it was only a matter of time before Alicia would change her mind.

"Claire!" Caleb's voice rang out through the house. Claire heard him come in and called that she was in the kitchen.

"Claire," Caleb said as he rushed in, "was that Paul Vickery I saw walk onto the ranch with Alicia?" Claire watched him walk over to her, his eyes large and pleading for answers.

"Yes, it was," she said calmly.

"Well?"

"Well, what?" she asked, clearly enjoying the fun she was having at Caleb's expense.

"What was he doing?"

"It was all quite innocent on Alicia's part. She told me that she was going for a walk and all of a sudden Paul joined her. She was intending to go to the meadow but then decided to come here after Paul decided to tag along with her."

"So did she seem interested in him?"

"No." The look of relief on Caleb's face was unmistakable.

"She told me that she was aware of his attraction to her, but that she did not share it," Claire stopped. "She also said that she does not want to be romantically involved with anyone right now." She watched Caleb carefully to judge his reaction. He remained stoic and then slowly began to smile.

"Good," he said. Claire looked at him in surprise. "If she is not attracted to anyone and does not want to be at the moment, then I have as good a chance as anyone. For the moment, though, keeping her thoughts away from men might be a good thing." He went on to explain. "Her thoughts will not be so distracted, and there may be more room for her to think about God and allow him to work."

Claire was impressed with her brother's reasoning and agreed wholeheartedly. Caleb stood.

"Oh, by the way," Claire added, "Alicia's staying for dinner." Caleb smiled, nodded, and went on his way. Claire began to hum as she continued preparations for dinner.

Dinner that night was relaxed and pleasant. The three adults chatted and laughed all evening. It had been a month since they had met, but they already acted and spoke as if they had known one another for years. Alicia kept the Carters in stitches as she recounted some of the children's antics. After dinner, they played cards for a while, and then Alicia announced that she had to go. As had become routine, she hugged Claire good-bye with the promise of seeing her the next day, and Caleb began to walk out with her. He always saw her safely back to her little house on the evenings that she spent at the ranch.

She was completely relaxed with him as they walked toward town. It dawned on her that it was nothing like how she felt when she was walking with Paul. Paul made her nervous and feel as though she had to continue a conversation or say all of the right things. With Caleb, silence was not awkward or uncomfortable, and when they did speak, she did not have to keep her guard up. She surprised herself even further with how much she was beginning to enjoy their evening strolls back to town. She quickly pushed those thoughts from her mind as she began to speak.

"So when do I get to ride Knight or Midnight?"

Caleb dreaded that question. He was uneasy with the idea of her handling one of his stallions alone. They could be quite unpredictable and very difficult to manage. "Well, maybe one day soon. I have to be with you, though. I don't want you taking one of the stallions out alone."

"Cocoa rode pretty well today," she commented.

"She really seems to enjoy the stables here and the new environment. I think it's about time for her to be reshod."

"All right, I'll check on it in the morning."

"Thanks."

They always reached the house much too quickly for Caleb. Alicia did not seem to notice as she turned to face him. Caleb wondered if she was completely oblivious to his feelings for her and then quickly decided that for the moment it was for the best that she was.

"Thanks for walking with me, Caleb." His stomach did a quick flip.

"Anytime."

"See you tomorrow," she said as she went inside. Caleb turned to go back to the ranch with a lighter step. He was unaware that Paul Vickery was watching them from the window of the sheriff's office.

Chapter 8

Sunday dawned fresh and clear, and Alicia was glad for the sunshine. It stormed the day before and prevented her from riding. She now sipped some coffee and enjoyed the view from her window. On one side of her little house was the schoolhouse/church, but on the other side, the view stretched out over the prairie lands that were behind the town. As she sat for a while, she began to think about church that morning. In spite of herself, she was actually coming to enjoy Sunday church. She loved all of the townsfolk and enjoyed the fellowship that she had with everyone on Sundays. Almost all of her students and their families attended, and she was growing to love Pastor Tyler and his wife more and more. Aside from that, Alicia found herself actually interested in the sermons. Pastor Tyler was taking them through a series on the life of Joseph, and Alicia had found herself captivated by it all.

Last Sunday, the pastor read from the book of Genesis, chapters 37 through 39. Alicia felt great relief that she had thought to pack her mother's Bible before she left. She was able to follow along as Pastor Tyler read of Joseph's fine beginnings and being his father's favorite son. He went on to read about Joseph's betrayal by his own family, being left to die in a well, and then being sold. Pastor Tyler continued to emphasize God's mighty hand at work in every situation, no matter how bad. Alicia was skeptical of his remark. Was God really at work in her life? Did he care? She pushed away the thoughts that continued to nag at her. But she had been fascinated by Joseph's story and was eager to see what Pastor Tyler would present this morning. She pushed herself up from her chair and readied for church.

Alicia walked into the church and quickly spotted Caleb and Claire sitting up front. She went to join them. She found herself sitting with Claire on her right side and no one to the left of her. The two women were chatting away when she heard a male voice approach.

"Good morning, ladies." Caleb turned to find Paul Vickery gazing down at Alicia. He turned to face the front, reminding himself that Alicia was not his and that she was a very attractive woman. Naturally the men would want to approach her. His reasoning made him feel no better.

"Good morning, Paul," Alicia and Claire said almost simultaneously.

"May I sit with you?"

It was the question Alicia had dreaded. She quickly glanced around to find every pair of young woman's eyes on them.

"Of course," she replied out of courtesy. After all, they were in church. How could she refuse? However, she could feel the stares on her back and wondered how badly idle tongues would gossip over this. She wished he would turn his attention to one of the other young ladies because she simply wasn't interested. In her mind there were plenty of them and on top of that, they would be thrilled.

"Morning, Caleb." Paul extended a hand to Caleb. Caleb reached over the two ladies to return the shake.

"Morning, Vickery." Most of the men in town referred to the sheriff and his deputy by their last names. "How's it going?"

"Can't complain. It's been pretty quiet lately."

"Good to hear."

The service started, and Alicia found herself squirming uneasily and wishing that it would soon be over.

An hour later, everyone filed from the church building. Alicia stayed by Claire's side as they moved to greet Pastor Tyler and his wife.

"Excellent sermon, Pastor," Alicia heard Caleb say.

"Thank you, son. How are things on the ranch?"

"Doing well, thanks."

Caleb moved on, and soon Alicia found herself in front of the Tylers. She gave Gloria a quick hug before she shook the pastor's hand.

"It's good to see you today, Alicia," Pastor Tyler said kindly.

"Thank you, sir. I hope to see you both later in the week." Alicia occasionally ran into Gloria and would sometimes see Pastor Tyler as well. She smiled and bid them good day as she followed Claire to the waiting buggy.

"Miss Barnes." Paul's deep voice stopped her in her tracks. "Sheriff Holding and his wife have invited me for lunch, and I was wondering if you would escort me?" He was quite charming when he made his request, and Alicia's mind whirled. She had already told the Carters that she would lunch with them. She knew that, of course, she could change her plans, but she really did not want to. Wouldn't that be rude to her two friends? Still, would it be rude for her to refuse the deputy's invitation? What would Sheriff Holding and his wife think? All of these thoughts were racing through her mind when she finally spoke.

"Well, I don't know," she said with uncertainty. "That would be very lovely, but I promised the Carters to lunch with them this afternoon." Caleb watched the entire exchange in silence, desperately wanting to refuse for her but willing himself to remain still. He would only make the situation more awkward for Alicia.

"Of course," Paul graciously replied. "It would be rude to cancel your previous plans. Perhaps another time."

"Yes," she said softly.

He tipped his hat and smiled before turning to leave.

⁓

"But why?" Alicia asked after lunch. The silence had long been broken, and Alicia was thankful that she had chosen not to go with Paul. The three were now comfortably seated in the living room discussing the morning's sermon.

"Why was Joseph not resentful toward his brothers or angry with God?" Alicia persisted. She tried hard to understand what tormented her own thoughts. Joseph had been worse off than she, yet she was the one pushing God away instead of Joseph. Alicia wanted to understand what it was she was missing. Why did she feel such thoughts of anger and abandonment when Joseph did not?

"Joseph trusted in God," Caleb gently tried to explain. He prayed for the right words to speak. He had no desire to confuse or anger her with a poor interpretation.

"Every time a bad situation came up in Joseph's life, he trusted God to provide and take care of him. And God proved to Joseph his love and mercy throughout it all. Joseph was left to die in the well but instead was sold into slavery and lived. God spared his life, and Joseph was grateful. What's more, God gave him a kind master who eventually made Joseph his attendant. Joseph's life as a slave could have been much worse, but God kept some of the more evil elements of slavery away from him." Caleb paused and searched her face for understanding. Her eyes remained glued to his in full interest as he continued.

"After the betrayal from Potiphar's wife, Joseph was put in prison. But I believe that he did not feel resentment because he knew that God was sovereign and still in control of the situation. I think he was sad and burdened over Potiphar's wife and the poor decisions both of them made, but he loved God and that was more important than holding a grudge. Now, the Bible does not tell us whether or not Joseph ever got angry or if he questioned God at any point. He very well may have. But he did not dwell in his anger or his doubts. He left his life to God, and God proved faithful over and over. The prison warden even made Joseph in charge of those in the prison. God was still taking care of Joseph." Caleb stopped and looked over at Alicia. They were still at chapter 39 of Genesis in the sermon. Alicia's eyes had moved to the window. She had a distant look in her eye.

"Thank you for explaining it to me, Caleb," she said as she continued to stare out the window. Much was churning in her heart as she processed Caleb's words.

Caleb exchanged a glance with Claire. They were both greatly encouraged by Alicia's questions. They sat in silence, waiting for Alicia to speak again. When she did, it was about the horses, and they wisely let the matter drop for the time being.

Chapter 9

The days passed swiftly for Alicia, and October soon became November. Alicia, feeling confined, restlessly paced the floor of her house and finally decided to head to the ranch. She grabbed her coat and made her way for the door. As she opened the door, the brisk autumn air blew heavily against her. She was surprised at how cool the weather was becoming. She firmly shut the door and walked as swiftly as she could toward the ranch.

She was relieved when she finally came in view of the Blue Star. It was not a long walk or a difficult one, but with the windy weather, it seemed to last forever. She could see smoke rising from the chimney of the house and hurriedly made her way to the door. As had become custom, Alicia did not knock but simply turned the knob to let herself in. She quickly stepped in and shivered. The warmth of the house was a welcome feeling to her stiff body.

Claire was in the kitchen and felt the cold air rush in and sweep through the house.

"Hello?" she called, fairly certain that it was Alicia.

"Don't worry, Claire; it's just me," Alicia called back as she stripped off her coat and gloves. She hung them up and made her way to the kitchen.

"Well," she said as she looked around at the abundance of delicious food, "what's all this?"

Claire looked excited as her own eyes swept over the kitchen.

"Mark is coming for dinner."

"I suspected as much." Alicia smiled at her beaming friend and offered to help with the finishing preparations. At any other home, Alicia would have felt like an intruder and immediately excused herself at the mention of other company, but she had become such good friends with the Carters that it was a given in all of their minds that she was welcome no matter what. Claire gratefully accepted her offer, and together the two of them quickly finished the preparations for supper.

An hour later, the four adults were gathered around the table as Caleb led the blessing.

"Thank you, Lord, for this food that you have blessed us with. Thank you for your goodness and love and all of your many blessings. Please help us to be mindful of you in all that we do. In Jesus's name, amen."

There was an echo of "amens" around the table before everyone began to help themselves to the food. There was no doubt that Claire had outdone herself. There were lamb chops, mashed potatoes, biscuits and gravy, green beans, and fried okra.

"Claire, this is absolutely delicious," Mark declared for the third time that evening. "You have me eating like a king." Claire beamed at his praise and Alicia and Caleb watched as she began to blush. Alicia put her napkin to her mouth to hide her smile.

"So how is school coming along?" Mark asked Alicia.

"It's very well. The children are doing excellent work and are good students. But a good deal of praise also goes to their parents. They do such a wonderful job of encouraging their children and participating with them. I have found that the support of the parents is as vital as the individual effort of the students."

"That makes sense," Caleb chimed in. "I remember

that our parents were very adamant of our education—and supportive."

"And how is the bank doing?" Alicia asked in return. She really had no notions of the workings of a bank.

"Very well," Mark responded with a wide grin. All eyes turned to Alicia as everyone began to laugh. They were all aware of her financial knowledge. She shrugged and kept a very innocent look on her face as they continued to laugh.

After dinner, they all retired to the living room to drink some coffee and chat some more. Caleb and Mark became engrossed in a very competitive game of checkers, and Claire picked up some sewing. Alicia excused herself and made her way out to the barn.

She put her coat and gloves back on before opening the front door, and when she did, she felt something soft bump against her.

"Hello there, Rebel," she said as she bent to pet the German shepherd. "How are you boy? Are you being the fierce protector out here in the cold?" She smiled at the dog that wagged his tail in delight. To a dog, any attention was welcome. He remained on the front porch as Alicia walked toward the stables.

She opened the door and stepped inside to find that it was surprisingly warm in there. She unbuttoned her coat and slipped off her gloves. She walked past the stalls and spoke soothingly to the horses. She gave Midnight, Ginger, and Knight extra pats as she passed them before she reached Cocoa's stall.

"Hello, Cocoa," she said softly and soothingly. "How are you? Did you miss me?" She picked up a brush and began stroking the horse's soft mane. She loved to brush her horse. She found it almost as soothing as the horse did. She began to hum softly to herself and did not hear the door to the stables open. She continued with her task, and then suddenly her arm seemed to slow down with its even strokes of the brush. There was someone behind her, and she was fairly certain it was not Caleb.

She slowly turned to find Dirk Kindred standing right outside Cocoa's stall. He was the newest hand at the ranch. Caleb hired him about two months ago. Dirk got the job that brought Alicia to Darby in the first place. Dirk was tall and handsome. He was only twenty years old, and Alicia had the impression from previous encounters with Dirk that he was used to having his way with women. He approached Alicia on several occasions, and she was always quite cold toward him. She did not have a good feeling about him, nor did she appreciate his boldness.

"Good evening, Alicia," he said in a charming voice.

Alicia inwardly sighed. She did not want to speak with him. Surely he had figured out by now that she was absolutely not interested. She turned back to Cocoa and continued to brush the horse. Dirk remained still, and finally Alicia responded.

"Good evening. And it's Miss Barnes."

"Ah, Miss Barnes." Dirk swept off his hat with one smooth move and dramatically bowed. "It is always so good to see you."

Alicia rolled her eyes and wondered when this charade was going to end. She hung Cocoa's brush and exited the stall. She walked calmly toward the stable door with her head held high. The sound of Dirk walking right behind her made her nervous, but she was determined not to let it show. Suddenly Dirk's hands were gripping her upper arms as he spun her around to face him.

"Let me go!" she practically shouted in his face. His grip tightened on her arms, and she flinched.

"Alicia, run away with me. We could have such a good life together. You would not have to teach school anymore. I would take care of you, and we would be together forever." Alicia looked at him as if he had taken leave of his senses.

"Of course I will not go anywhere with you," she said between gritted teeth. "I'm not one of those girls who will just fall all over themselves for you. Now let me go." She was met with a tighter grip and tried hard not to show how badly her arms hurt as they began to pulse under the pressure of his hold.

"That's part of the fun." He smiled in a way that caused a shiver of fear to run up Alicia's spine. "You're a new challenge for me."

Alicia gathered her wits and in a burst of energy kicked Dirk hard in the shin. Stunned, he let go of her but only for a second before he grabbed her again and swung her around, landing her hard on her back against the stable wall. This time she let out a loud shriek, which left Dirk so startled that he slapped her hard on the face for silence.

Alicia was stunned at his slap as her face began to sting severely. She kicked with all of her might and tried to punch, but he had her arms firmly pinned. He was doing an expert job dodging her kicks and laughed when Alicia lost her balance and fell to the ground. He went down with her and continued to hold her. Fear shot through Alicia as she felt his weight on top of her. She continued to struggle, but he was so strong. She then heard Rebel bark and heard more than saw him enter the stable and hurl himself onto her assailant. Following Rebel were Caleb and Mark.

Caleb grabbed Dirk by the front of his shirt and slung him into the barn wall. Mark helped Alicia to her feet and held onto her to keep her steady. The foreman, John, and several other hands also came running into the stables to see what was going on. All were shocked into silence as they surveyed the scene.

"What are you doing, Dirk?" Caleb growled at the man as he strongly held him against the wall.

"Just trying to have a friendly chat with Alicia. But she would have none of it. Silly girl." His tone was dripping with sarcasm, and Caleb found it vile. Anger boiled up within him, and he worked to stay levelheaded and not run his fist through Dirk's face.

"Get out," Caleb said firmly and loudly as he roughly let him go. No man in his right mind would take on Caleb at this point, and Dirk made his way to the door. But not before turning to smirk at Alicia. She shivered, and Caleb pushed him through the door.

"Get out, and never come back, or I'll have the sheriff out here. John," he said, turning to his foreman, "see that Dirk gets packed and out of here tonight." John led Dirk away, and Caleb moved to go back in the stables. He found Mark still supporting Alicia, and he reached out for her. As he gently put his arms around her, he could feel her trembling violently. She clung to him, and he felt his heart turn over.

"It's all right. You're safe now," Caleb said softly as he gently moved to help her walk back to the house.

Claire had grabbed her coat and was making her way to the stables just as the three were walking out. She ran to Alicia.

"You poor thing." She took Alicia's other hand and felt the same trembling that Caleb did.

As soon as the group entered the house, Claire turned to Alicia and softly gasped. She had just caught a glimpse of Alicia's red cheek that was swelling slightly. Caleb saw it too and felt fury wash freshly over him again. Claire moved to the kitchen to get a cool rag to place over it. Caleb went over to the fireplace, where he rested one arm against the mantle and ran his hand through his hair. *How could I have been so blind? Alicia was hurt tonight on my ranch by one of my hands.* Caleb's shoulders sagged. The fact that she was hurt on his property by one of his men was almost more than he could bear.

Alicia continued to shake slightly until she began sipping some fresh coffee that Claire brought to her.

"Alicia, I'm so sorry," Caleb finally said as he turned from the fireplace.

"It's not your fault, Caleb." Alicia could sense Caleb's feeling of responsibility and worked to put his mind at ease. "He was a fine hand and excellent with the horses. Who would have thought that he could be so vile? I'm just glad that you came when you did." Alicia put a hand tenderly to her face. The swelling was worse, and her cheek was turning a shade of purple. She placed the cool rag that Claire brought against her cheek and winced.

"Did he do anything else to hurt you?" Caleb asked, fearful of her answer.

"No." Everyone breathed a sigh of relief. "The only other thing was that he held on tightly to my arms." Caleb's eyes slid shut. He couldn't believe this was happening. "It's all right, Caleb," Alicia said again in an attempt to reassure Caleb. She caught the contrite look in his eyes.

After about half an hour, Alicia felt well enough to head for home. Mark left as well and headed off on his horse, while Caleb hitched up the buggy to drive Alicia home.

The ride was a quiet one. Caleb was still struggling with feelings of anger and responsibility over what happened. Alicia wasn't sure how to reassure him that everything was all right, so she remained silent.

Her cheek continued to throb as she readied for bed, but Alicia hardly noticed. She realized that today was the first day she wasn't overwhelmed with the ache of losing her parents. Naturally she missed them tremendously, but the pain no longer threatened to engulf her every time she thought of them. As she reflected back on the day and the incident with Dirk, she realized that she wasn't as alone as she thought she was.

The ride to the ranch was a silent one that Sunday after church. Lately Alicia seemed intent on the sermons but very disconcerted when it was all over. She was left wondering about how much she knew to be true and why she was fighting against it with all of her might. She asked herself if God would want her should she turn to him. Then she wondered about the ache she seemed to have inside of her lately. She thought she had everything she could want. She had a good job, good friends, and her faithful horse. What was missing? The question tormented her for the entire ride to the ranch and continued for the better part of the day.

Caleb and Claire wisely remained silent during these times when they could sense that Alicia needed to be alone with her thoughts. They fervently prayed for her daily, turning her over to the Lord. The waiting was hard sometimes, but they determined to trust God wholeheartedly with this one. They knew God cared about Alicia's eternity even more than they did.

"I don't understand it," Alicia remarked after lunch. They were all comfortably settled in the living room when her voice broke the silence. She sat staring out the window and was unaware that she spoke aloud.

"Understand what, honey?" Claire asked.

"What?" Alicia turned to face her, and the Carters watched her face turn a deep shade of red. "Oh, I'm sorry. I was just thinking."

"Anything you'd like to share?" Claire's question was asked so gently that Alicia turned fully to face her. Claire caught the tears standing in her eyes.

"Well," she began, "I still don't understand Joseph." Caleb and Claire nodded in understanding. Pastor Tyler was still preaching on the life of Joseph.

"He was imprisoned, but yet God was still with him, and he trusted. Then he interpreted the dreams of the cupbearer and the baker accurately and gave God the glory. He then waited another two years for the cupbearer to remember his promise to speak to Pharaoh on Joseph's behalf. Joseph was sent off by his brothers at seventeen and finally given power by Pharaoh when he was thirty. That's thirteen years! What kept him so faithful? Why was he put through that? I just don't understand any of it." Alicia's shoulders slumped in defeat. She knew the real reason why she was confused was because Joseph trusted his life to the Lord in spite of all he went through, and Alicia was still fighting. While the pain of losing her parents was not as strong as it once was, she still spent nights crying into her pillow. She could not bring herself to understand how God could allow this to happen to good people who loved him.

Claire walked to Alicia and put an arm around her dear friend.

"Alicia, Joseph did not run from God." The words were tenderly spoken. "God rewards those who are faithful. I don't think all of those thirteen years were completely miserable for Joseph as you seem to think they were. He trusted God. He turned his life over to the Lord, and therefore, I'm quite certain that Joseph felt contentment in all of his circumstances. What's more is that even during his slavery and prison time he was given great positions of authority and was well respected. Everyone goes through trials, and some are worse or longer than others, but God is still God. He is sovereign and always with us. We are never alone. Joseph was not alone. The key is to not run from God but trust in him during our lives whether we have good times or bad."

Claire stopped talking and looked over at Alicia, who had tears coming down her face. She was feverishly wiping at them with the back of her hand. Claire's own eyes held tears, but they never fell, and Caleb looked on with tenderness. He prayed so hard for Alicia to feel a need for a personal relationship with God's Son, Jesus Christ. He wanted her to feel the void of being without him. Caleb was beginning to think that she may be experiencing that feeling of longing.

They sat in silence for a while, and then Alicia challenged Claire to a game of checkers. The three of them spent the afternoon laughing and in high spirits, but the question of what was missing in her life still gnawed at the back of Alicia's mind, while Caleb and Claire's thoughts were joyous and prayerful over her desire to learn more about the workings of God.

The beginning of December was now upon them, and it became harder and harder for the children to settle down as Christmas approached. It was finally Saturday, and Alicia was relieved for the day off. Never had the children wore her out more than they had these last few days. Christmas was still three weeks away, yet their excitement was insatiable.

The day was chilly, but the sun was shining and the air

was crisp and clean—a perfect day for a ride. She quickly buttoned up her coat, tied her shawl securely around her head, and put her gloves on. She walked out of her house and was greeted by the brisk air. It was cool but not freezing. Alicia would enjoy her ride.

She made it to the ranch in good time and swiftly mounted the porch stairs and entered through the front door. Claire was reading in the living room and stood to greet her friend.

"It's good to see you today. It's a lovely day. Too bad it's so cold."

Alicia laughed and then told Claire that she thought it would be perfect for a ride. Although Claire loved to ride, she despised cold weather and was quite content to remain indoors through the whole of winter.

"What's Caleb up to?" Alicia inquired. "I was hoping that he would go on a ride with me and let me ride Knight."

"Oh, he's out with several of the other hands to look at some horses in the next county. He won't be back before sundown."

"Oh." Alicia's face revealed her disappointment. "I'll just go and check on Cocoa and see if she's up for a ride."

"Okay. Stop back by for coffee when you're through."

"Sounds good." Alicia quickly moved for the door and made her way to the stables. She noticed how quiet the ranch seemed with most of the men gone, and it felt rather strange. She walked into the stables and up to Cocoa. She fed her some oats and then looked around to see which of the horses the men had taken. Aside from the horses the men took, several were left in the pasture and there were several left in the stables.

As Alicia's eyes roamed the stalls, she was surprised to see Knight in his stall.

"He won't be back before sundown"; Claire's words rang through her mind.

Should I risk it? she wondered. She walked to Knight's stall and began stroking his soft mane. *He's been promising to let me ride Knight for months, but he never has time to go with me on a ride. Why not just take him for a quick ride? Caleb's not here … he'll never know.* Alicia's thoughts finally convinced her to saddle up the stallion. She made quick work of it and soon found herself soaring off on the back of the magnificent horse.

Claire heard the front door open and came from the kitchen, smiling.

"Oh. Hi," she greeted her brother. "I didn't think you were coming back until sundown."

"Who were you expecting?" he said with a grin.

"Alicia, actually," she admitted.

"Alicia's here?"

"Yes. Well, at the moment she's out riding, but she promised to come in for coffee when she gets back."

"Great." Caleb moved toward the stairs. He had to clean himself up before Alicia's arrival.

Alicia rode Knight as though she had not a care in the world. The horse fairly flew over the land, and Alicia expertly maneuvered him as they went along. The ride was smooth, and Alicia discovered that Knight was the most magnificent horse she had ever ridden. He was high-spirited and ran like the wind.

After a while Alicia reluctantly steered the horse back to the stables. The house and stables came into view, and as Alicia rode up she noticed the stable door open. She slowed the horse down. Wasn't everyone gone? Then, Caleb's tall figure appeared in the doorway.

Oh no, she inwardly groaned. *What's he doing back now?* Alicia's heart sank as she realized she had been caught. She felt just like a child getting caught stealing a cookie from the cookie jar. One look at Caleb told her that he was upset, and she was sorely tempted to turn Knight right back around and head for the hills. She slowed Knight to a walk and made her way toward Caleb. She slipped out of the saddle, and Caleb took the reins and led Knight inside. Alicia timidly followed.

He began to strip off the gear and give Knight a thorough brushing. Alicia stood silently by, wondering when Caleb was going to let her have it. She studied his eyes, searching intently for anger, but what she found was worse than that. Disappointment. She could see the disappointment radiating off of Caleb as shame washed over her.

Why did I take Knight so deceitfully? I've let Caleb down, and he has been nothing short of wonderful to me. Will he be able to forgive me? Alicia's thoughts whirled. *Will he ever trust me again?* The thought made alarm slam through her. She had not even thought about trust. *Why would I betray his trust like that?* Alicia was thoroughly disgusted with herself. She shuffled her feet slightly and cleared her throat. Caleb pretended not to notice as he continued to steadily brush Knight.

"Caleb, I'm so sorry." Caleb continued to brush. "I was wrong, and I've betrayed your trust. There is no excuse for what I did. Knight is your horse, and I should not have taken off with him." Alicia stood motionless as she waited.

Caleb turned to fully face her.

"You're right. You should not have taken Knight. I

forgive you, but in the future I would like for you to only ride Cocoa." With that he hung the brush up and left the stables. His words shook her, and she slowly sat down on a bale of hay. She often rode other horses that belonged to Caleb, and now she was forbidden to ride any of them. *I deserve it,* she thought.

She didn't know what to do. If she had been in Caleb's shoes, she knew she would be angry. Trust and forgiveness didn't come easily to Alicia these days, and she wondered how she could be so foolish as to break the Carters' trust. *Well,* she thought, *I'm not just going to sit here and feel sorry for myself. I have to rectify the situation, and there's only one way to do that.* She stood, squared her shoulders, and made her way toward the house.

———

"I wonder what's keeping Alicia?" Claire said to Caleb. He was standing over the fireplace resting one arm against the mantle. Claire could tell that he was troubled, but she didn't know why.

"What's going on?" Claire stood with her hands on her hips, waiting for Caleb to explain.

"She took Knight out to ride," he said simply. There was an unmistakable sadness in his eyes. "She knew how I felt about that, and when I was gone she snuck him out for a ride. What if something had happened out there while she was riding? No one would have known. Neither I nor any of the hands were here."

"Did anything happen to her?"

"Well, no, but that's not the point."

"What is the point, then?"

"Claire, you know I'm concerned for her safety. She didn't even tell anyone she was taking him out. It was deceptive."

"You should have taken her before."

"So you're blaming me for this?"

"No, but she's been asking you for months for a ride on Knight, and you're always too busy. She's not a child anymore. She has proven that she can handle horses as well as any hand you have. She handled Knight all on her own. You should give her some credit for that."

"I told her she could only ride Cocoa in the future."

"Oh, Caleb." Claire sat down in one of the chairs, and Caleb followed suit. "She really should not have taken Knight without permission, but we need to resolve this. She was really beginning to open up to us and share with us."

"I'm going to go find her and talk with her."

Caleb was already leaving his chair as he spoke the words. But before he could even take a step, he heard the front door open. He watched as Alicia walked into the living room and stood right in front of him.

"I just wanted to apologize again, Caleb. What I did was wrong and I'm sorry." She never broke eye contact and watched Caleb's eyes soften.

"My sister's been trying to talk some sense into me. I shouldn't have put off riding with you for so long. You're great with horses, and the sooner I realize that the better," he said with a wink.

Alicia was pleasantly surprised at this admission and threw a grateful glance Claire's way.

"Thanks," she said as she reached to give Caleb a hug. "That means a lot to me. Now what about that coffee?" Claire got up, and the two started for the kitchen.

"Oh, by the way." Alicia and Claire turned at the sound of Caleb's voice. "Feel free to ride any horse anytime." Alicia nodded her thanks and followed Claire into the kitchen.

Chapter 10

Christmas morning dawned bright and early. Alicia felt chilled as she moved to add more wood to her stove that served to heat her small home. She pulled back the curtain to her living room window and gasped. The town was covered in a beautiful blanket of sparkling white snow. The sight was absolutely breathtaking.

After a few moments she turned to put some coffee on and ready herself for the day. She was to spend it with Caleb, Claire, and Mark at the Blue Star. She put on the new festive dress that she made of dark green velvet with lace decorating the cuffs of the sleeves and neckline, and brushed her hair until it shone. She looked back out the window and wondered how deep the snow was. Several inches at least. She dreaded the thought of walking. It would ruin her new dress. But what choice did she have? She put on her coat and was buttoning it up as she heard the jingle of a sleigh.

She opened the door as Caleb climbed down. She smiled, excited over a ride in the sleigh. Caleb rarely got it out. He stood to his full height and looked at her in the doorway. His heart skipped a beat, and then his pulse suddenly started to race at the sight of her in her new dress for Christmas. The green made her auburn hair glow and her green eyes sparkle like emeralds. He stood there for a moment in the cold, and Alicia's eyes began to dance with delight.

"Merry Christmas, Caleb."

"Merry Christmas."

"Come in before you freeze." She laughed as she stepped aside so he could enter.

"I'm so glad that you brought the sleigh. I thought for sure I would ruin my new dress walking to the ranch." Her eyes still sparkled as they held his. He finally found his voice.

"Of course you were not going to walk in this snow and ruin your beautiful new dress."

Alicia's face blushed an attractive shade of pink.

"Stop grinning at me, Caleb Carter." She feigned a rebuke. He smiled all the more, and she found herself enjoying his attention. Most of the men who tried to catch her eye were too bold or coarse, but Caleb was neither of those. He was a gentleman, and Alicia appreciated it.

She finally broke the spell as she began to speak again.

"Let me get my things." She had several neatly wrapped gifts to take. She gathered them and put on her scarf and gloves. Caleb helped her into the sleigh and secured her gifts in the back. He then nestled all of the blankets around her to shield her from the cold as they made their way to the ranch.

⁓

"Merry Christmas!" Claire greeted her as she walked through the front door. Claire looked beautiful in a red dress with a red satin bow tied on the back. Her hair was piled atop her head with little ringlets caressing her face. She always complained about how plain her brown hair was, but Alicia thought it looked beautiful. Today was no exception.

"You look lovely, Claire. Am I to assume that you're expecting someone else?" she said with a wink.

"Only the most handsome man in the whole of

Kentucky. And what about you? That new dress is stunning. Are you trying to impress anyone?" Claire responded smugly.

Alicia crossed her eyes and made a funny face at Claire, making her laugh, and they both made their way to the living room. Alicia looked around and smiled. There was holly hanging from the mantle, and there was a beautiful tree decorating a corner of the room. Presents were spilling out from underneath it, and Caleb had already added Alicia's to the bunch. The blazing fire filled the room with warmth. They were not seated long before a knock was heard at the door. Caleb went to answer it as Claire began to fuss with her hair and the folds of her dress. Alicia chuckled at the flustered mess Claire always became whenever Mark was coming.

Caleb brought Mark into the living room, and the room became full of noisy chatter.

"Merry Christmas, Claire," Mark said as he reached for Claire's hand. He held it briefly and placed a soft kiss on the back of it before letting go. "You look beautiful today."

"Thank you," she responded with a shy smile.

"Merry Christmas, Alicia." Mark walked over to Alicia and gave her a momentary hug before he went to place his gifts under the tree.

The four sat down and began to visit. Alicia was always amazed at how easily the conversation came to them. They were all such good friends and so comfortable with one another. Alicia felt a brief pang of loneliness creep upon her when she realized that this was her first Christmas without her mother. Christmas was her mother's favorite holiday, and she always made the day extra special for the family. She spent hours baking and decorating and making sure everyone was happy. Alicia quickly pushed the feeling aside and tried to concentrate on her friends. She was truly fortunate this day. Here she was on Christmas day surrounded by the people who loved her. But there it was again—the thought that something was missing continued to haunt her. She squashed it down and focused on enjoying the day.

Christmas dinner was extraordinary, and by the early evening the four were once again cozy and settled in the living room. The fire continued to roar, and they all held steaming cups of apple cider. Caleb sat in a comfortable armchair, while Mark and Claire sat on the sofa, and Alicia took a smaller chair. Caleb then cleared his throat, and everyone turned to face him.

"As has become tradition in our home, Claire and I read the Christmas story from the Bible every year before we exchange gifts. We feel that it is extremely important to remain mindful and thankful of the greatest Christmas gift we have ever received, and that is God's Son, Jesus Christ. We're so honored to have you both here with us to share the holiday and this special time." He made brief eye contact with Alicia and Mark before he continued. Caleb reached for the Bible that was beside his chair and began to read the story of Jesus's birth.

Alicia was caught off guard by his little speech and was impressed that they took time to read. She realized with a start that this was the first Christmas where she did not have her own Scripture reading time. It was a tradition in her family too. This year she seemed to completely push the true meaning of the season from her mind. Guilt washed over her as the realization fully dawned on her that she was not embracing what Christmas really means.

Her parents instilled in her the importance of Christ's birth, yet she chose to ignore it this year. *What is the matter with me?* she asked herself. *Does God play a role in my life?* Alicia knew the answer was no. *Shouldn't he play a role in my life? Isn't that what my parents always taught me? Why can't I seem to trust like Joseph did?* Her thoughts were whirling through her mind, and she forced herself to focus as Caleb read.

Afterward they all exchanged presents and had a marvelous time laughing and fully enjoying one another's company. They received very handsome gifts as hugs and thanks were passed all around. Night was swiftly approaching, and the adults were having such a wonderful time that they did not want to pull themselves away. Alicia finally stood from her chair.

"Caleb, I'd like to go see Cocoa. It may sound silly, but I got her a new brush for Christmas. Will you go out there with me?" Alicia blushed slightly when she told of her gift to her horse and was rewarded with one of Caleb's hearty laughs. She rarely went to the stables at night alone anymore after her incident with Dirk. Caleb was only too happy to escort her, and tonight was no exception.

"Of course," he said as he stood up. The two of them bundled up and made their way through the snowy ground to the stables. Alicia tried to keep her dress as clean as possible but decided that she would just give it a good wash later and not worry about it for the moment as they made their way out.

Mark and Claire were left indoors, and they were both glad for a few moments of privacy. He turned to face her and was met with a smile.

"This has been a wonderful Christmas."

"Yes, it has," she agreed.

"There is only one thing that would make it even more wonderful."

Claire's breath caught in her throat as she watched wide-eyed as he descended to one knee in a smooth, easy motion.

"I love you, Claire Carter. Will you marry me?"

"Yes!" She leapt to her feet and was in his arms in an instant. She had never felt such happiness as she did at that moment. He twirled her around once and then set her down to look at her.

"You do realize that you've made me the happiest man in Kentucky, don't you?" he said with a wide smile on his face.

"And I'm the happiest woman," she replied. She felt as if she could squeal in delight. He ran a finger down her smooth cheek and gently brushed a loose curl aside.

"I love you," he whispered right before he gave her a delicate kiss.

The front door opened a moment later, and Caleb and Alicia walked back through. They stopped in the doorway to the living room and looked first to Claire then to Mark. They were fairly glowing.

Alicia burst into a smile just before Claire said excitedly, "We're getting married!" Alicia squealed and ran to embrace Claire. Caleb shook Mark's hand and offered his congratulations. It was the best Christmas gift any of them received. The rest of the evening was spent in excited chatter as the four talked long into the night. It was one of the happiest days Alicia had spent in Darby.

Chapter 11

The year 1870 quickly melted into 1871, and plans for Claire and Mark's upcoming wedding were heavily underway. It was set for late June, and already Claire was overwhelmed with sewing and planning out all of the details. Alicia helped her as much as possible. It was already decided that she was to be Claire's bridesmaid, and one of Mark's brothers was going to be his groomsman.

Mark had two brothers and one sister, and his whole family was expected to arrive from Virginia in early June and stay through the month. Claire had never met them before and was greatly excited about their visit. However, it was now only January, and she and Alicia walked through the general store looking for just the right material for her wedding dress.

"Claire, I really don't think you'll find anything suitable here," Alicia said for the third time. "You should order some nice material from the city."

"You know how expensive that can be. Besides, on occasion they have excellent material that would be perfect." Claire walked toward the counter to speak to Mr. Levi Thomas. He and his wife, Matilda, or Mattie as most people called her, ran the store. They were both fine people and had two daughters, whom Alicia loved to teach.

"Well, well, what's this I hear about you getting married?"

Claire turned to find Mrs. Thorne nailing her to the

ground with her penetrating stare. No one could push Claire's buttons like Mrs. Thorne. She was the town gossip and snippy with everyone. Her husband died young, and her son died in the Civil War. It was very tragic, and the townsfolk blamed her sour attitude on her bitterness. Claire always found it a struggle not to allow the woman to get under her skin. She determined that today she would be just as friendly as possible with the poor old woman.

"Good afternoon, Mrs. Thorne. How are you?"

"Far from well." Mrs. Thorne snorted.

"I'm sorry to hear that. Is there anything I can do for you?"

"Stop trying to butter me up. Are you getting married?" Her eyes were pointed as she stared Claire right into the floor.

"Yes, as a matter of fact, I am. To Mark Brewer."

"Well, good for you." With that she turned and left. Alicia turned questioning eyes to Claire, who only answered with a shrug. Usually Mrs. Thorne left with a biting remark. *Perhaps she was having a good day today*, Claire thought wryly. She turned again and went to the counter.

"Hello, Mr. Thomas."

"Well, Claire Carter, it's good to see you. You too, Miss Barnes. The kids sure do enjoy your teaching." Mr. Thomas was a kind-hearted man who always sported a smile and a friendly word. His family had been in this business for years, and he was quite comfortable and stable.

"Thank you." Alicia acknowledged his compliment.

"Mr. Thomas," Claire leaned across the counter and whispered conspiratorially to him, "Mark Brewer and I are engaged." He let out a whoop as he jumped in the air. Claire and Alicia both laughed.

"Well, it's about time. I was just telling the missus what a fine pair you two make."

"Thank you," Claire beamed. "I was looking for some material for a dress. Do you have anything in that might do?"

"Mattie!" he called toward the open door that led to their living quarters. She came in a flurry into the room. She was short and round and always had her hands busy with something. She was a rather anxious woman but one of the sweetest in town.

"Oh, Claire and Alicia! It's so good to see you." She embraced them both warmly before her husband gave her the news.

"Well, as a matter of fact, I may have just the thing. It only just arrived and is still in my living area waiting to be sorted. Come with me." Claire smiled back smugly at Alicia as they followed Mattie into their living quarters.

"Here we go." Mattie lifted up a beautiful creamy white satin material.

"Oh, it's beautiful," Claire breathed. Alicia raised her brows in surprise. She would never have believed that a general store could carry such fine material. Then Mattie held up a bag full of delicate pearls to match.

"These would be perfect to sew around the cuffs and the neck, or just anywhere you'd like." She beamed with pleasure at the look on Claire's face. She decided to purchase the material but come back for it later. She was so excited that she nearly floated out of the store and back to Alicia's house.

"That material was simply extraordinary," commented Alicia. The two were enjoying cups of coffee by the window and watching tiny snowflakes fall. It would still be another hour or so before Caleb would bring the buggy to get Claire. "I'm amazed that they had such material there."

Claire simply smiled dreamily. Alicia was hesitant to change the subject. The moment was so peaceful, and Claire was so happy. But something was weighing heavily on Alicia's mind, and she felt sure that her friend would not mind if she shared.

"Claire?"

"Yes."

"Do you remember last Sunday's sermon?"

Alicia had Claire's full attention now as she leaned forward slightly.

"Yes. Is there something you'd like to talk about?"

"Well," Alicia began thoughtfully, "do you remember how you and Caleb so easily forgive me of my shortcomings, and everyone else for that matter? For instance, when I snuck a ride on Knight?"

Claire nodded.

"Well, Joseph was that way too."

Pastor Tyler had just finished his messages on the life of Joseph. Alicia found it all very fascinating, but the ending especially held her attention.

"Joseph forgave his brothers. After all those years, he forgave them wholeheartedly. He gave them what they needed, and he cried when he saw his brother Benjamin. He was never bitter or resentful toward them or tried to make them feel bad. He even told them that the Lord planned the bad things to happen to eventually bring him to that place. It was all for the greater good of everyone and Egypt. Joseph understood this." Alicia stopped then and looked at Claire, who had been watching her intently.

"Oh, I don't know." She shrugged. "It's just that, does God always let bad things happen to lead to eventual good things? And how could Joseph still remain so loving and willing to forgive?"

Claire sat and thought and prayed for a moment.

Alicia asked some big questions, and Claire wanted to be sure that her answers were not hasty.

"God brings trials into our lives to teach us dependency upon him and perseverance. He loves his children, and yes, all things happen to bring glory to God. What matters is how we deal with our struggles. We can learn from everything in life if we choose to, and we can let it all bring us closer to God. All things work for his glory, whether they are good or bad. We have to decide how we are going to allow our trials to affect us. Does that make sense?"

"Yes," Alicia slowly responded. "Joseph loved God, and that is what made him able to forgive and to see past the present and give all glory to God. He knew that God would see to his future needs. I just don't understand why I can't." Claire reached across the table to give Alicia's hand a quick squeeze, grateful that God was working on Alicia's heart.

Chapter 12

The month of April was drawing to a close. To Alicia, the winter had simply flown by. Now the weather was warm and beautiful. The children began wading through the creek and fishing again. Alicia had a hard time keeping their attention in the afternoons. The school year would soon be over, though, leaving the children free to help out their parents with the planting, and to fish to their hearts' content.

Alicia was walking through the town and crossing over into the meadow when she stopped in her tracks.

"Good afternoon, Alicia," a deep male voice said from behind her.

She turned to find herself staring into Paul Vickery's chest. "Good afternoon, Paul." She tilted her head back to look up at him.

"Going for a stroll?"

"Yes, the weather is so beautiful that I just had to go for a walk." She smiled as her eyes roamed the open land. The sun was shining, and there was not a cloud in the sky. Everything was beginning to turn green, and the wildflowers were blooming with extraordinary colors. Paul watched her, fully enjoying her presence.

"Would it be too bold to invite myself along?"

She glanced over at him and inwardly shrugged. She still had no romantic feelings toward him, but some company might be nice.

"Sure," she responded. He quickly fell in step with her.

"Are you feeling relief about the end of the school year?" he asked.

"Yes and no. I will miss the children terribly, but some time to rest and relax will be nice too. I have also been meaning to devote more time to my vegetable garden, and that's so hard while I'm teaching." They chatted pleasantly as they walked. Alicia was completely unaware of the things she was doing to Paul's heart. This was the first time that she had ever allowed him to really get near her. If she had realized how hard he was falling for her just then, she would have immediately excused herself. As it was, she remained ignorant of his feelings, and so they continued.

They eventually reached a lake, which was the largest one in the town and the one the children loved to swim in the most. Today the sun was shining down on it, making it sparkle as if challenging everyone to take a swim.

"Miss Barnes!" Alicia heard some children shouting her name and looked toward the lake. She spotted about eight of the children on the bridge and smiled and waved. She and Paul walked over toward them in time to hear the dare.

"Go on, chicken." Logan, a boy of ten who was the big shot with all of the other boys, was challenging Zeke to dive from the bridge into the lake. Zeke was seven and afraid of water but even more afraid of the older boys. More than anything, he wanted to fit in with their crowd. Zeke already had his shirt and shoes off and was poised on the rail. A look of sheer horror was on his face as he looked down at the water below, which seemed to be taunting him.

Paul and Alicia quickened their pace. This looked like the making of trouble. But before they could make it to the bridge, they watched as Zeke took a breath and jumped. They ran the rest of the distance and looked down at the water below.

"Can he swim?" Alicia breathlessly asked Logan.

"Well, I think so, ma'am." Logan began to look contrite over his dare and being caught, and then fearful when Zeke still had not surfaced. Murmurs began to ripple through the children, and before Paul could even blink, Alicia had kicked off her shoes and executed a perfect dive off the bridge into the water. In a matter of seconds, she resurfaced with young Zeke. Paul ran down to the shoreline and helped Alicia get Zeke out of the water.

Paul was horrified when he realized that Zeke was not breathing. He covered Zeke's little mouth with his own and blew in a few breaths of air. Nothing happened. He tried again, and this time Zeke began to spew water out of his mouth and cough fiercely. Relief washed over Paul and Alicia. Paul scooped him up, and they walked swiftly to town, straight to Dr. Clarke's office.

"The water is still freezing, Paul," Alicia quietly told him as they made their way through town. Zeke's lips were blue, and he was shaking uncontrollably. Alicia's own body was chilled to the bone, but at the moment all she could think about was the safety of that little boy.

Alicia sat wrapped in a blanket sipping coffee in Dr. Clarke's office, waiting to hear the report on Zeke. Paul sat with her and finally turned to speak.

"You were amazing today, Alicia. You saved his life." There was pride and awe in Paul's voice as he spoke. He had never met a woman as capable and beautiful as Alicia Barnes.

Alicia looked over at him.

"I love the children," she said simply. "I would do almost anything for them." She turned her anxious eyes back to the door. She had no clue that she just awed Paul again—this time with her humility. His feelings for her seemed to grow by the minute.

Dr. Clarke finally emerged and sat down in front of Alicia.

"How is he?" she asked anxiously.

"He's fine and resting comfortably," he quickly assured them both. "It's a very lucky thing that you happened along when you did, though. If he had been in that water much longer, he could have suffered permanent brain damage."

Alicia gasped as her hand went to her chest.

"You saved his life, Alicia. Now, how are you?" The doctor gave Alicia a quick inspection before he allowed her to leave. She was fine, but he advised that she stay plenty warm for the next day or two. She and Paul were leaving just as Zeke's parents burst through the door. Alicia's heart went out to his mother, whose face was pale and distraught.

"Zeke will be just fine. Miss Barnes saved him from drowning."

They both turned grateful eyes to Alicia, who stood awkwardly. His mother grabbed Alicia and held her as tears poured down her face, and she tried to express their thanks. Alicia spoke soothingly to them, and they hastily went in to see Zeke. Relieved, Alicia turned to walk home.

Paul saw her to her door, but before he left, he again told her that he was proud of her.

"Thank you, Paul. But anyone would have done what I did. I'm not a hero; I was just in the right place at the right time. And I'm very glad you were there. I could not have carried Zeke all the way to town by myself." She smiled and then went inside. Paul's heart thundered in his chest. She told him she was glad that he was there! A surge of joy went through him as he made his way back to the sheriff's office.

Chapter 13

Caleb was walking through town at a slower pace than usual. He had much on his mind. He was just at a meeting of the elders at church but found that it was hard for him to concentrate on anything but Alicia. She had been on his mind for so long. He continued to pray that she would soon come to know Jesus Christ as God's Son. The waiting was so hard for him. He never breathed a word of this to anyone except his sister and Pastor Tyler, but apparently his actions did not go unnoticed by some of his friends at the church.

Steven, a friend since childhood, had discreetly pulled him aside tonight and said in a low voice, "God's timing is perfect. Just trust him." Before Caleb could even respond, Steven was gone and mingling with some of the other elders. Caleb stood in wonder for a moment that his friend could see through him so easily.

Caleb now prayed as he walked down town, thanking God for his wonderful friends who he knew were also praying for the situation. He also prayed to trust the Lord. The waiting was so hard for Caleb, who found that every day he saw Alicia made him care for her even more. Suppressing his feelings for her became harder by the minute. He prayed for strength and God's wisdom. He knew that God was in control, and Caleb surrendered himself to God's will.

Caleb continued to pray as he walked, but something caught the corner of his eye, and he stopped dead in his tracks. He turned and found himself facing the sheriff's office. On the bulletin board right outside his door was a wanted sign. The picture was of four rough and dirty men with scowls and one smaller male with an almost frightened look on his face. Caleb continued to read as the advertisement went on to say that they were criminals at large and wanted for crimes including theft, murder, horse thievery, and train hold-ups. That last crime caught Caleb's eye and he could only stare in disbelief. Could it really be that these are the same five men that killed his parents and Alicia's father? Caleb was certain that the men would forever go unpunished. But apparently the authorities knew who they were; they just had to be caught. Caleb quickly pushed open the door to the sheriff's office and stepped inside.

It was a small, neatly kept building with the cells at the back. Sheriff Tom Holding and his deputy, Paul Vickery, were able-bodied men who kept Darby a safe place to live. Tom was almost forty and slightly balding, but he was a tall, muscular man, and many found him quite intimidating.

Caleb knew that outside of work, he was a teddy bear. He had a wife and four daughters and was one of the kindest men Caleb knew. His deputy was a bit different. Paul Vickery only lived in Darby a little over a year and was quite young and handsome, though he was slightly balding. He grew up in Kansas and was a rugged man. It seemed as though all of the women had eyes for the young deputy. Caleb also knew that Paul had his eye on Alicia, which made him wary.

"Well, Caleb Carter, what can we do for you?" Sheriff Holding greeted him cordially as he walked in.

"Sheriff, there's a wanted sign outside your door for five men."

Sheriff Holding nodded in understanding. Everyone

in town knew the story of Caleb and Claire's parents. The sheriff stood and walked around his desk to stand next to Caleb.

"Your guess is right, son. They are the five men who were responsible for the death of your parents."

"How old is that wanted sign?" Caleb inquired.

"It's only a couple months old, so the likeness in the photo should be accurate."

Caleb's eyes turned stone cold, and the muscles in his jaw twitched. The sheriff continued.

"They were seen just a few miles beyond here in Longville stealing horses. Every town in the state of Kentucky has notices about them. Everyone is watching for them. We are closer than we have ever been to finding these men, Caleb. Justice will be done." The sheriff's eyes were determined. Just then, sudden realization jolted through Caleb.

"You said they've been stealing horses lately?" Caleb felt the hair stand up on the back of his neck.

"Yep, but it is unlikely they'll try and steal again until they are in another state. Every horse ranch and cattle owner in Kentucky is likely to be notified by now. Why, Vickery was just about to go out to your ranch to warn you to keep an eye out." Caleb looked over at Vickery, who looked rather defeated. Caleb knew exactly why Vickery wanted to come to the ranch. He wanted to catch a glimpse of Alicia.

Caleb balled up his fists but left them discreetly by his side as anger began to swell in him. Not anger toward Vickery, but anger over the five men who were still destroying lives and stealing possessions that people worked so hard for. Caleb waited a moment before he spoke.

"Thanks, Sheriff. I'll alert my men and keep an eye out." His voice was tight. He bid the two gentlemen good day and left for home, except this time he was covering the distance much more quickly.

———

Sheriff Holding hoped beyond hope that the men would be caught soon and not stir up any trouble in his town. The wanted poster had been up a month, and all remained quiet. The sheriff was bent over his desk working on paperwork, and his deputy was cleaning rifles when the shots were heard. They both grabbed weapons and bolted out the door. Once outside, they were not exactly sure where the shots came from. Then four masked men ran out of the bank and jumped on horses that a fifth man had ready. One of the men was dragging a woman with him. He threw her over his horse and rode off with the other men.

Holding ran for the bank, while Vickery moved for his horse. In the blink of an eye, Vickery was on his horse and riding hard in an effort to catch up.

Caleb almost knocked Sheriff Holding down as he tried to run out the door just as the sheriff entered. Holding caught his arm, and Caleb was breathless as he shouted, "They took her!" Holding watched Caleb jump on Midnight and ride hard in the direction Vickery went.

Holding's eyes scanned over the bank. Scared customers lined the wall. There were many women shaking and trying to soothe their crying children. Suddenly, Holding saw him. Mark Brewer was shot. Holding ran to him and shouted for someone to get the doctor. Mark was losing blood at an alarming rate from a wound in his side. Holding then noticed Claire sitting by him with tears flowing. She was whispering words of comfort and encouragement to the man she loved as she watched him fight for his life.

Dr. Clarke came rushing in, and within minutes, the other men helped him move Mark to Dr. Clarke's office.

Claire was forced to sit in the waiting room and endure the agony of waiting for news. Sheriff Holding sat next to her and placed a hand on her shoulder.

"He's in good hands, Claire. Dr. Clarke is one of the best, and Mark has God watching over him." The tenderness in Holding's voice was too much for Claire. She burst into tears. The sheriff was almost sorry he had said anything. But he had to find out what happened. "Claire, you must try to explain to me what happened. Please."

Claire's body shook as she tried to still the tears long enough to explain.

"It all happened so fast. Caleb, Alicia, and I went to take care of some business, and all of a sudden four men burst in with guns. They made us all line the walls. One of the men grabbed Alicia and held her at gunpoint and ordered Mark to fill up their bags with money. After Mark filled up one bag and was working on another, he tried to grab the gun that was hidden under the counter. He wasn't fast enough, and the man shot him." Claire's sobs were so uncontrollable at this point that Holding could barely understand her. She had severe hiccups as she continued.

"After the shot, Mark fell. I couldn't do anything. I had to just stand there and watch!" She wrung her hands helplessly. She looked to the sheriff, whose eyes were filled with compassion. "The man finished filling up the bags himself and ran. Oh no!" Reality hit Claire hard as she grasped the sheriff's arm. "They took Alicia with them!"

Sheriff Holding stood so quickly that he almost knocked his chair over. He ran for the door. "Vickery and Caleb have already started after them. Thank you,

Claire!" He mounted his horse and took off in the same direction the others had left only ten minutes earlier.

———

Alicia was tossed and jerked on the horse that ran through the woods. The path was not very clear, and the horse jostled her painfully. She was unable to steady herself because she was wedged in between her assailant and the saddle. His filthy arms were around her, and she could smell the foulness of his breath as she rode. She felt herself becoming nauseous. *No*, she told herself firmly, *you have to keep your wits about you to get out of this alive.* Her mind was reeling as she tried to watch and make mental notes of where they were. But the horses were moving so fast that she could not tell. All she could see was the blur of trees as they went by. She then remembered that she was wearing her favorite ring and the bracelet her mother had given her. She slid the ring off and dropped it. No one noticed it as it fell just off the path.

They kept riding and in a matter of minutes were out of the woods, and the horses were winding their way through the hills they had just entered. The hills were large enough that they could conceal large groups of men, and there were various boulders all around. She knew there must be caves in these hills. To the left the woods continued, and to the right the hills stretched out and eventually opened into a field. Alicia felt desperate as the horses slowed deep into the hills behind a large boulder. She knew her chances of being found were slim. She had already dropped her ring and bracelet as guides, but she knew she needed more. She did not know what to do. Fear began to crowd in on her, and the next thing she knew darkness overcame her.

Caleb was riding hard through the forest, trying to catch up. He pushed Midnight, and his stallion instincts began to kick in as he ran like a wild, free horse. Caleb saw someone just ahead and realized it was Vickery. He stopped Midnight just before they all collided. Vickery was off his horse and reaching to pick something up.

"What is it, Vickery?" Caleb said between breaths.

"It's a ring." Vickery held it up for Caleb to see.

"It's Alicia's!" Caleb nearly shouted.

Anger seethed through Caleb as they rode in search of Alicia. These men had already killed Alicia's father and Caleb's own parents. Caleb's jaw was locked in determination. They were not going to kill Alicia too.

Vickery's own thoughts were running wild. While Caleb cared only for the safety of Alicia, Vickery knew that he had to get those men too. They were dangerous criminals. How would they get Alicia out safely? His mind staggered at the thought of any harm coming to Alicia. He knew they needed more men, but there was no time to get them. Every minute was crucial.

They rode on and stopped when they made it out of the forest. They looked around as panic began to squeeze around Caleb's heart. He knew they had taken her into the hills. These men could watch and shoot at him and Vickery before they even started their search. The very thought that they had Alicia up there and he could not reach her knocked all of the breath out of him.

"Look!" Vickery shouted. He was over by the edge of the forest. He held up a delicate silver bracelet with the initials *AB* inscribed on the casing.

"It's the bracelet Alicia's mother gave her on her

eighteenth birthday." Just then Sheriff Holding rode up to them and jumped off his horse.

"What's going on?"

"They've taken Alicia up into the hills. She's left her bracelet and ring along the path as clues. We know they have brought her here." Vickery's eyes were cold as steel as he looked toward the hills. The sheriff stopped short. She could be anywhere, and they could all easily be shot before they could even take a stand.

"Sheriff, I need to go home and get Rebel. He can help us find her," Caleb suggested. Caleb's German shepherd was not only an excellent guard dog for the ranch but also had the best nose in the county. Rebel had proven his ability to track anyone or anything time and again.

"All right, that's good. Vickery, we need to go back to town and gather more men. We have to take these kidnappers by surprise." Sheriff Holding quickly jumped into the saddle of his horse.

"Let's go." The three men rode off, Caleb heading home and the sheriff and his deputy toward town. There was no time to lose.

Chapter 14

Alicia slowly opened her eyes. Her head was pounding, and she looked around in bewilderment. *Where am I?* Panic squeezed her heart as she remembered what happened. Her arms ached terribly, and as she tried to move them, something chafed her wrists. She was tied up. She stopped moving and slid her eyes shut as she heard men talking. They were sitting a few feet away from her and were huddled close together.

"What are we gonna do, Buck?" she heard a man gruffly ask. "We ain't never kidnapped people before. And a woman to boot. What are we gonna do with her?"

"I don't know," Buck stiffly replied. "What choice did we have? We had to take her if we wanted to get out of that bank alive."

"I don't want to kill her." Someone in the bunch spoke up timidly.

"Oh, and what do you think we should do with her, Rigby?" a fourth man snarled. "Let you run off and marry her and live happily ever after?" The four men began to hoot over that thought at Rigby's expense. Alicia heard someone's feet shuffle and lay very still.

"Pop, we shouldn't have taken her. Let's just leave her here and go. She'll be found." Rigby addressed Buck. He seemed to be the ringleader of the gang.

"No," Buck responded slowly. "She's comin' with us. She may be of some use to us later on. Once we get a safe distance away, we'll put a ransom out for her." The men snorted and chuckled.

Alicia heard the whole exchange, and fear coursed through her body. What exactly did he mean? What did they plan to do with her? And what would happen if no one answered the ransom? She shivered slightly and soon realized her mistake. The men turned suddenly, and Buck already had his gun out. Alicia was shocked over how quick his draw was. The man slowly stood and began to walk toward her. Alicia trembled as she watched. Even though he could not have been any taller than Caleb, he seemed like a giant to Alicia. He was a rough-looking man with unkempt hair and two missing teeth. He stopped right in front of Alicia and bent until he was eye level with her and only inches away from her face.

"I should be thankin' ya, missy," he snarled as his foulness invaded Alicia's nostrils. "You made fer us an easy escape from that bank with loads of money to boot." Alicia cringed and held her breath as he spoke. The other men laughed cruelly and all made their way to stand around her. They looked just as coarse and mean as the first man except for one, whom Alicia noticed was considerably younger and had a look of misery on his face.

"Allow me to introduce us all, missy. My name is Buck, and these here are my boys, George, Bob, Cotton, and Rigby. Boys, this is Miss—" Buck stopped for a moment. "Why," he said overly polite, "I'm afraid I don't know your name, missy."

Alicia was frozen. A mixture of fear and anger seared through her. She was angry that these men had so much control over her that she was scared out of her mind. She was angry that they had destroyed so many lives, including her own already. She knew these were the same five men who held up the train and killed her father and the Carters' parents. Despite the fear that was so strong in her that she wanted to faint again, she promised herself to live through this and be brave. She quickly found that being brave was easier said than done.

"What's your name, lass?" Buck shouted the command this time and watched in satisfaction as Alicia shivered.

"Alicia Barnes," she said quietly but firmly.

"Welcome, Miss Alicia Barnes," Buck said sarcastically as he began to laugh. The others joined in with him, and Alicia merely sat where she was, bound and looked helplessly at the men, hoping with all of her might that someone was searching for her right now. She continued to look around, and she noticed that the only man who wasn't laughing was young Rigby.

Midnight came up on the ranch fast, and Caleb quickly lowered himself out of the saddle. The ranch hands ran up to him, curious as to what was going on. Caleb shouted for them to get Midnight ready to take out again and signaled John into the house.

"John, something terrible has happened." Caleb slowed down enough to explain what was going on to his foreman as the men walked into the ranch house together. "The five men robbed the bank and shot Mark. Claire is with him now at Doc Clarke's. If she's not back by sundown, I want you to send Robby for her, and if she wants to stay at Doc's, tell him to stay with her until morning." Robby was one of the Carter's most loyal ranch hands. John nodded in understanding and waited, knowing there was more to the story.

"They took Alicia," Caleb said finally in a quiet voice. "They held her at gunpoint in the bank, John, and then they took her." Caleb slammed his fist into the wooden kitchen table. "I had to just watch. If I had tried to move, they would have shot her. They've taken her up in the hills, and I'm going after her. I'm taking Rebel with me. I don't know when I'll be back, but you're in charge until I do."

John nodded. "Don't worry, boss. You'll get her back." His voice held more confidence than he felt. He watched the muscles in Caleb's jaw lock.

"Yes," he said strongly, "I will get her back even if I have to give my own life to do it." There was a brief pause and then Caleb said, "Take care of the ranch and Claire while I'm gone. Make sure she stays safe and that she's okay." With that, Caleb dashed up the stairs to get his rifle and his knife. He was already wearing his pistol.

When he came back down, John handed him a large sack of food to put in his saddlebag.

"Thanks," Caleb said hurriedly. He whistled for Rebel. He tried to calm his beating heart that threatened to pound out of his chest. The dog's hair went up. He always knew when something was wrong.

In quiet tones, Caleb kneeled and spoke to his faithful dog, "Rebel, we have got a big job ahead of us. They have taken Alicia, and we have to find her. We have to be quiet and careful and not let anything happen to her. I don't think I could take it if anything happened to her, boy." Caleb shuddered on those last words; then he raised his chin and looked his dog straight in the eye. While he was upstairs, he grabbed one of Alicia's handkerchiefs that she left in Claire's room. He now held it to his dog's nose and allowed Rebel to fully make note of the scent.

"Find her, boy!" Caleb commanded with steel lining his voice. He jumped on Midnight, and, with Rebel running alongside, flew off in search of Alicia and her captors.

Chapter 15

Claire watched Mark vigilantly all that day. Dr. Clarke was able to remove the bullet, and Claire finally began to relax as she saw Mark resting comfortably. The entire afternoon had been difficult and burdensome. After Mark was brought in, Dr. Clarke had to use some chloroform to make sure Mark would stay asleep for the operation. The bullet was lodged in his back and had to be removed immediately. It was one of the most delicate and painstaking surgeries Dr. Clarke ever encountered. It was hours before the surgery was over and Claire could see him. The wait to her seemed like an eternity. There was no guarantee at that point whether or not Mark would make it out alive.

Dr. Clarke could see where the bullet entered his side, but finding it was a different story altogether. Once in surgery, Dr. Clarke could see that the bullet entered through his side and bounced off his spinal column. Beads of perspiration dotted his brow as he delicately removed the bullet, being careful not to add any further damage to his spinal cord.

Claire now leaned over her sleeping fiancé and remembered Dr. Clarke's words as he came out of surgery.

"I successfully removed the bullet, but let me be honest with you. It's pretty bad, Claire. The bullet hit his spinal cord, and I had to remove it. There was damage, but we will not know how severe until he wakes up. He could have nerve damage, or he could be paralyzed. Or even a combination. We just won't know for a while." Dr. Clarke washed his hands and then collapsed into a chair. Never had a surgery been so physically, emotionally, and mentally demanding for him.

Claire sat in a state of shock. Her eyes were wide and round as she listened. She slowly stood and made her way to the door. She turned and gave her beloved one last look before she left the room.

As she walked out of his room, Dr. Clarke met her in the hallway and addressed her. "Claire, he won't wake up for a while now, and when he does, it is imperative that he remain perfectly still. You'll need your strength for when he wakes up. Why don't you go rest and get some food? He will need you to be strong later," Dr. Clarke gently advised Claire, whose eyes were brimming with tears. She nodded and swallowed hard as she made her way out of the doctor's office. But instead of heading for home, she began walking toward the church.

The small white church building stood facing the town. As she slowly made her way toward it, the church bell suddenly starting ringing in loud, clear tones. The bell was put up five years ago for school and church use. It was a real town effort to see the establishment of the bell. Teachers used it to summon children, and it was always heard on Sunday morning to let everyone know that church was starting. But it was also used on rare occasions when an emergency arose and the townspeople needed to be gathered immediately. Claire quickened her pace as the other townsfolk began to rush toward the church. Apparently all had heard the news of the bank and were anxious to hear what was going on now.

Sheriff Holding and Deputy Vickery were standing by the church, waiting for everyone to arrive. Their faces were grave, and everyone stood in reverent silence until all were present.

"Everyone," Sheriff Holding's loud voice boomed over the crowd as he began, "there was a hold-up at the bank this afternoon. I think we all are aware that the five notorious criminals who held up that train from Texas three years ago are in this area. They robbed the bank and shot Mark Brewer. They have also kidnapped our schoolteacher, Alicia Barnes." Holding heard gasps resound through the crowd. He waited as mothers began to take their children inside so they would not hear the rest of the story. The men watched him, some with eyes wide in astonishment and others whose looks were penetrating with anger. The men of Darby felt a strong sense of pride for their land and were willing to protect it and all of its members with their lives if necessary.

"Men," Holding continued seriously, "we need your help. They have taken Alicia into the hills, where it will be almost impossible to find her without being shot at first. We will split into groups and search different areas of the hills. We will meet back at the woods every few hours to check on each other's progress. We have to be careful, men. Alicia's life is in grave danger." Holding eyed each of the men hard to drive his point home. His look was met with nods and determined faces.

The sheriff was satisfied that these men would take every precaution to make sure Alicia would not be harmed. He and Vickery quickly teamed the men off, but dusk was coming in fast. It would be foolhardy to search in the dark. They were all told to meet back at the church at sunrise ready to go out.

As the men began to disperse, Holding saw Claire standing a few feet away. His heart was ready to melt at how young and forlorn she looked. Her shoulders sagged with a burden she was much too young to have to bear. Her eyes were puffy and distant as she watched the exchange. The sheriff made his way over to her and Vickery joined him.

"Claire," Holding said softly as he put his arm around her, "it will be all right. We will get Alicia back." Claire looked down at her shoes and nodded slightly.

"How is Mark?" he gently asked.

"The doctor does not know yet." Her voice was barely audible. "The bullet bounced off of his spine, and he may have suffered severe permanent damage." Tears streamed down her face, and she muffled the sobs that were rising from her throat. Holding and Vickery exchanged a look. These criminals would stop at nothing to get what they wanted. The thought sent shivers up and down Vickery's spine. More than anything, he wanted to find Alicia right now and prevent her from having to spend the night in the hills with those men. But he knew that he would be of better use to her in the daylight. He balled his fists up in anger.

"Excuse me, please," Claire suddenly spoke. "I'm going into the church for a bit." Sheriff Holding moved to let her pass, and she walked quietly into the church building. Holding and Vickery slowly made their way back to the sheriff's office, both extremely anxious for morning to come.

Claire sank into the front pew and allowed herself to sob freely. She never felt so helpless in her life. The sobs racked her body as she began to pour out her thoughts to God.

"Mark has been hurt so badly, Father," she prayed through her tears. "He loves you, and I know you love him. Father, I want to see him healed more than anything.

Please heal him and give him the extra strength he needs to pull through this." Claire stopped for a moment as she began to think about Caleb. She realized that she had not seen him since the robbery. "Lord," she continued, "please be with Alicia. Please do not let any harm come to her and keep my brother safe as he tries to rescue her. Be with all of the men in town." She continued to pray until she had given everything up to the Lord. She put everything in his hands, and after all of her tears were spent, she slowly rose to go back to the ranch and eat and sleep as Dr. Clarke suggested.

As she was leaving, she felt as if the huge burden had been lifted off her shoulders. She knew there were still hard and uncertain times ahead, but she also knew that it was all in God's hands and that he would take care of them. She knew that no matter what kind of damage Mark suffered, she would stay by him, love him, and help him. Her chin rose slightly with determination as she walked out of the church.

"Claire," a male voice called. Claire jumped nearly a foot off the ground as she turned to see who it was.

"It's just Robby. I didn't mean to scare you." He smiled at her as she began to calm down. She almost slapped him on the arm for startling her like that, but his mischievous smile made her stop and smile herself.

"What are you doing here?"

"John sent me. He said Caleb wanted me to come to town and watch over you tonight. He didn't know if you'd be staying at Doc's or not."

"Oh. Well, that was nice of you to come, Robby. Dr. Clarke suggested that I go home for the night and eat and sleep because the next few days will be rough." Claire's eyes misted over slightly but only for a moment. Robby brought Ginger, and she resolutely mounted her horse, and she and Robby began to fill each other in as they headed back for the ranch.

Chapter 16

Alicia woke with a start. Her hands remained bound behind her, and she had finally drifted into a restless sleep. She looked around her and strained to see. Everything was completely dark, and she knew it was the middle of the night. Her eyes finally began to grow accustomed to the darkness, and she could see the five men swiftly packing their gear. One of the older men—Cotton, if she was remembering correctly—came and roughly untied her and grabbed her forearm in a tight grip. Suddenly, Alicia felt a blade press up against her back.

"If you even think of screamin'," he growled in her ear, "or tryin' to get away, yer gonna be met with this." He pressed the knife slightly into her to make his point and felt her shudder. She nodded.

"Cotton," Buck bellowed as loud as a whisper would allow, "that'll do. She's ridin' with Rigby. He's smaller and lighter, and it will be easier on the horse."

Alicia's chest heaved in relief to not be riding with Cotton, who at the moment smelled distinctly of liquor. Cotton roughly maneuvered her over to Rigby and his horse and gave her a final push toward him. Rigby caught her as she almost hit the ground. He glared at his brother, but for only a moment. Cotton returned the look with an even darker one, and Rigby lowered his eyes in intimidation. During this exchange, Alicia quickly tore off the last piece of jewelry she was wearing—a simple silver chain—and let it drop from her fingers.

Rigby faced her then and helped her onto his horse and took his place behind her. The five horses went galloping off into the night. Alicia was disoriented as to where they were before, but now she was completely clueless. She tried to take it all in, but it was nearly impossible in the dark. At one point, they stopped to take a break by a large stream and debated over whether or not it was safe to cross. Alicia took advantage of the moment to see herself to the bushes to take care of personal needs. Rigby stood close by with his back to her, and Alicia quickly tore off a piece of her petticoat and left it on the ground. The men decided to cross, and so on she rode helplessly; they did not stop again until morning.

Caleb's heart was pounding as he knew that he was close on their trail. Rebel very easily picked up on Alicia's scent and was leading Caleb deep into the hills. They stopped just behind a large boulder and looked down. Anger and frustration rose up in Caleb. He could tell the men had been there. From the looks of things, they had been there for quite a while before they set off again. Caleb was fighting the panic that was squeezing his heart. *Where could they have taken her in the night?* Fear rose up in him, and he pushed the awful thoughts away. Alicia needed him to stay calm and think clearly.

He quietly made his way to the camp and looked around. He then noticed Rebel sniffing the ground and let out a low growl. Caleb came and stooped down to where Rebel smelled. At first he didn't see anything and had to search for a moment. Then he saw it. A glimmer of silver. He lifted it from the ground and realized that it was Alicia's necklace. Another clue! And now at least

Caleb knew that she was still alive. Caleb inwardly praised her genius under such frightening pressure.

Caleb turned to Rebel and allowed him to smell the necklace and urged him to keep searching. After a couple hours, Rebel led Caleb out of the hills and into the forest on the other side. *How far have they taken her?* He wondered as once again fear began to overcome his senses. He swung off Midnight and stood for a time, silently praying for Alicia's safety and for her rescue. He looked around for a while but could see nothing out of the ordinary.

He got back on Midnight and once again followed his faithful dog. It seemed like an endless ride before Rebel stopped. Caleb's heart sank. They were at a large stream. The current was rather rough, and Caleb wondered if they even dared to cross it. But he knew with a look at Rebel that they had, and the trail was lost. Caleb walked around for a moment then looked down and noticed fresh horse hoof tracks. *They must have crossed here last night!* At least he knew he was in the right direction. It wasn't much, but every little bit helped.

Rebel continued to walk around the area when Caleb noticed that he was behaving as he did at the camp where he found the necklace. He sniffed intently and then let out a low growl. Caleb rushed over and bent down. A piece of white petticoat was lying on the ground. Caleb knew it had to be from Alicia, and once again silently thanked God that she was still alive.

"Good job, boy." Caleb patted Rebel's head in appreciation and admiration. Caleb would still be searching in the hills if it had not been for Rebel. *The hills!* The other men from town were certain to be scouring them all day. Caleb realized that they would be of no help to Alicia there and that they stood a better chance of getting her back if there were more than just he who knew where to continue to search. He jumped into the saddle and galloped toward the hills with Rebel at his side to inform the men what he discovered.

Sheriff Holding, his deputy, and more than half of the men in the town had been searching through the hills for hours. They covered almost the entire area. Sheriff Holding began to suspect that she might have been moved. He was about to voice as much to Vickery when Caleb rode into view from the opposite direction with Rebel at his side. The horse had barely stopped when Caleb swung out of the saddle and practically ran up to Holding.

"They moved her in the night," he managed between breaths.

"I suspected as much." Holding was grim. Caleb took a few deep breaths before he continued. All the men gathered around.

"Rebel and I went in the night and found their camp. They were already gone, but I found this." Caleb opened his hand to reveal her silver necklace. "It's Alicia's. They took her through the forest, and it eventually leads to a rather large stream. They crossed there. There were fresh horse prints to prove it, and Rebel lost her trail. But he did find this." Caleb opened his other hand to reveal her torn piece of petticoat.

"She's leaving a trail for us." Vickery stated the obvious. His face went pale when Caleb began, but now he was regaining some color.

Sheriff Holding and the men had been prepared for this. They left with enough food and supplies to last them for days. Holding knew that they could not keep backtracking to town.

"Caleb," he said loudly and firmly so that all would hear, "take us to the stream. We'll have to cross and pray that we find more clues from her."

———

Alicia was on the verge of hysterics. It had been almost a week since she was kidnapped, and she had no idea where she was. Her petticoat was a torn mess. She left pieces everywhere they stopped. Rigby eyed her once, and she knew she had been caught in the act. He watched as her face blanched in fear. He simply turned and pretended not to see a thing.

Now it seemed as if they had stopped for a while, at least for a few days, and Alicia was terrified. Where were they? What were they going to do? Every night she heard their muffled voices discussing what was to be done with her. None of them seemed too keen to have a woman under foot, or that they kidnapped her in the first place. But it seemed as though now that she was here, they were stuck with her. Alicia didn't even know if they had sent a ransom demand yet or not. Alicia hoped every day that they would release her and just be on their way. They could leave her in the middle of nowhere for all she cared; she just wanted to be free.

They all pitched tents, which was something they had never done before. Alicia had the feeling they may be scoping out a new town to see where they could make a move. Alicia was grateful to have a tent to herself, although it was guarded at all hours of the day. Initially, the men all took turns watching her, but they seemed bored with the task. They were restless and ready for the rush that breaking laws brings. Alicia was repulsed by their despicable behavior. She found it impossible to understand why they would want to be criminals.

Eventually, Buck handed over the job of guarding Alicia to Rigby. His other sons were rough and liked to tease and mess with Alicia, which made Buck nervous about her caving in and making a scene. She was a bit more comfortable with Rigby, and Rigby hated being a criminal anyway. Buck saw this as the best solution.

Alicia woke up one morning a little after a week since she had been taken and felt a terrible ache from deep within her. She felt so lost and helpless under the domination of these men. They completely destroyed her world once, and now they were trying to destroy it again. Alicia felt a surge of desperation well up inside of her, and she threw herself on the blankets in her tent and wept. The tears were coming so fast and so strong that her entire body shook and the tent shook with her. Her sobs were loud and heart wrenching.

Rigby sat outside in misery. His father and brothers had taken off toward the town, and he alone knew the full emotional beating this was taking on the girl. He watched the tent shake and listened as her sobs rang out, and his heart tore in two for her. *Surely there must be something I can do,* he thought. He just wasn't sure what.

His mother died giving birth to him, and soon after his father turned to drinking to drown out his grief. He enlisted the whole family in outlawing, and now they were all wanted criminals. Rigby wanted nothing to do with this life, but he was stuck now. What's more, he was only sixteen years old. He had lost his childhood, so what kind of a future could he possibly have? His own sobs caught in his throat as he swallowed them down and looked back toward the tent.

The shaking stopped, and Alicia was silent. Rigby

quietly opened the flap that hung loose as her door and poked his head in. He took one look at Alicia all crumpled on the floor with her red, tear-stained face and felt fury rise up in him against his father and brothers. Never had he been more ashamed than he had this last week.

"Is there anything I can do fer ya, miss?" His voice sounded as helpless as he felt.

Alicia wanted to throw something at him. *What kind of a question is that? Let me go!* She wanted to scream at him.

Instead, Alicia finally asked the question that had haunted her since the day they took her, "Rigby, did you know that you and your family killed my father?"

Rigby's eyes grew round as he stared at her in horror. "No, miss," he answered just above a whisper.

"About three years ago your family robbed a train." She watched his face carefully and knew he knew what she was referring to. "My father was on that train and never made it off. My best friends' parents were on that train too, Rigby. Your family has shattered so many lives."

"I'm so sorry, miss." Rigby hung his head in shame. Alicia watched him for a moment then remembered his question, and she had an idea. For the last few days, she had begun to talk to God. She found herself wanting to believe that he was watching over her.

"Rigby," she said quietly, "I want to leave, but you already know that. Since you are not going to help me with that, I would like to ask for a Bible."

Stunned, Rigby lifted up his head to look at her. He did not expect her to want a Bible. He closed the flap and went to his own tent. Alicia slowly emerged, and Rigby came out to find her sitting on a stone watching his tent. He tentatively approached and then thrust out his hand. In it was a small, leather-bound Bible.

"It was my ma's," he said as if to answer the confused

look on her face. "Look, I don't like what my pa and brothers done. We spent our whole lives like this, and I hate it. I want out, but Pop keeps remindin' me that I'm a wanted criminal. I don't know what to do. I'm sorry we done wrong by you, miss." He quickly stood and went back into his tent.

Alicia was so thankful that he was with her and not one of the other brothers. They never let her out of her tent except to attend to personal needs, and they would never have left her alone and gone to their own tent. Alicia's expression remained emotionless during Rigby's speech, but she knew he was sincere. His actions spoke volumes. He was so unlike his brothers. Every night he would sneak extra food to her because what Buck gave her was barely enough to survive on. She was rapidly losing weight and growing weak.

She now turned her eyes toward heaven and prayed.

"God, I don't know if you're there, or if you want to hear from me, but please help me. Please send someone for me." She stopped then and opened the Bible Rigby gave her. She spent the remainder of the afternoon reading. She read through the story of Joseph in Genesis and tried to remind herself of what Pastor Tyler and Claire and Caleb tried to teach her. In the midst of all of the hard times in Joseph's life where it seemed as though there was no hope, Joseph trusted in the Lord. He stayed strong in his faith and was rewarded.

She then flipped over to the book of Romans. That was always one of her father's favorite books in the Bible. As she started reading through Romans, her eyes landed on a passage in chapter five, verses three through eight. She silently began to read to herself.

And not only so, but we glory in tribulation also: knowing that tribulation worketh patience; and patience, experience; and experience, hope. And hope maketh not ashamed; because the love of God is shed abroad in our hearts by the Holy Ghost which is given unto us. For when we were yet without strength, in due time Christ died for the ungodly. For scarcely for a righteous man will one die; yet peradventure for a good man some would even dare to die. But God commendeth his love toward us, in that, while we were yet sinners, Christ died for us.

Alicia slowly read the words over to herself again and felt tears sting the back of her eyes. This passage was telling her to rejoice in her sufferings. Not only that but that God uses the suffering to help people grow. He used the sufferings in Joseph's life to develop his character and help him to become a good leader. Christ himself died for all men while they were still sinners—just like Alicia. Alicia realized with a start that while she turned her back on God, he didn't turn his back on her. Understanding was finally beginning to dawn on Alicia. She closed the precious Bible in her hand and went back into her own tent. She was scared and uncertain about the future.

But one thing was becoming clear: God was with her.

Chapter 17

Claire spent nearly every waking moment with Mark. She stayed by his side, talking to him, helping the doctor clean his wound and change his bandages, reading Scripture to him, and praying over him. She even began taking her meals in the sickroom because she could not bear to be away from him. Robby was ever faithful to stay close by to monitor her safety and well-being. On two occasions, she was so tired that her hands trembled just lifting her spoon, and Robby gently made her come back to the ranch for a good night's sleep.

It was a little over a week now, but to Claire the days blurred together. Every day seemed to stretch a little longer, and she became more and more aware that she had no news of her brother or Alicia. She began to feel fear squeeze at her heart, and her mind would think the worst until it felt like everything was suffocating her, and she had to force the thoughts away and focus solely on Mark. He needed her now. He had not woken yet. The doctor remained positive, but Claire began to fear more with each passing day.

Claire sat in a chair by the bed, barely awake herself, when she heard a faint rustling sound. She quickly jumped out of her chair and leaned over Mark. He stirred slightly, and Claire felt a surge of renewed hope. She anxiously watched him as he tried to open his eyes. They were slowly fluttering and finally opened a crack. Claire could have jumped and screamed for joy, but Mark's frail state kept her in check. The wound was still fresh and could begin to bleed again.

Mark looked around with a bewildered look in his eyes, finally seeing Claire beside him. She smiled down sweetly at him.

"Welcome back, sweetheart." She carefully took hold of his hand and entwined their fingers together.

"The bank," Mark managed to get out.

"It's all over. You are going to be fine." Tears shone in her eyes as she talked. "Just rest now, my love." His eyelids slid shut, and within moments he was sleeping deeply again. Claire closed her eyes too, and with her hand still in Mark's, she lifted a prayer of thanks to her heavenly Father.

Twelve hours later, Mark stirred again. Claire was relieved. She was getting worried because Mark had not eaten in over a week. He was so weak, and she knew he simply had to stay awake until she got some nourishment in him. He slowly opened his eyes to see Claire leaning over him just as she had earlier in the morning.

"Hello, sweetheart." She smiled down at him. He found the strength to smile faintly back at her.

"How are you feeling?"

He groaned in response.

"Well, before you go back to sleep, we have to get some food in you."

"How many days?" he said softly.

"Nine. You've been asleep for nine days. You were hurt pretty badly, but you will be better now." She brought a steamy cup of broth over to him.

"Here now," she said soothingly. "This will help you gain some strength back." She reached to help him sit up better, and as she bent over him, she stopped and stared at him, completely terrified with what she saw. His eyes held horror and panic. Every muscle in his face was tightened, and he was turning deathly pale.

"*Doctor!*" Claire screamed. "What's wrong, Mark?" She began to gently shake him as her own fear grew. "Honey, what's wrong?"

The doctor rushed in and ran to his side. He tried to calm Mark and make him slow down his breathing because he was on the verge of hyperventilating. Suddenly Mark's arms, chest, and head began flying in all directions, and the doctor was sure he was going into convulsions. Mark grasped the front of the doctor's shirt with both hands and looked at him with wild eyes.

"My legs!" he shouted as loud as he could in his condition. "I can't feel my legs!"

———

For thou, O God, hast proved us: thou hast tried us, as silver is tried. Thou broughtest us into the net; thou laidst affliction upon our loins. Thou hast caused men to ride over our heads; we went through fire and through water: but thou broughtest us out into a wealthy place.[2]

Alicia silently read these words from Psalm 66 as she sat outside the camp with Rigby.

"Hmm ... that's interesting," she murmured.

Rigby turned from his whittling to look at her.

"What is it, miss?" Rigby frequently asked Alicia to share what she was reading. At first Alicia found the entire situation very strange. Here she was, being held captive and reading from the Bible. At home she did not even pick her own Bible up except for church. Could this be why she was kidnapped in the first place? Had she become so stubborn that nothing short of criminals kidnapping her would open her eyes to the truth of God's Word and his perfect will for her life?

What is more, she was sharing what she read with one of her captors. Rigby seemed captivated with the Scriptures. He confessed to her that he did not believe that God would want him after all of the horrible crimes he was associated with. Alicia felt sure that was not true, but she did not say anything. Her thoughts ran along those same lines with her own life. She was still uncertain about God and his role in her life, and whether or not he would still want to be a part of her life after she had been running so hard from him. She did hope, however, that one day Rigby would find someone like Pastor Tyler to talk to about this.

Now as she was being held prisoner, she was reading Scripture again and with one of her captors. She smiled to herself as she remembered her father saying that God works in mysterious ways.

"Miss?" Rigby asked again. She pulled herself from her reverie with a start.

"Oh, I'm sorry, Rigby. I was just thinking." She looked up and smiled slightly at him. She felt such compassion for this boy, who had been sucked into a world of crime from birth.

"I was just reading from Psalm sixty-six." She began to read to him what she had just read. "I find it interesting because I think that may be how Joseph must have felt after Pharaoh promoted him to second-in-command."

At the look of confusion on Rigby's face, Alicia began to recount what Pastor Tyler said about Joseph's life. Rigby let out a low whistle.

"That sure is interestin', miss." He stood and began to pace. He finally turned to face Alicia and found her looking up at him.

"Thank you, Miss Barnes," he said quietly as he walked

back to his own tent. He went in and sat down, but his thoughts were in a complete jumble. *Could I come to know this God that Joseph knew? Would God want someone like me? Would I ever find a wealthy place?* He desperately wanted peace, but he still felt so sure that God would never want him. He finally decided to drop the matter for the time being.

His thoughts then turned to Alicia. She was so kind and innocent. *She does not deserve to be held here like this against her will. What of her family? They must be worried sick.* In that moment, Rigby firmly decided one thing.

He was getting Alicia Barnes out of that camp alive even if it took his own life to do it.

A week later Alicia was reading outside of her tent with Rigby when they both heard the other men approach. Alicia quickly ducked back into her tent and slid the Bible under some blankets. She sat motionless and strained her ears to hear what was going on outside. She soon found, however, that she did not have to strain very hard. The men were in a drunken stupor and talking quite loudly.

"It's time to go, Rigby," Buck bellowed. Alicia judged him to be only a few feet away from her tent. "We got two nice new horses. They look like thoroughbreds. Stupid ranchers don't got enough sense to keep a watchdog or somethin' to protect their prize animals. Takin' these was like takin' candy from a baby." He laughed cruelly, and Alicia felt shivers run up and down her spine.

"We got to move, boys. Get these tents up, and let's get outta here!" He was as ornery and bossy as ever. Alicia quickly moved to fold up her blankets, being careful to make sure that the Bible stayed safely preserved inside the folds. The flap of her tent suddenly flew up, and she felt the man who was called George grab her roughly by the arm and drag her out. He threw her down, and she landed hard on her side in the dirt. George was by far the largest and strongest man. He rarely spoke, though, and Alicia tried not to even look his way.

She slowly stood and began to rub her side. She could tell there would be bruises in the morning. It was beginning to grow dark, and she dreaded another night being forced to ride on a horse alongside one of the men. She hoped it would be Rigby. At least he would not say crude things in her ear all night as they rode.

The men were packed in a matter of minutes and ready to move. Alicia quickly excused herself and moved to the woods to take care of personal needs before they went. She had to leave more of her petticoat. She was beginning to wonder if anyone even found anything, but she knew it was all she could do so she had to keep trying and pray that someone would pick up on her trail. If they knew she was alive, they might keep looking. But if they thought she was dead … Alicia couldn't finish the thought. Buck motioned for Rigby to follow her and keep an eye out. She stood behind some bushes, and Rigby kept his back to her. He heard a slight rip and knew what she was doing. He knew from the beginning that she was leaving things. He would never say anything to his father because he secretly hoped they would be caught and Alicia would be rescued.

Alicia quickly dropped the piece of her petticoat and stepped out from behind the bushes. She and Rigby exchanged a knowing glance. She also knew that Rigby was aware of her actions and that he was allowing it. She sent up a quick prayer for safety as they made their way back to the waiting men.

She found herself once again in front of Rigby in the saddle and being swept away in the night. Every time they moved, Alicia grew more fearful and in more despair.

Tears trickled down her face as they rode on. She was

thankful that it was dark and no one could see her. She was not aware that even though her back was to Rigby, he knew that she was crying. His heart broke for her and, as so many times before, he tried to think of a way to help her escape.

———

Sheriff Holding, Vickery, Caleb, and two other men were all that was left in the search for Alicia and her captors. It had been two weeks, and the other men had to see to their families. Everyone understood, but Caleb felt sharp disappointment. After two weeks, they were still not able to find them. Rebel continued to find clues that Alicia left, but they had covered so many miles that it was hard to stay on her trail. They crossed the Missouri border a week ago and now were all beginning to wonder if maybe she was still in Kentucky.

They came to a small town and decided to stay there and rest for the night. They took their horses to the livery then made their way toward the hotel for a hot meal before going to sleep. As with every town they stopped at, Holding always checked with the local sheriff's office to see if they had any word on the criminals. He also normally stopped at the news office as well.

He slowly made his way up to the sheriff's office and was truly not expecting to hear any news. They had no leads and all but decided to return to Kentucky in the morning. They were sure they were headed in the wrong direction. He took off his hat as he walked inside.

"What can I do for you sir?" the sheriff asked Holding.

"My name is Tom Holding, and I'm the sheriff in Darby, Kentucky. Two weeks ago there was a hold-up at the bank and a kidnapping by five men. We have been tracking them down and believe they may be in this region somewhere. Do you know anything about them?"

"Well, Sheriff Holding, this is indeed a surprise. Just this evening we had one of our wealthiest ranch owners come to complain of two horses missing. He did not say who took them because he didn't see it happen. He just knew they were gone. Are you talking about these five?" The sheriff held up the same wanted poster that was posted in Darby.

"Yep, they're the ones. It seems that poster is up all over. They stole some horses up our way too."

The sheriff stood from his desk and walked around to face Holding.

"My name is Don Roberts," he said with an extended hand. Holding took it with a firm shake. "I can't claim that those are the same men, but it looks as if it could be their work. You said you've tracked them to this area. What makes you think they might be here?"

"They kidnapped our young schoolteacher. She left jewelry and pieces of her petticoat on the trail, and we've got a German shepherd with us to track her. We finally made it to this town." Holding stopped then and waited for the other man to speak. For the first time in two weeks, he began to feel hopeful.

"Well, that's good enough for me. In the morning I'll send notices to the neighboring towns to keep an eye out, and my deputy and I will help you search."

There was no mistaking the relief on Holding's face.

"Thank you, Sheriff Roberts," he said and extended his hand, signaling his farewell. "We're staying at the hotel here in town. We'll meet you here at daybreak." With that, the men shook hands, and Holding made his way down to the hotel, eager to tell the men the news.

"They were here?" Caleb's heart pounded in his chest with the thought of being so close to finding Alicia.

"Hold it, son," the sheriff gently cautioned. "We don't know for sure if she was here. But this is the best news we've had in two weeks. We're meeting Sheriff Roberts and his deputy in the morning. They are going to help us search the area for her." The men all looked relieved. Everyone was exhausted and discouraged.

"Excuse me," Caleb said as he rose from the table, "I need to get some air."

The men watched as Caleb made his way to the door and stepped outside. He began to walk around the town. He spotted a small church at the edge of town and made his way toward it. He needed a place of solitude and peace to collect his thoughts and pray.

He slowly pushed open the door and made his way inside. He walked quietly to the front pew and sat bent over with his head in his hands. His thoughts were a jumbled whirl. *Is she all right? Are they feeding her? Has she been abused? Is she still alive?* All of these thoughts were beginning to overwhelm him.

He began to fervently pray. He prayed for Alicia's safety; he prayed for wisdom to find her and the strength to carry on; and he prayed for Claire. He had not seen her in two weeks and prayed for her safety and for Mark's health. He wondered if Mark even survived the shot.

"Father, please give me strength. We're all so tired and discouraged. Help us to trust you, Lord, because I know that you are sovereign and your plan is best. Help me to hold onto that because when I think of something happening to her—"

His prayer was interrupted when he heard the door creak open. He sat as a statue until he felt someone sit down next to him.

"We will find her, Caleb," he heard Holding's voice firmly say. He rested a hand on the younger man's shoulder. "We won't give up until she is safely back with us."

"You're right. We will find her," Caleb agreed. His voice was lined with steel as he spoke. "I won't go back unless she is with me. I just pray that she is all right. When I think about how those men could hurt her..."

"You must think about her as being safe. She needs us all to think clearly." Holding's fatherly presence at the moment was like a tonic to Caleb. He often thought about his own father these last two weeks, wishing that he were here to help him and give him some wisdom.

"Come on, son," Holding urged. "You need to get some sleep tonight. We have a long day tomorrow." The men rose and made their way back to the hotel. Caleb felt a huge load lift off of him as he committed the situation into the Lord's hands.

Chapter 18

The next morning, Alicia found herself in another strange place in the middle of nowhere watching the men build another camp. The routine was becoming old and frustrating. At least this time there was a creek nearby. Alicia was allowed to walk to it and quickly bathe. Rigby was once again assigned to guard her. The other men wanted nothing to do with her, and Rigby was almost useless to the men as a thief. He was slow and hesitant.

Buck often would yell and hit Rigby out of spite and resentment. He wanted no son of his to have a soft heart. Rigby was constantly ridiculed over the way that he took pity on Alicia. Alicia would hear all of their remarks and hoots of laughter from inside her tent, and it made her blood boil. How could a family be so cruel to each other? Rigby took it all quietly. Alicia knew that he was almost as afraid of his family as she was.

Rigby's back was to her while she was in the creek, but even with that, Alicia remained fully clothed in her undergarments. She never knew a time when she was more humiliated than in the presence of these men. She was even unable to get a decent bath. She knew she was filthy, and it made her feel horrible. She hastily cleaned herself as best she could and made her way toward the camp.

They were almost to her tent when a large root caused Alicia to trip. She fell and landed face first on the ground. She was furious with herself because she knew she would not be allowed to go back and clean up again. In her anger, she did not realize that her dress had flown almost all the way over her head. The men roared in laughter at her expense when Buck suddenly stopped. He rushed toward her and yanked her up.

"What's this?" he growled as he lifted her dress to reveal her tattered petticoat. "Have you been trying to leave a trail?" Alicia tried to back away. Everyone could see the terror in her eyes. The other men smirked, but Rigby watched in horror. Alicia was unable to move because Buck's grip on her was so strong. Suddenly, the back of Buck's hand came hard across her face. He let go, and she fell to the ground.

"Guard her, Rigby." He tossed Rigby a rifle. Rigby caught it and stared in disbelief. "We've got to scope out this town, and I gotta figure out what to do with our little schoolteacher." He glared toward Alicia and smiled to reveal his decaying teeth. "You may think you are pretty smart, missy, but you done landed yourself in a great heap of trouble!" With that, he signaled for the other boys to leave with him. They jumped onto their horses and galloped off after him.

Rigby threw down the rifle in disgust and ran to Alicia.

"Are you all right, miss?" he asked. He wanted to help her up but was afraid to touch her. He did not want to hurt her anymore.

Alicia's entire body stung from the impact, and her face felt as if it were on fire. She turned slightly to face Rigby, and he grimaced. There was a large cut under her right eye where she had been hit. It was bleeding, and the eye and cheek were already beginning to swell.

"Hurry, miss," Rigby ordered. "We gotta get to the creek to clean this up." He gently helped her up and held her unsteady arm as they walked toward the creek.

The water stung as Rigby tried the best he could to clean her wound. The bleeding was not stopping, so he had her hold a cloth over it.

"Come on," he said and moved toward the camp. He looked back and saw Alicia slumped against a tree. She did not have enough energy to move. He went back to her and helped her walk back to camp.

"I've been thinking a lot, miss. I'm takin' you back to your town, and I'm gonna turn myself in." Alicia had never felt such relief.

"The Bible," she managed through quivering lips. Rigby quickly packed it and a few other essentials into a small bag and helped Alicia onto one of the stolen horses before mounting his own horse. Alicia was weak, but she was an experienced rider, and Rigby knew they would make better time if she were on her own horse. He knew there was a chance his father could catch them first, but it was a chance they had to take. They rode off hard, and this time Alicia was not riding off in the night. She was leaving her prison. Relief flooded her stinging body as they made their way out of sight.

Sheriffs Holding and Roberts, along with their deputies, Caleb, and the other two men, had been riding for the better part of the morning. Rebel was making a noble effort to find Alicia's trail, but it had been difficult. The pieces of the petticoat that she managed to leave were so few and far between. The men finally found themselves along a ridge that overlooked one of the valleys. They climbed down from their horses for a brief rest.

Rebel had been sniffing nearby and suddenly his head shot up, and he let out a low growl. Caleb was all too familiar with that sound. He jumped and ran to Rebel.

"What is it, boy? Another clue?" He followed as Rebel slowly sniffed and walked along. Caleb was sure that he must have picked up on something. He was right. Just then Rebel stopped and stayed with his nose to the ground. Caleb looked down and spotted it. A small white piece of cloth. He snatched it up and ran back to the other men.

"She was here!" he exclaimed as he thrust the piece at Sheriff Holding. "They had her here!"

"Well, at least we know we're on the right track," Holding responded as he fingered the piece of cloth. "Reckon after they stole the horses, they made off again." He looked thoughtful for a moment.

"I think we may finally be getting close to finding her, men. The horses were stolen just yesterday, which means they don't have much of a head start on us." The men exchanged looks of relief and determination. Their pursuit might soon be over. They quickly mounted their horses and continued on their way.

———

Alicia and Rigby had only been riding for an hour, but to Alicia it seemed like an eternity. Her entire body screamed at her to get off the horse and rest, but she knew that was simply impossible at this point. She had to continue on— her life depended on it. Her cheek continued to sting badly, and her eye was nearly swollen shut. It made her all the more uncomfortable, and the thought of sleeping in a real bed weighed heavily upon her.

They continued to ride and finally came through a clearing in the woods. Alicia squinted with her one good eye and was sure that she saw riders in the distance coming toward them. It looked like several men, and panic gripped her for a moment before she realized that these were not her captors. They were coming from the opposite direction, and there were seven of them. They rode closer to them, and Alicia suddenly spotted him. Caleb was leading the way with Rebel by his side! Alicia nearly shouted with joy and relief.

They rode closer together, and then Alicia practically threw herself off her horse and began to run toward Caleb. He was off Midnight in a flash and running toward her as well. She flung herself in his arms, and he held her tightly and twirled her around once, causing her feet to lift from the ground.

She stayed locked in his arms, so thankful that he found her. Her heart swelled with joy, and she never wanted to let go of him. For the first time in a little over two weeks, she felt safe. Here in Caleb's warm and safe embrace, Alicia knew that she would be all right.

However, the sound of several guns cocking broke her reverie, and she slowly let go of Caleb. She moved to face him and the other men and was greeted with gasps on all sides. They were all staring wide-eyed at her face. One entire cheek was red and puffy, the cut had dry blood surrounding it, and her eye was completely swollen shut and was already turning a deep shade of purple. In her excitement of being rescued, she had completely forgotten about it and now put her hand to it in embarrassment. Rage filled Caleb toward the man that was responsible for this. Never had he seen a woman who had been hit so severely before, and it made his blood boil. He put his arms back around her and held her tightly. His eyes moved to the man on the horse.

"Who are you?" Holding's voice said sternly. Alicia then turned, but Caleb kept one arm firmly around her. She looked to see that all of the men that rode with Caleb had their guns focused on Rigby.

"My name is Rigby, sir." His voice faltered, and Alicia

felt compassion toward him and knew she needed to intervene.

"Sheriff Holding, this is Rigby. He was responsible for my escape." At Holding's nod, the men lowered their weapons.

"His father and brothers are responsible for all that has happened. Together they make up the five men that have wreaked havoc on the region." Alicia stopped for a moment. She took a breath and continued. "But Rigby is different. His father forced him into this life after his mother died and has been physically forcing him to remain ever since. While no one was looking, he took care of me while I was being held prisoner. He made sure I was well fed and taken care of. After I was struck by his father, he decided to risk his own life to take me out of the camp." Alicia ended her speech, and the men looked rather taken aback. Was she really defending one of her captors? Caleb looked at her in wonder. Was he just imagining it, or did he see a change in her?

"Sir," Rigby timidly addressed Sheriff Holding, "I'm here to turn myself in. Like Miss Barnes said, I don't want no part in this kind of life. I never did," he ended quietly. Holding did not quite know what to do. The father in him saw a scared boy who did not know where to turn or what to do. The lawman in him saw a criminal who had aided in a kidnapping, among many other serious crimes.

"Thank you for returning Miss Barnes to us, son. You'll have to come with us, though. There will be a trial in Darby for the bank robbery and the abduction," Holding firmly stated. Rigby lowered his eyes and nodded. He never came down from his horse. Alicia knew fear kept him firmly rooted to the saddle, and Holding suspected as much as well.

"We need to know where your father and brothers are," Vickery added. Alicia looked over and saw Paul

Vickery there for the first time. He looked at her, but his expression remained unreadable. As he had watched her jump into Caleb's arms, he finally realized she would never be his.

"Yes, sir," Rigby acquiesced. "We've only been ridin' an hour. They left to scope out that next town."

"Excellent," said Sheriff Roberts. "After we find them, we'll send them on to Darby." Holding nodded.

"Excuse me, but you need to take this horse with you," Alicia interjected, motioning to the horse she rode. "The men stole it yesterday."

"She can ride back with me," Caleb added.

"Great. Thanks," said Sheriff Roberts as he took the reins of the other horse. "I know his owner will be relieved to get him back."

Then Holding sent Caleb and the remaining two townsmen on toward home with Rigby in their charge. The two sheriffs and their deputies rode off in search of the other four men.

When they turned to leave, Alicia quietly asked Caleb where they were.

"We're in Missouri, Alicia," he responded gently, and he watched her one good eye grow wide.

"And you continued to search for me? I suspected that we were over the Kentucky line, but I wasn't sure. Thank you, Caleb. Thank you for not giving up." Alicia was moved beyond words. She had secretly been afraid that after all this time, the search would have been called off. Her heart soared with the knowledge that Caleb continued to search for her.

He helped Alicia onto his horse, and when she was comfortably settled in front of him on the saddle, he reached for her hand and gave it a firm squeeze.

"You know I would never give up on you." She turned

to look at him, and his eyes were tender as he gazed into hers. "I won't let anything happen to you again."

He gave her hand another squeeze before he released it and spurred his horse on. Despite all that she had been through, Alicia felt as if she was riding on air after hearing Caleb's words.

Chapter 19

Claire walked slowly into town, trying to think back on the last few weeks. It seemed such a horrible blur to her. Caleb was still not back yet, and Claire had no idea where he was or how Alicia was doing. Every day she fervently prayed for their safety and was beginning to become very fearful for them both. Already several men from the teams sent to search for Alicia had come back defeated. They had to continue to provide for their families and told Claire very little. The search was taking them farther west, and they found clues from Alicia but still had not found her.

Claire struggled with fearing the worst and forced herself to push those thoughts aside. She continually reminded herself to trust the Lord and remember that he was in control. Her thoughts drifted back to the present in town. School had been called off for the remainder of the year. It was already so close to the end of the school year, and Alicia had been gone for almost three weeks. The children were now needed to help their parents with their farms. Sheriff Holding's brother, Carl, had been filling in as sheriff when necessary. Carl Holding owned the hotel in town, and whenever his brother was sick, he would also fill in as sheriff. The town had been pretty quiet since the bank robbery, though, and for that everyone was grateful.

Claire walked past the doctor's office, where she had spent some of the worst weeks of her life. Mark was released only a week ago, and Claire spent most of her days with him at his house just a few hundred yards outside of town. On this day, memories of the last few weeks that brought them to today flooded her memory.

After Mark first cried out that he could no longer feel his legs, Claire felt her own legs go out from beneath her. Mark immediately lost consciousness, and Claire sank into the chair by his bedside and sobbed. She watched as Dr. Clarke examined him and said that he fainted from shock and exhaustion. Tears poured down her face as Mark's words echoed through her mind. *"I can't feel my legs! I can't feel my legs!"* Dr. Clarke helped her to her feet and guided her out of the room and into his office.

She worked hard to stifle the sobs that clogged her throat as Dr. Clarke began to speak.

"I was afraid of this. I was afraid he may be faced with paralysis." His face was pained. He hated this part about his job. Claire sniffed and looked at him through red, puffy eyes.

"Is this permanent?"

"Most likely. We'll know more when he wakes again." Claire stared at him completely speechless. She slowly rose from her chair and turned to leave the office.

"Claire." His voice stopped her as she reached the door. She turned slightly, and he spoke to her profile. "You need to deal with this before you come back. Mark will need your strength and support, not your tears." He said the words as gently as possible, but it was so difficult. How do you tell a woman that the man she loves is paralyzed? He watched as her chin rose in determination, and she quickly strode out of his office.

She left from Dr. Clarke's and immediately went to the small house that Pastor Tyler and Gloria lived in. It was a stone's throw from the church. It was a small, white house, but it was tidy, cozy, and forever welcoming. Claire walked up to the front door and knocked. Gloria Tyler opened the door, and as soon as Claire saw her, she burst into tears. Compassion swelled Gloria's heart as she took Claire's arm and gently led her into the living room.

Gloria held Claire and allowed her to cry for as long as she needed. Gloria knew how difficult it was for Claire dealing with Mark's uncertain state and not knowing where Caleb or Alicia were or if they were safe—or even alive. Pastor Tyler and Gloria prayed often for Claire, Caleb, Mark, and Alicia and were amazed at the strength Claire was showing throughout the whole ordeal.

When Claire's sobs finally began to abate, Gloria gently pushed some loose strands of her hair aside and patiently waited for her to speak.

"Oh Gloria, I just don't know how to handle everything. Everything seems to be spinning out of control, and I feel stuck in the middle and can't do anything to set my world right or make the spinning stop." The crying caused hiccups, and Claire tried to speak through them. She sniffed, and Gloria watched her intently so as not to miss anything.

"Mark woke up this afternoon and said that he can't feel his legs." Claire watched as Gloria's eyes opened wide and her expression was full of sympathy. She continued. "After that, he passed out, and Dr. Clarke said the condition was most likely permanent. He'll be so crushed when he finds out. How do I help him? What can I do for him? My heart breaks for him." She paused for a moment and stared out the window. "I don't know where Caleb is. I have not heard from him. I don't know where Alicia is or if he found her or if they're safe or hurt or even alive!" With that she burst into tears again, and Gloria gently put her arms around her.

"I know this must be so hard for you, honey. Pastor Tyler and I are so proud of the way that you have been clinging to God in your time of need. You know that he is still with you, and is crying right along with you. He won't leave you now, and his mighty hand is still in control. His plan is perfect, and you never know what he wants to come of all this." Claire nodded, and Gloria continued. "It will be hard with Mark, but you will both get through it and be all the stronger for it, both as a couple and as individuals. I wish I could say that Caleb and Alicia are well and on their way home, but we don't know. We just have to trust them into God's hands. And Claire, Pastor Tyler and I will always be here for you. Come whenever you like. We'll help you in any way we can." Gloria smiled at Claire, who finally had herself back under control.

It was always such a help for her to sit under the wisdom of Gloria Tyler. Claire sent up a quick prayer of thanks that God had put this wonderful couple into her life and into the life of the town. The two continued to talk for a while, and then Claire decided she should head back to Dr. Clarke's. Before she left, Gloria prayed with her, and Claire felt as if a huge weight had been lifted off her shoulders as she made her way back to Mark.

The next couple of days proved to be torturous. Mark finally came out of his state of unconsciousness, and he was able to get some nourishment in his system, something for which Claire was greatly relieved. But upon being told of his condition, he was filled with rage. He shouted and forced everyone to leave his room. Claire stood by wanting to comfort him, but with cold eyes, he firmly told her to leave. She and the doctor stood outside Mark's door as they heard something crash. Dr. Clarke grabbed Claire's arm when she tried to go inside, but he told her to give Mark some time alone to adjust.

Alone in his room, Mark tried to sit up and used all the strength he had left to use his arms to push him up.

He slumped against the headboard in defeat and looked up to the ceiling.

"Why God? Why did this happen to me?" he shouted feeling as helpless as a child. He was not a man prone to reveal many emotions, but now while he was alone, he let tears claim him. The sobs shook his large frame as he came to grips with the fact that he would never walk again. He was a man who was to be forever crippled. His pride was wounded and he wondered what Claire must think of him. Then a horrible thought raced through his mind. *What if she no longer wants to marry me?* He then felt a gentle peace and a verse that he read popped into his mind.

Be still and know that I am God.

Mark knew God was speaking to him. He finally began to relax against the pillows and pray.

"Father God, I don't know what your plan is for me. I hate that this has happened to me, but please help me to trust you and remember that you are in control and my life is no longer mine, but yours. Please get me through this."

With that, he closed his eyes and rested against the pillows. He had to trust God. He was thankful that he was even alive after all that happened. He was given a second chance, and in that instant, he determined that he would not take that for granted. He knew it would be a struggle, but he also knew he was not alone. God would get him through. He once again let sleep claim him.

When he awoke, Claire was sitting by his bed. He reached for her hand, and Claire breathed an inward sigh of relief. She was not sure what he would be like when he awoke. But she now saw an unmistakable peace in his eyes. They held each other's eyes for a while before Claire spoke.

"How are you, dear?"

He smiled despite his aching body. "I'm all right. How are you?"

"I'm fine." A long silence followed.

"I'm just glad to be alive," he finally said quietly. He then looked to Claire and spoke rather hesitantly. "I'm glad that I have another chance to be with you. But Claire"—his grip tightened slightly on her hand—"I'm a crippled man now. I'll understand if you want to call off the wedding."

"Are you crazy?" she practically shouted at him. He smiled wide in relief.

"I love you," she said emphatically. "I prayed for your recovery, and I'm so thankful you are alive. It doesn't matter to me if you can't walk anymore. The important thing is that we are still together. And we'll get through this together."

She leaned over and kissed him gently. He put his hand under her chin and looked deeply into her eyes.

"I love you too," he said tenderly. He momentarily forgot all about his accident and being paralyzed as he gazed at the woman he loved. He was so thankful that God had put Claire into his life, and he breathed a prayer of thanks.

The doctor surprised them both when he told them that he had taken the liberty of already ordering a special chair from the city for Mark. It was called a wheelchair, and rightfully so. It was simply a chair with wheels. It had a high back with handles on it so that he could be pushed, or he could wheel himself around. Mark and Claire were relieved at Dr. Clarke's insight and thanked him for his help.

Pastor Tyler had announced Mark's situation in

church, and all of the men rallied to build ramps to put in Mark's house, the bank, the Carter ranch, and various other sidewalks and buildings in town. The couple was moved beyond words and felt proud to know that they were forever in debt to the kind people of their town. The women provided continual refreshments for the men who worked shifts in the town building ramps while they were not working at their own farms. Within a week, everything had been successfully built and installed, and Mark was able to move home.

His first day home proved to be a bit of a challenge for him. After Claire left that evening, Mark was alone for the first time since his accident. The doctor wasn't nearby ready to lend a hand, but Mark wasn't worried about that. He had always been an independent man and thought nothing about being left alone. He wheeled himself to his bedroom and realized that the drawer that held his pajamas was too high for him. He stretched his arm and was able to grasp the handle. With his other hand, he wheeled backwards and finally got the drawer open enough to get out his pajamas. He reached his hand up and felt around. He pulled out his pajamas, closed the drawer, and wheeled over to the bed.

Putting on the button-down pajama top was the easy part. Now he had to put on the pants. But first he had to get off his regular pants. It took a combined effort of hoisting himself up with his arms then pulling off the pants. This routine went on and on until he was finally free of them. Then he started to put on the pajamas—first one leg, then the other. Then once again the combined lifting of his body and pulling up the pants inch by inch. The effort left him exhausted. Sweat beaded his forehead, and he still had not made it into the bed yet.

He turned his wheelchair so that he was facing the bed. He placed his hands on it and tried to lift himself enough to pull himself onto it. He used his arms to lift his body and then shuffled his hands forward to pull his body on the bed. As he started to come out of the wheelchair he lost his balance and fell hard on his side on the floor.

Mark gritted his teeth as pain seared through his body. He rolled over on his back and looked up. The bed and wheelchair seemed as if they were mocking him, daring him to get back up and try again. *I'm not a quitter.* He placed his arms on the seat of the wheelchair, took a deep breath, and, using all of his strength, hoisted himself up and back into the wheelchair. At this point sweat was running down the back of his neck, and he was panting from the exertion. Frustration threatened to overwhelm him, and he punched his fist into the mattress.

"God, I can't do this!" he cried out in anger. "Why me? Why?" He punched the mattress over and over. When all of his energy was spent, his chest slumped over against the mattress. He was so tired and wanted to sleep so badly—just enough motivation to try to get onto the bed one more time. He gripped the mattress and pulled with all of his might and finally plopped onto it. He rolled over on his back and stared at the ceiling.

"I sure hope this gets easier," he muttered to himself as sleep rushed in to claim him.

Mark squinted against the sunlight that was pouring into his room the next morning. He used his arms to push himself into a sitting position. He leaned his back against the headboard and sighed. All of the little tasks that he took for granted were such a challenge now. He reached out a hand to grab the handle on the back of the wheelchair and pulled it so that it was right up against the bed. He carefully worked to maneuver his body onto the chair and instead ended up flat on the floor.

"Blasted wheelchair! I hate this!" he shouted. He lay

against the floor in defeat and heard a knock at the front door. *Oh, no,* he thought. *I don't want Claire to see me like this.*

But it was too late. He didn't have time to try to lift himself onto his wheelchair before Claire let herself in.

"Hello?" she called. When there was no answer, she started to walk toward the bedroom, afraid that something had happened to Mark. "Hello?" she said as she knocked on the door.

"Go away," Mark barked at her.

"Mark, are you all right?"

"Go away!"

"What's wrong?"

"Nothing. Just go away."

But Claire wouldn't be dissuaded that easily. She turned the knob and gasped. "Oh honey," she cried as she knelt beside him. He turned his head away from her humiliated. "Have you been like this all night?"

"No."

"Let me help you," she said as she grabbed under his shoulders. He shook free of her grasp.

"I don't want your help. Just leave me alone."

"I most certainly will not leave you alone, Mark Brewer. I'm not going to just leave you here on the cold floor. Now stop being so stubborn and let me help you up." She wheeled the chair over to Mark, and together they were able to get Mark into the chair.

"I'm just a pathetic cripple, Claire."

"Don't you ever say that again," she ordered, standing with her hands on her hips. "You just need to give yourself time to adjust."

"Is this really the kind of life you want? Helping your pitiful husband get off the floor or get into the bed or get on his clothes?" He voice grew louder with each task he listed off. "Well, it's not the kind of life I want for you. You don't deserve to be saddled with an invalid. I'm calling off the wedding."

"No, you can't do that. I don't want to call the wedding off. You're not an invalid. It seems daunting, even impossible, right now, but in time you'll adjust. Haven't you heard of a thing called unconditional love? Would you stop loving me if I were in your place? Would you not want to marry me? Loving you unconditionally means that I love you no matter what, and I'll be here no matter what." He refused to look at her.

"Look at me," she cried out in frustration. "Do you understand what I'm telling you?" Mark wouldn't respond. He turned his wheelchair around so that his back was to her. He heard her stifle a sob and leave the room. She slammed the door so hard on her way out that the whole house seemed to shake. Mark hung his head miserably. He didn't want to lose Claire. But he honestly thought that letting her go was the best thing he could do for her.

Claire marched resolutely toward Dr. Clarke's office. She was not going to give in to Mark's stubbornness. She opened the office door and saw Dr. Clarke sitting at his desk.

"Hello Claire," he greeted warmly. "How is Mark today?"

"Not well." The doctor nodded.

"I was afraid of that. It's going take time to adjust."

"Time he doesn't seem willing to allow himself," Claire added. She paused for a moment, lost in thought. "I have an idea. Will you help me?"

———

Mark sat in his living room listlessly. The newspaper sat on the table, but he didn't feel like reading about "normal" people's lives. He knew he shouldn't be sitting around feeling sorry for himself, but he didn't have the energy to fight it. A knock at the door pulled him from his reverie. He wheeled over to the door and opened it. His mouth hung open and he stared.

"Hello, Mark," Claire said as she wheeled her way past him and into the living room. "Stop staring at me. Do you like it when people stare at you?"

He shook his head, completely speechless. Claire was in a wheelchair!

"What in the world?"

"Oh, this," she said, motioning to the chair. "It's my wheelchair. Dr. Clarke ordered three in case of other injuries that would require one, and he loaned it to me."

"Why?"

"Because you're not going to go through this alone," Claire said as tears began to form. Her voice was shaky. "Even Dr. Clarke said you need time to adjust. Being in a wheelchair isn't the worst thing in the world. Remember when you told me you're just glad to be alive? Can't you be grateful for that? Caleb and Alicia might not be that fortunate." Sobs overtook her as she put her head in her hands.

Filled with compassion, Mark wheeled over to her and put his arm around her.

"Please don't cry," he consoled. "We can't give up hope. Caleb and Alicia might be on their way home even now."

Claire hiccupped and looked up at Mark. He cupped her face with his hands and used his thumbs to wipe away her tears. Leaning forward in her chair, she wrapped her arms around him and held on tightly.

Claire's tears finally began to subside and she released her hold on Mark. She reached for some knitting that she had left and began to expertly maneuver the needles while Mark simply watched in wonder. He still couldn't believe that Claire was in a wheelchair. As the afternoon hours slipped away, Claire's stomach began to rumble. Mark looked up from the paper he finally decided to read and chuckled.

"I guess I'm a little hungry. How about I fix us some supper?" Claire suggested.

"Sounds good to me." Claire turned her wheelchair and headed into the kitchen. Mark shook his head in disbelief. She had been in that chair all afternoon! He went back to his paper. It wasn't long before a loud bang caused him to nearly jump out of his skin.

"What happened?" he called as he made his way toward the kitchen.

"Oh, I just dropped a pot," Claire answered. When Mark reached the kitchen, he burst out laughing.

"What's so funny?" Claire demanded. But Mark was laughing too hard to answer. If only Claire could see herself sitting in that chair with a pot on the floor, flour everywhere, bowls scattered, and spilled milk, she would probably be laughing too.

"Oh, for heaven's sake," she said as she leaned down to retrieve the pot. "These biscuits aren't cooperating with me tonight." She reached up for a towel on the counter and began wiping up the milk that had spilled from the counter to the floor. As Mark watched her, he realized that only the love of a truly good woman would go through all of this just to help him understand that he's not alone and that she would never leave him. He wheeled over to her and took the cloth out of her hand. He lifted her hand up to his mouth and brushed a gentle kiss across it.

"Thank you," he said, his voice husky with emotion.

"Oh Mark," she said as she gripped his hand, "you know I would do anything for you. When I say I love you, I mean I love you unconditionally."

"This isn't going to be easy."

"I didn't sign on for easy. I signed on to go through life with you through good times and bad."

Mark's instinct was to jump up and hug this precious woman but his paralysis prevented him from doing that. So instead he reached over and put his arms around her and pulled her close. She allowed herself to be drawn into his embrace and leaned her head against his chest.

"I'm sorry about what happened this morning," he said against her hair as he continued to hold her tightly against him. "This is going to be a difficult and painful road to walk down, but I'd be a fool not to walk down it with you. So if you're still willing, I'd be honored to have you as my wife."

"Mark Brewer," Claire said as she pulled away just far enough to be able to look him in the eyes, "would I have sat in a wheelchair all day if I wasn't willing to walk down this road with you? Of course I still want to be your wife."

Love shone through Mark's eyes as he leaned in for a kiss. It was gentle but filled with meaning. It took Claire's breath away.

"And you'd better not change your mind again," she warned.

"Not a chance," he answered, covering her lips with his own.

⁓

Caleb and Alicia rode slowly back onto the ranch. Never had Alicia been so glad to see any place in her life. She did not realize how weak she was until she sat in front of Caleb in the saddle, and he kept his strong arms firmly around her to keep her from falling. She practically collapsed against him and fought to stay awake. But sleep claimed her for a good deal of the journey home. Her eye remained sore to the touch and painful to look at.

It was still quite swollen with shades of purple and blue surrounding it.

Rigby was turned over to Carl Holding, and now Caleb and Alicia were finally at the ranch. Caleb helped Alicia off of the horse, and they stood staring at the house for a moment.

"I never thought I would see this place again," she said thoughtfully. Caleb noted the slight tremor in her voice and put an arm around her shoulder.

"You're safe now," he assured her in a strong, quiet voice.

They turned at the sound of whoops coming from all directions. All of the ranch hands were running toward them, smiling and hollering. Caleb and Alicia smiled in return as they were surrounded by hands sending questions flying. They answered the best they could. John then stepped forward.

"Welcome back, boss," he said with an outstretched hand. The men shook hands, and John let out a low whistle when he saw Alicia.

"You got yerself quite a beauty there, miss."

Alicia put her hand self-consciously to her eye and smiled slightly. It was so good to be back.

"How's Claire?" Alicia asked the only thing that had been on her mind during their torrent of questions. Caleb's eyes told of his anxiety to know about his sister too. He noticed that she had not come out when they rode up, so he knew she must be in town.

"Well, it's been a mite rough for her, boss. Robby here has been watchin' over her and makin' sure she was safe." John motioned with his eyes to Robby, and Caleb and Alicia glanced at him. He shyly met their gaze before he lowered his eyes again. "She'll probably want to tell you the rest herself, though. She's over at Mark's place now."

"Then he's alive." Caleb sighed in relief. The men

soon disbursed after that, and Caleb steered Alicia into the house.

"I'm going to get cleaned up, and then I'm going to go see Claire and Mark," Caleb said.

"I want to go with you," Alicia stated. Caleb looked at her and knew she was still exhausted. The strain had really taken its toll on her. She was drawn and pale and so thin. He hesitated for a moment. Alicia gently laid her hand on his arm.

"Caleb," she began firmly, "I have to go. I have been just as worried about her as you, and I need to see her for myself." Caleb knew he could not refuse her this and nodded.

"Thank you. I'll be ready shortly."

The two then parted to clean up before going into town in search of Claire.

Claire was busy bustling around Mark's kitchen getting his lunch ready. Mark didn't let Claire stay in the wheelchair after that first day. As much as he appreciated her gesture, he wanted her to use the legs God blessed her with. Lunch was the simplest meal of the day for Claire. Mark had never been one to eat much for lunch. Claire was slicing some thick pieces of bread when she heard Mark wheel into the kitchen.

"Claire?"

"Yes," she answered. Her back was to him, and she continued to slice.

"What happened to my shirt, dear?" He grinned as Claire turned around. He held up one of his white shirts that had a large black print in the shape of an iron right in the middle of it.

"Oh my." Claire jerked it out of his hands. "You weren't supposed to find this. I threw it out."

"I know." He chuckled. "But I found it." He watched as color began to rise from just above her collar and go up to her cheeks. She was mortified. She had not stained a shirt she ironed since she was a little girl. Mark reached out and grabbed her hand and pulled her to him. He was laughing hard at Claire's red face and his stained shirt.

"It's not funny, Mark Brewer! I didn't mean to stain your shirt. I was trying to iron it for you so that it would be fresh when you went back to work. I guess my mind has been a little preoccupied lately." Claire sat down in one of the kitchen chairs beside him, still holding his hand. She did not want him to think that she did not even know how to iron. Tears filled her eyes. Mark saw them and all laughing stopped.

"Claire, honey, it's really okay. I think it's rather amusing to see my shirt like this, but it doesn't matter. I have several." He stopped then, and with two fingers he turned her face to his. He waited until their eyes locked before he continued. "I know that Caleb and Alicia are heavy on your mind. They are on mine too. They'll be all right." He smiled at Claire, and she held up the shirt and stared at it in disdain.

"Well," she said, eyeing the poor shirt, "I guess I could use it as a dust cloth." Mark could no longer hold back his laughter and threw back his head and howled. Claire began to chuckle too, and soon they both had tears in their eyes from laughing so hard.

A knock at the door made them pull themselves together, and they looked questioningly at each other. They both made their way to the door, and Claire slowly opened it.

She stopped suddenly as her hand flew to her mouth. Tears began to fill her eyes. Mark swung the door fully open and stared for several seconds before any words would come.

"Caleb! Alicia!" Claire cried as she threw herself into her brother's arms. He held her tightly as tears poured down her face. Her beloved brother was back safely, and so was Alicia. She was overwhelmed by how wonderful it was. She then turned to Alicia, and both women hugged tightly. Claire continued to cry and laughed with joy through her tears. Alicia's hurt eye could not bear tears, so she swallowed down the ones that were threatening to spill over.

Claire quickly ushered them into the living room, and they all sat and began to talk at once.

"How are you? What happened? How did you escape? Are you all right?" Claire's questions came endlessly at Caleb and Alicia, and they told her everything, ending with Rigby turning himself in. Claire and Mark sat back in amazement when they heard the whole story.

"I can't believe it," Claire said for the third time. "Thank goodness you're both safe. I was so worried. Alicia, I think there is some cream in one of the kitchen cabinets that might make your eye feel better. Let me see if I can find it." Claire was back shortly and gently rubbed some of the cream on Alicia's eye. It had a cooling sensation, and Alicia inwardly chastised herself for not thinking to put something on it while at the ranch.

Alicia had some questions of her own. Words could not describe the shock that she felt over seeing Mark sitting in a wheelchair at the door. She naively expected to come back and find everything as it was before.

"What happened with you two while we were gone?" she inquired. Caleb leaned forward. He was anxious himself to hear what happened.

"After I was shot, the bullet damaged my spine. I was out of it for a week, and when I woke up, I could no longer feel my legs." Mark was calm as he told the story. Caleb listened intently, but Alicia was growing very upset.

Why Mark? she thought. *Why do such horrible and unfair things happen to good people?* She forced herself to pay attention as Mark finished the story. "The doctor said that it is most likely a permanent condition, and for a while I was very angry. Then I realized that I should be thankful that I was still alive. These last few weeks haven't been easy, that's for sure. Every day that goes by we consider a victory. But we're taking life one day at a time." Mark and Claire exchanged a knowing glance. They had had time to make peace with the situation and were completely unaware of the bitterness that was going through Alicia upon hearing of Mark's accident.

Caleb was moved and proud at the peace that the two of them felt, and their ability and desire to be thankful for what they had rather than dwell on what was different now. He said as much and volunteered to lead them all in a prayer of thanks for their safety and for allowing them all to be together again.

Alicia shifted uncomfortably in her chair. She did not understand why everyone was feeling so thankful over Mark's condition. He would never walk again. He was such a good man, and instead of being angry he was praising God. Alicia felt confused and hurt and angry over all that had happened in the last month.

Chapter 20

Gloria Tyler was busy dusting when she heard a knock at the door. Brushing her hands against her apron, she threw the dust cloth on the windowsill and made her way downstairs. She sported another cloth on her head to keep the dust off and was wearing old work clothes. Cleaning days always seemed to find her a mess. Of course, her naturally pleasant disposition never allowed her to be upset over someone finding her in disarray, so she did not give it a thought as she opened the front door.

"Alicia!" she cried, as she pulled her into a tight embrace, "I'm so glad to see you. Thank the Good Lord that you're alive. Come in, dear."

It did Alicia's heart a world of good to see Gloria Tyler again. She often spent time with the elderly woman and found that her wisdom was just what she needed to continue on in her daily life. While Gloria could never take the place of her own mother, it was wonderful to have a matronly figure around to guide and advise her.

"Gracious, child! I'm covered in dust!" Gloria laughed as she continued to hug Alicia.

"It's so good to see you again," Alicia responded as she held the woman at arm's length. They walked together into the small living room and sat down.

"Let me run get us some tea." Gloria quickly moved to the kitchen and was soon back carrying a tray with two cups and saucers and the teapot. She poured them both a cup and then settled back on the chair and looked at Alicia.

"I prayed for your safe return every day, honey."

"Thank you. I appreciate all of the prayers. I must admit that there were times when I was sure that I would never make it back." Alicia sipped her tea and smiled. How delighted she was to be home!

"Well, I had heard that was quite a black eye you got, but it was hard to believe it was real. Now I can see that it is most definitely real. And they were all right. That's one of the worst I've ever seen."

Alicia's good eye sparkled.

"I think I must have set a record or something. I should be proud. Most men can't boast a beauty like this one." She delicately touched her eye and smiled dramatically. Gloria laughed.

"You know," Gloria put in, "I was quite impressed with Claire during the whole ordeal. She was so strong and courageous."

"But she was afraid too. I know that I was scared to death being dragged from place to place and never knowing where I was or if I would survive."

"Ah yes, Claire was very fearful. For Mark and his health, and for you and Caleb. But the Lord says that his power is made perfect in weakness and his strength really shined through Claire during those horrible weeks." Gloria continued to sip her tea. Her eyes held contentment and peace. Alicia watched her for a moment.

"I started reading my Bible again," she said simply. Gloria sat up a bit straighter and looked directly at her.

"And?"

"That's all. One of my captors was rather nice, and he gave me his mother's old Bible. I began reading it, searching for comfort. I'm still sorting out my own feelings, but I just wanted you to know." Alicia ended the topic there, and Gloria felt sharp disappointment. She wanted to continue to discuss this matter with Alicia and invite her to ask questions. She knew, though, that this was a big step for Alicia. A step in the right direction. She wisely decided not to press the matter.

"You know, I was actually a bit surprised that Caleb and the other men continued to look for me. I guess deep down I thought that they might, but I have never really seen myself as much before. Perhaps that is why I was surprised at how quickly Caleb and Claire befriended me and how fiercely they protect me. Don't get me wrong,"— she was looking right at Gloria, and her voice was gaining passion. Gloria inwardly smiled as Alicia continued—"I would do anything for the Carters. I just never expected them to do anything for me. They have such great love for people. It really amazes me. I know that it is because of their faith in God, and I have to wonder if I would ever feel like that if I had faith in God." Her musings brought her to an abrupt end but only for a moment.

"I have never paid much attention to the men in town before, but Caleb does strange things to my heart." Her voice took on a rather dreamy quality, and Gloria smiled as she put her cup down. Alicia's own was in mid-air, seemingly forgotten.

"I don't understand it, Gloria." She then looked to Gloria with young, innocent eyes that took Gloria back to her own youth. Douglas Tyler had done strange things to her heart too.

"It reminds me of how Claire used to act before she and Mark were engaged. She would get all giddy and clumsy. She is not a clumsy woman, but she would become very clumsy in his presence. She never knew which way was up. And she blushed often at the mere mention of his name. I'm afraid that I find myself doing some of these same things with Caleb." She looked helplessly to Gloria, who let out a small laugh.

"Yes, I remember what that was like," Gloria said fondly. "It is difficult to be yourself around someone you're in love with."

Alicia's mouth dropped, and she stared at Gloria. *Did she just say what I think she said? I am not in love with Caleb Carter! I'm not in love with anyone.*

"Oh no, Gloria," she quickly began but stopped as Gloria raised her hand.

"Honey, just listen to me for a moment."

Alicia closed her mouth and sat still.

"You have allowed past experiences in your life to control your future. You know firsthand the pain that comes with losing someone that you love dearly, and you have determined not to let that happen again. In doing so, you have closed off your heart to love others and to be loved. Perhaps that is why you are so amazed with Caleb and Claire's ability to love. Their hearts did not harden after their own loss. They allow themselves to love God and others, and to be loved in return. Now, you may not be in love with Caleb. You have to work through those feelings for yourself. But you do need to allow yourself to feel and accept love again. Do not allow the past to control your future." Gloria took Alicia's hand and gave it a slight squeeze. Alicia was left speechless. She knew that Gloria was absolutely right and wondered why she did not realize it herself. *Why am I so blind to things that seem to be staring right at me?*

The two women chatted a while longer before Alicia announced that it was time for her to head back home. Both women had thoroughly enjoyed the visit and were sorry to see it come to an end.

Alicia began to head for the ranch. Since the abduction, the Carters wanted her to stay with them until everyone was caught. Alicia was only too happy to oblige. The thought of staying at her home alone was a bit frightening to her. She walked slowly, processing all that Gloria told her.

Why am I such a fool? she wondered as she walked along. *I survived an abduction with five men who wouldn't think twice about killing me.* The very thought sent shivers up and down her spine as she continued to think. *Like Mark, I have been given a second chance at life. Am I squandering it by keeping a lock on my heart?* The answer came to her in a rush and was a resounding yes. It stopped her in her tracks as she reflected on the truth of it.

Why am I keeping such a barrier around my heart? Is it making me any happier? No, it certainly isn't. The revelations were a lot to take in as she wondered again about the role of God in her life. There was a constant ache in her that she could not seem to shake. She quickly pushed the feeling aside as she always did and began to walk more swiftly to the ranch. She did not know how to deal with her thoughts and feelings. She had run for so long and had fought so hard.

But why? Why do I run? Especially in light of all that I've been through. I read some amazing things in the Bible during my captivity. All of these thoughts swirled through her mind as the ranch came into view. As had become custom, she pushed the thoughts from her mind and walked swiftly toward the house.

"Hi," Alicia called as she burst through the front door of the ranch. She heard movement from the kitchen and went in search of Claire. She found her in the kitchen bent over some pots and pans in the sink.

"Wonderful! You're just in time to dry." Claire smiled mischievously toward her.

"Bad timing," Alicia said dryly. "I think I'll go back

to Gloria's and come back in a few hours." She quickly turned and pretended to head out the door.

"Don't even think about it, Miss Barnes."

Claire chuckled as Alicia grabbed the drying cloth and began to work on the pile of wet pans.

"So how was your visit with Gloria?" Claire inquired. Alicia glanced toward her. She never revealed all of the soul-searching that took place with Gloria Tyler. The woman seemed to have a way with making people see and face up to their fears or struggles.

"It was really nice," Alicia responded honestly. "We chatted over some tea. I forgot how wonderful it was to just sit and visit with her. She is so wise."

"It's the same way with me. She was there for me every step of the way with Mark's accident. I hope that I'll be that wise when I'm older and can guide younger women the way she does." Claire's voice was wistful. Alicia looked over and saw that Claire's hands had momentarily stopped in the water and were now resting in suds. She knew that they were both thinking toward the future.

Alicia knew that Claire was already wise and special and a dear friend to everyone. How much more would she be thirty years from now! But as for herself, Alicia found the thought troubling. Would people want to come to her for help and advice? Or would she end up alone and miserable and unable to deeply love anyone? *Surely not*, she reasoned with herself. Her musings were interrupted as Caleb walked through the door.

"My two favorite women!" he gushed as he gave them both hugs. "How was your day?" The question was directed at both of the women as Caleb made himself comfortable in one of the kitchen chairs.

"It's been rough." Claire took on a dramatic voice and sighed deeply. Alicia turned to face the pile of dishes to dry in order to squelch the laughter that was threatening to spill over.

"This girl here"—Claire motioned with her head toward Alicia—"has given me nothing but trouble all day. First, I was sweeping out the front room when she opened a window and let a burst of air come through and scatter the dust everywhere." Caleb feigned a shocked look as Alicia stood with her hands on her hips to hear what Claire would concoct next. "Next she got Rebel all riled up, and he went trampling through my vegetable garden! Then, while *I* was out brushing down some of the horses, Alicia came to cook and left an atrocious mess for me to clean up. Do you see all these dishes?" Alicia turned and gave her a playful slap on the arm.

"I didn't do any of those things!" she cried. Caleb let out a hearty laugh.

He felt that nothing could be better than seeing his sister and Alicia together again, laughing and not feeling afraid. He would take on the world for them if he could. It was moments like these when he realized just how precious life was and the people in his life were to him. Claire's thoughts were running along the same lines as her heart wanted to sing for joy. It felt like ages since they were able to laugh together and simply enjoy each other's company.

The girls turned to finish with the dishes as Caleb spoke.

"I spoke with Pastor Tyler today."

"I saw Gloria Tyler today," Alicia commented.

"Really? And how is she doing?"

"Fine."

"Good. So is Pastor Tyler. In fact, we've decided that it's time to pay a visit to Rigby in jail." Alicia whipped around so fast that a pan nearly fell from her hands.

"Really?" she asked with a hopeful smile.

"Yep."

"Oh, I'm so glad." The Carters both looked at her in surprise.

"He's really not a bad guy," she admitted. "He's only a boy. His father just led him astray, and he needs someone to help him get his life back in order. He shared a lot of things with me while I was being held captive." Alicia put up her cloth and went to sit down at the table. Claire joined them, and Alicia continued. "He told me that after his mother's death, his father turned to alcohol and then forced his sons into a criminal life." Alicia paused for a moment. Caleb and Claire waited silently for her to continue. "He asked about God. I remember thinking how I wished that he had someone like Pastor Tyler to talk to. And now you're both going to see him! I think that's wonderful, Caleb. Please, try to help him find God and peace in his life." Alicia stopped, and Caleb and Claire both exchanged a glance. Her speech confirmed their suspicions. God was working on Alicia's heart and breaking down some of the walls that she had put up.

If Caleb had any doubts of going to see Rigby with Pastor Tyler to share the gospel, they were laid to rest at that moment. He knew beyond a shadow of a doubt that it was the right thing to do. God forgives sins—what right do they have to do any less?

"In fact, wait just a moment." Alicia quickly dashed up the stairs. Caleb and Claire both looked at each other questioningly.

"Here," she said as she thrust a small, black object in Caleb's hand. He turned it over to read *Holy Bible* written in faded gold letters on the front. He looked to her with questions in his eyes.

"It's a Bible." Claire stated the obvious.

"It belonged to Rigby's mother," Alicia informed them. They both looked to her and then the Bible with surprised eyes. "Rigby gave it to me in the hopes that I might find some comfort while I was their prisoner." Alicia did not mention that she actually read any of it, and that it really did help to calm some of her fears.

"I think it might be nice if you took it back to him. Maybe even mark some important scriptures down in it." Alicia smiled.

"Alicia, I think that's a wonderful idea," Claire said as strong emotion gripped her. She could tell God was at work in Alicia's life.

"I agree. That's a splendid idea." Caleb was just as touched that Alicia was so concerned and cared for one of her former captors enough to lay bitterness aside and think of his soul. "In fact, let's pray now that God will prepare Rigby's heart and give Pastor Tyler and me the right words." The three joined hands and bowed their heads as Caleb led them in a prayer.

"No! No!" Alicia's screams of terror rang through the house. Claire jumped out of bed, and without even bothering with her robe, ran into Alicia's room. Caleb burst through the door seconds later and watched as Claire quickly moved to the bed. Alicia was thrashing under the covers and continued to scream for help as Claire tried to wake her in soothing tones.

"No!" she screamed again as she sat up straight. Beads of perspiration dotted her face, and she looked around first in bewilderment, then in relief. She collapsed into Claire's arms. Claire held her as Alicia shook and fought to regain calm.

"It was awful! They were dragging me into the woods. There was no way to escape. They all snarled and laughed, and I couldn't run or scream or do anything. The harder I tried to fight, the worse it got." Alicia let out a small sob.

Caleb had been standing in the doorway witnessing the whole scene and stepped forward and stood directly behind Claire. For the first time, Alicia noticed his presence and released Claire to grab Caleb by the shirtsleeve.

"Caleb, don't let them get me!" Her voice was desperate, and the look in her eyes caused Caleb's heart to squeeze with pain. "Don't let them take me again! Don't let them come back for me!"

He gently removed her hands from his shirt and held them in his own. He looked her directly in the eyes and spoke with a quiet passion.

"Don't worry, Alicia. Those men will never get you again. I promise to keep you safe." With that, Alicia began to relax and slumped back against the headboard in sheer exhaustion. Caleb quietly exited the room, and Claire sat with her a few more moments. She helped Alicia get settled back down on the pillows and waited until her breathing was deep and regular to leave the room. She tiptoed out and quietly shut the door behind her. She turned and started when she saw Caleb still standing outside the door.

"Poor thing," she said softly. "She tries so hard not to let it show just how badly the situation has traumatized her."

"I know," Caleb murmured.

"I'm so glad that she's staying with us until everyone is caught. I feel so much better knowing she's right here."

"So do I."

"Caleb, has she told you any details of what happened out there?"

"Only what she told you about Rigby and then about her eye the day we found her. I don't know anything else."

"Well, I hope they did not do any other physical harm, but the emotional scars can be even worse and last longer."

Caleb nodded in agreement. "You know, perhaps it would make her feel better if Rebel began sleeping in her room at night."

"That's a good idea. You should ask her about it in the morning." With that in mind, they both turned to go to their separate rooms. But both of their hearts and minds were full. They did not know the best way to help Alicia. It broke their hearts to see her so scared and in pain. They knew that they were going to have to trust her over to God.

Chapter 21

"Rigby, you have visitors," Carl Holding said as he got the keys off of their peg and moved to unlock his cell. Rigby sat up a bit straighter. Who in the world would be visiting him? He had no friends or even relations that he knew of. He aided in kidnapping the town's schoolteacher, and his brother was the reason that Mark Brewer was to remain in a wheelchair.

The thought made him nauseous. He was so ashamed that he played any role in helping his family to destroy other people's lives. The guilt weighed heavily upon him like an anchor resting on his shoulders.

He lifted his head at the sound of the key's jingle to see two men. Carl opened the cell door to let them in and then closed it firmly behind them. Rigby looked up at them and shrank back on his bunk. They were sizing him up as well, and Rigby felt intense intimidation.

He lowered his eyes to the floor as the older man took a seat beside him on his bunk and the taller man took a chair that Carl put inside the cell for him. Rigby recognized the tall man as the one whom Alicia rode back with.

"Hello, son. My name is Douglas Tyler. I'm the pastor of the church here in town. This"—Pastor Tyler gestured with his hand toward Caleb—"is Caleb Carter. He owns a ranch just outside of town."

Rigby quickly glanced toward both men and mumbled "hello" before he dropped his eyes again. Not only was he ashamed, but he was afraid. He was afraid of the townspeople, facing his father and brothers when they were caught, and he was afraid of dying. *Is that why these men are here?* He wondered. *Am I going to die soon?*

Caleb looked to Pastor Tyler, who turned sympathetic eyes to the boy. It was obvious that he was afraid. Pastor Tyler knew that he would have to proceed gently with him. Pastor Tyler and his wife never had children, and he felt a deep fatherly compassion over this boy. He lifted a hand up and easily laid it on Rigby's shoulder.

"We just came to visit with you a while, son." Rigby slowly looked up and turned his head to look Pastor Tyler directly in the eyes. He seemed sincere enough. But Rigby was really worried about Caleb.

"I'm Caleb." Caleb made an instant decision to offer his hand. If someone had told him just days ago that he would shake hands with one of the criminals that kidnapped the woman he loved and killed his parents, Caleb would have laughed in their face. But secure in the knowledge that God was in full control and that revenge was his, he fought hard to lay aside his own feelings and be the godly example this young man needed. The gesture, though small, also helped to extinguish some of the feelings of resentment that Caleb had been quietly harboring and struggling with. In his effort to turn all things over to the Lord, he was being freed from the bonds of bitterness.

Rigby stared at him for a moment in surprise. He then took the offered hand and shook it slightly.

"I need to thank you for returning Alicia safely to us," Caleb said. Again Rigby stared, though this time wide-eyed and stunned.

"It was very brave of you to defy your family for her safety," Pastor Tyler added.

"Well, sir, I...um, well." Rigby stumbled around in

complete confusion. These people were supposed to hate him, not thank him. "I don't deserve yer thanks at all. I done some horrible things before, and I wanted out. I hate that life. It ain't right and, well, she was just so sad and scared, and I didn't want nothin' bad to happen to her is all." Rigby again hung his head. "I'm awful ashamed and would do anything to make things right."

Pastor Tyler and Caleb both studied him carefully. There was no doubt that the boy truly was filled with regret and shame.

"How is Miss Barnes?" he timidly asked.

"She's holding up pretty well." Caleb would never reveal to them just how traumatized she had been or about her nightmares that caused blood-curdling screams to resound throughout the house.

"Here," Caleb said as he handed over an object. Rigby recognized it immediately. He carefully turned it over in his hands.

"My ma's Bible," he said softly.

"Yes. Alicia wanted you to have it back."

"Rigby, if you don't mind, I've taken the liberty of marking a few of the scriptures in there that I thought may be of particular interest to you," Pastor Tyler said as he gently took the Bible from Rigby and began flipping through the pages. "See." He pointed to some underlined verses. "I thought you might find these helpful." He handed it back to Rigby and pulled out his own.

Rigby looked through some of the pages and stared. The gesture moved him beyond words.

"Much obliged," he whispered. "I wonder," he cleared his throat, "if you would mind tellin' me about 'em, please."

"Of course, son." Pastor Tyler opened his Bible and directed Rigby to where he was. "I marked these particular verses to show you how much God loves you and everyone, and he is waiting with open arms to forgive *anyone* of *anything*, and that salvation is a free gift from God through his son, Jesus Christ."

"Really?" Rigby said quietly. "I didn't think I could be forgiven. I done so much wrong." He hung his head again and looked pitiful.

"Of course you can be forgiven." Pastor Tyler almost shook Rigby to get him to raise his head. "You just have to confess your sins and believe on Jesus Christ as Lord. Here, let me show you." He found the book of Acts in Rigby's Bible and pointed out some verses. "For example, read what this says in Acts, chapter ten, verse forty-three."

Rigby looked at it for a while and then read very slowly.

"To him give all the prophets witness, that through his name whosoever believeth in him shall receive remission of sins."

"That verse is talking about believing that Jesus is God's son, and that he came to earth, was crucified, and then raised to life to save you from your sins and grant you forgiveness if you believe in him," Pastor Tyler said. Rigby did not look up from his Bible but nodded. Pastor Tyler pointed to another verse—Acts 13:38—and Rigby read once again.

"Be it known unto you therefore, men and brethren, that through this man is preached unto you the forgiveness of sins."

"Rigby," Caleb said quietly, "that means you too. That means all sins are forgiven. In God's eyes, a sin is a sin no matter how small or big. We're all sinners saved by grace." Caleb stopped then forced the next words from his throat. "To God, my sins are just as great as yours." Caleb struggled over those words. He had never killed anyone or knowingly destroyed someone's life. But he knew that deep down it was true. Sin was sin. Once again, some of the bitterness in him melted away.

Rigby's eyes flew to his to see if he was telling the truth. Caleb stared back unflinchingly, and Rigby began to understand the truth of his words. Pastor Tyler showed Rigby a few more verses and listened quietly as he read them all slowly, drinking in the words.

"'If we confess our sins, he is faithful and just to forgive us our sins, and to cleanse us from all unrighteousness.' That's from First John 1:9. Let's see, the next ones are in Romans. Chapter three, verses twenty-three and twenty-four say, 'For all have sinned, and come short of the glory of God; being justified freely by his grace through the redemption that is in Christ Jesus.' Then in chapter five, verse eight it says, 'But God commendeth his love toward us, in that, while we were yet sinners, Christ died for us.'" Rigby stopped and stared at the words, unable to fully grasp the truth of the scripture. No one ever cared about him before. Could it be that there was a God who actually loved him?

Pastor Tyler broke his silent musings when he flipped the pages and pointed again.

Rigby continued to read. "'That if thou shalt confess with thy mouth the Lord Jesus, and shalt believe in thine heart that God hath raised him from the dead, thou shalt be saved. For with the heart man believeth unto righteousness; and with the mouth confession is made unto salvation.'³ It's from Romans 10:9–10. Pastor Tyler—" He suddenly jumped up and began pacing through the confined room between the two men. "Is that true?" He raised his arm to the back of his head and scratched slightly as he turned to stare at the elderly man.

"Every word of it, son." Pastor Tyler's gaze was intense as he looked at Rigby. Rigby sat back down and put his head in his hands, but only for a moment. He raised it to find two sets of eyes focused on him. They both noted the tears they saw in his eyes but never let on.

"Thanks. I need time to think this through."

"Of course, son." Pastor Tyler gave Rigby's shoulder a slight squeeze. They signaled for Carl, and he came to let them both out. Rigby sat motionless for a long time as his mind raced. Was this really the truth? Could he really be forgiven? Was there really a God who loved him and still wanted him? The questions swirled through his mind as he reached for the Bible and began to reread all that was marked.

Chapter 22

Dusk was swiftly approaching as Caleb and Alicia brought their horses back into the stables. Alicia needed to go on a ride to clear her mind. Lately it was all she could do to pull together a coherent thought. Everything seemed to swirl in her mind over Mark's accident and the way that he and Claire were so peaceful over it. Life was difficult for them; every day was a challenge, but they were learning how to cope. With the exception of just a few townsmen, everyone was treating him the same way.

Alicia also reflected on the recent events in her own life. She had been kidnapped and had moments when she was sure that she would never see her beloved new town again. Caleb came to her rescue and was wonderful to her. He and Pastor Tyler even began making trips to see Rigby and share the gospel with him. Caleb told her that he seemed happy and receptive to hear all that God had to say about sinners, forgiveness, and salvation. This brought Alicia's thoughts back to her own life and what was missing and why it was that she continued to run from God. Alicia found that she could not even answer her own questions. She did not know why she ran anymore. She gave herself excuses such as she had been running for so long that she was not sure how to stop. Or, like Rigby, she was not sure if God would still want her.

All of this consumed her every waking moment, and she finally went for a ride. Caleb insisted on going too—he rarely let her go anywhere alone anymore. He even let her take Knight. So they saddled up the two stallions and went flying off onto the prairie land. They rode long and hard.

It was now nightfall as they walked their horses back to their stalls. The couple had barely said two words to each other the entire trip. Caleb sensed Alicia's need to be alone with her thoughts. He now watched her as her fingers gently caressed the stallion. Her auburn hair fell softly against her shoulders, but the twinkle in her eyes was missing. Caleb's heart squeezed with pain at the sight of her troubled eyes, and he longed to help her. Her back remained to him and he just watched and prayed.

He lit a lantern and set it up on his small desk in the stables. He turned to guide Midnight into his stall as Rebel ran in and let out a small yelp, wagging his tail in anticipation of his master's attention. The brown mare closest to the door, which was Caleb's most skittish horse, let out a whinny and kicked her back legs out at the sound of the yelp.

Alicia started and quickly turned to see what was going on. She watched as the mare's hoof hit the desk and the lantern began to tumble toward the ground. Caleb dropped Midnight's rope and dove for the lantern. He caught it before it hit the floor full of hay and blew it out just before he himself crashed into the floor.

"Caleb! Caleb!" Alicia's cry of panic reached Caleb's ears, and he jumped up hurriedly. Memories flashed through Alicia's mind as she stood terrified in the darkness of the stable.

"Alicia, it's okay." Alicia barely heard Caleb through her panicked state.

"Caleb! Caleb! Where's the door? Where are you? Caleb!" Alicia was in a near state of hysteria. She began groping all around, trying to find her way out, and tripped over Knight's front hoof. She landed face first in a pile of hay and quickly sat up, more frightened now than ever. She spat hay out of her mouth and began screaming for Caleb. There was unmistakable terror in her voice, and the horses all began to tense and shift uneasily. Caleb had been searching for a match, and with hands that shook out of worry for Alicia, he quickly lit the lantern again.

He turned to find her crumpled on the floor just outside of Knight's stall. Her eyes were wide with fear and panic. Caleb's own heart skipped a beat when he saw that all color had drained from her face. He ran to her and came down beside her. He scooped her up in his arms, and she clung to him as if her life depended on it.

"Oh Caleb!" She sobbed as she continued to cling to him. Her small frame shook, and Caleb held her tightly.

"Don't leave me, Caleb," she begged him. The look on Caleb's face was as surprised as he felt. Of course he would never leave her. He did not say a word but held her all the more fiercely until he began to feel her relax in his embrace. After several moments, she finally moved until she could look him in the eyes. He stared down at her tear-stained face and was filled with compassion. She sniffed and, with a voice still trembling, began to speak.

"I'm sorry for my outburst, Caleb." She pulled a handkerchief from the sleeve of her dress and dabbed at her eyes. He stared at her for a moment. *What does she have to be sorry about? And what was it that scared her so badly? Was it her abduction or is there more?*

"There's nothing to be sorry for, Alicia. You've been through so much. It's all right. You're safe now. I wish I could help you." He spoke softly and tenderly as he felt Alicia relax a bit more in his arms.

"You help me more than you know." She smiled. "But I must explain to you the cause for my outburst just now. It's not because I was attacked by Dirk or because I was kidnapped." She stopped and looked straight ahead.

Caleb watched her intently. When she continued, her voice became very wistful. "I have never told you how my mother died. We were in the barn putting up the horses after an evening ride. Mother had hung the lantern from the same hook that it always stayed on. There was a stray dog who stayed in our town. No one wanted to claim him, so he moved from farm to farm. This particular night he came running into the barn and started barking loudly. Mostly we figured that he was really hungry. Anyway, mother's horse jumped and reared her hind legs, and they kicked the lantern. It landed with a crash in the hay, and it started a huge blaze in the barn." Alicia stopped as tears filled her eyes. She had never spoken of her mother's death until now, and she was not prepared for the emotions that came spilling back. Caleb's arm tightened around her, but she did not seem to notice as she continued.

"We were trying to get all of the animals out of the barn, but we did not realize how fast a fire spreads. I was closest to the doors, and Mother was toward the back. She had just freed the remaining horse and a cow when the large middle beam collapsed. It crashed to the floor and with it, the entire back end of the barn. I tried to get to her, but there was nothing I could do. Moments later the rest of the barn collapsed, and I just had to stand there and watch." Tears now poured down Alicia's face.

The pain of that horrible night rushed upon her and caused her whole body to tremble anew. She covered her face with her hands as she cried, and Caleb sat quietly beside her. His own eyes held tears. Alicia suddenly jumped up.

"I can't do this anymore, Caleb!" She began frantically pacing through the stable. He stood, and she practically flung herself at him. She grabbed his shirtsleeves and held them as she looked into his eyes. Her voice rose an octave as she spoke.

"Caleb, what's the matter with me? I can't do this anymore! I can't keep running from God! I know that something is missing in my life. I have known that for months! It's a void that only he can fill. I was just so angry over the death of my parents that I did not want anything to do with him. But he spared me when I was kidnapped. I actually started reading my Bible again! Did you know that?" Caleb shook his head slightly and listened in awe.

"I came back here and was filled with anger and bitterness over Mark's accident, yet he and Claire are happy and at peace. I want that too. Why have I been so foolish?" She quickly let go of Caleb's arms and ran out of the stable. She ran hard and finally stopped under a large oak tree. A brook gently made its way along, and the noise had a calming effect on Alicia. She sat on a stone that was to the right of the tree. This had become her favorite spot, and she often went there to find solace. She now came in her misery to try and make peace with God.

Caleb was only a step behind her. He was not sure how far she would go, and he was determined not to let anything happen to her. It was nearly completely dark outside now, and he was not going to leave her alone in the dark. He came up behind her and leaned against the tree.

She heard him approach and was thankful for his presence. She turned to find him watching her closely. She reached out her hand for him.

"Help me." Her words were simple, but her eyes were pleading. He took her hand and sat next to her. She looked at him, her eyes boring into his own.

"Will God still want me? I have run for so long and fought him for so long. I've been so angry and bitter. Will he still want me?" She had his hand clasped tightly in both of hers as her eyes searched his for help.

"Of course he does, Alicia." He felt her grip relax as relief washed over her. "He still wants everyone. It does not matter how far you have run or how hard you have fought or what sins you have committed. God longs for you to be his child and to turn to him. He's waiting with open arms to forgive you and accept you. All you have to do is believe and surrender your life to him." Alicia watched him for a moment and knew in her heart that he spoke the truth.

"I want to surrender my life to God," she said firmly. The words rushed over Caleb as a smile appeared on his face. How he had prayed for this moment when Alicia would accept Jesus Christ as her personal Lord. And he was here to share the moment with her! His heart felt as if it would overflow at any moment. He closed his eyes as Alicia did and sat motionless as she began to pray.

"God, I am so sorry that I have run so long and so hard from you. Please forgive me. I want to give my life over to you. I want you to be the Lord of my life. Thank you for your saving grace on the cross and for saving me. Amen."

Alicia spoke the words from her heart and immediately felt a peace steal over her entire being. She had finally stopped running. The deep ache that constantly lingered was now filled. She felt lighthearted and, for the first time in months, at peace.

She turned her beaming face to Caleb, who had a grin so wide it nearly split his face. She watched a tear roll down his cheek and threw herself into his arms. They hugged for a long time and finally pulled away and smiled at each other. Neither spoke, because words could never adequately express the joy that they both felt at this moment. Caleb kept one arm around her, and they looked out toward the brook. The moon had just come out and was now shining down, casting beautiful silver rays all across the brook. The stars were shining brightly and the entire sight was breathtaking. Here, beneath the oak tree, with Caleb by her side and God in her heart, Alicia knew that this was a moment she would always remember.

———

Rigby sat in his cell in quiet reflection. He peered out of the barred window and saw the moon casting silvery hues over the prairie land. So much had happened to him in the last couple of months. His world had been turned upside down, and he now found himself in strange and completely foreign territory. The only family that he had was out there somewhere, and for the first time in his life, he was not with them. Rigby found himself surprisingly glad that he was not with his father or brothers.

He thought back over his time with Alicia Barnes and found it to be a kind of turning point in his life. He found the courage to do what he had wanted for so long—to get away. End the life of being a criminal. He was still surprised from Pastor Tyler and Caleb's visit. Yet they would never know the impact that they had on him. Rigby was moved beyond words and realized that he wanted to know God more than anything. He wanted God to love him, and he wanted to surrender everything. He knew that whatever punishment he would have to face for his previous crimes would be bearable as long as he had God.

He silently turned from the window and reached for the Bible. He opened it up, and it fell to the book of Matthew. Rigby then began to read from chapter 4 about the calling of the first disciples. He read the verses several times, and 19 and 20 stood out to him in particular.

"'And he saith unto them, "Follow me, and I will make you fishers of men." And they straightway left their nets, and followed him.'" Rigby read the last words a few more times as their meaning began to sink fully in. Jesus called, and they responded with no hesitation. They were only fishermen, but God had great plans for them. *And they straightway left their nets and followed him.* Straightway. They left their nets. They left all means of livelihood to follow Jesus. They left the life they knew to follow, trust, and believe.

The truth hit him like a blow to the chest. Jesus was calling him to leave his old life and follow after him. Rigby had been standing by the window to be able to read, and he now sunk down onto the bunk. He had already decided to leave his old life. Now all he had to do was decide to follow Jesus. The decision was made in an instant. Rigby knew that he wanted the love of God more than anything else, and his only desire now was to follow him.

Rigby moved to kneel beside his bed. He buried his face in his hands and began to pray.

"God, I know I led a wicked life up to now, but I want to change. I want to change somethin' fierce. I also want to follow you. I believe in you and that your son died to save me from my sins. I know I ain't worthy to be given a second chance, but Pastor Tyler showed me in your book where you said that I could still be forgiven, and I thank ya fer givin' me that chance. Help me to be worthy of your love."

He stopped praying and felt a peace that he had never experienced before in his life wash over him. His heart felt lifted in his chest, and he knew that he was now a child of God. His relief at being set free caused tears to fall silently down his face, and he remained kneeling by his bed for a long time. When he finally rose and lay down on his bunk, a peaceful sleep claimed him.

Carl Holding silently watched the whole scene. He was touched that he was able to witness such a joyful moment in this boy's life. Carl knew that Rigby had no idea that he was being watched. Carl looked at the sixteen-year-old boy sleeping peacefully for the first night since he had been in town and lifted up a prayer of thanks.

Chapter 23

Breakfast at the Carter ranch was a joyous one that morning. Claire had been asleep when Caleb and Alicia finally came back into the house, so Alicia had to wait until morning to tell Claire of her decision.

Alicia was up, dressed, and halfway through preparing breakfast when Claire came down the back stairs into the kitchen.

"My, you're up early this morning," Claire noted. It was unusual for Alicia to be up before Claire, much less ready to go.

"Have some coffee," Alicia nearly sang as she poured Claire a cup. Claire studied her carefully to try and figure out why she was so cheerful. Her first thought was of Caleb, but she quickly pushed that from her mind. She knew that Caleb would wait until the end of time if he had to, but he was not going to make any romantic intentions known to Alicia before she was a fellow believer. She took the cup that Alicia offered to her and only stared when Alicia gave a wide smile.

"All right," Claire said as she sat down at the table, "I give up. What's going on?"

"What do you mean?" Alicia asked as she turned innocent eyes to her.

Caleb chose that moment to walk into the kitchen whistling. Now Claire knew that something was going on. She furrowed her brow in frustration when they smiled at each other.

"Good morning, little sister," he said as he dropped a kiss on her forehead.

"Okay, that's it," she said with a defiant huff, standing from the table. Caleb and Alicia both turned to her with sweet smiles that Claire found unbearably annoying. "Someone tell me what's going on!"

"All right, I'll tell you," Alicia said with a wide grin. "Last night I realized that there was a huge void in my life that can only be filled by the love of God. So, I turned it all over to him." Claire let out a burst of delight and ran to hug her new sister in Christ. The two women met halfway and embraced. Claire let out squeals that reminded Alicia of the children at the schoolhouse. Caleb stood back for a moment then decided to participate in the celebration and join in the girls' hug.

Claire was rarely one to be at a loss for words during moments of great excitement, but today she simply hugged and squealed and delighted in what Alicia had just told her. She had been praying for so many months that Alicia would make this decision. Joy filled her heart until it felt as if it would burst at any moment.

The three of them finally made themselves sit down for breakfast, and Claire wanted to hear the full story. Alicia told her of the night before and the incident in the barn. As she told Claire about her mother's accident, Claire's eyes brimmed with tears. Alicia spoke now with peace instead of fear, and Caleb silently noted the change in her and his heart rejoiced. When Alicia finished her story, Claire was ready to squeal all over again. She had no words to express her utter delight upon hearing of her dear friend's salvation. Which caused another thought to cross her mind. Alicia was now a born-again believer. Caleb was now free to pursue her. The thought almost made Claire begin to squeal all over again, but she squelched it down knowing that now was not the appropriate moment, and the subject at the table switched to Rigby.

"Caleb, I meant to ask you how your meeting with Rigby went," Alicia said.

"It went very well." Alicia knew that going was a huge step for Caleb. He was trying not to be overcome by anger over this man and his family. Alicia's heart swelled with pride.

"I gave him his mother's Bible," he continued. "He seemed genuinely pleased to have it back. Pastor Tyler marked several verses for him and shared them with him. Rigby was very open and receptive. There were times when he seemed so much younger than sixteen. He is like a lost child trying to find his way on his own." Alicia nodded at this description. She knew it to be all too true. She had felt the same way during the weeks that she spent with him. He was a boy desperately trying to become a good man with no one to show him how.

"Caleb, I've been thinking," Alicia slowly began. "Would you mind going back there today?"

Caleb watched her in puzzlement for a moment.

"Well, no," he answered slowly. "But why?"

"Because I'd like to go and see him."

———

There was a loud commotion as seven men rode into town. The townspeople gathered outside on the boardwalks coming out of all the buildings and looked out toward the far end of town. A cloud of dust hid from view the faces of the men who approached, but it made quite a scene. As they drew closer to town, women could be heard gasping as four men held rifles trained on three men whose horses were situated in the middle of the bunch. The men in town stood and watched, most with expressions of satisfaction. Holding and Vickery were among the men with rifles, and the townspeople knew who the three men must be that they brought with them. Everyone watched as they rode up to the jailhouse.

Holding and Vickery ushered the men inside. The other two men with rifles walked in and stood toward the back, and the three men were shoved forward. Carl Holding stepped forward, and the two brothers shook hands.

From his cell, Rigby watched in shock. Although why he was surprised, he did not know. He knew that sooner or later the rest of his family would be brought in. They saw him and glared at him. He wanted to dive into a corner and hide but resolutely held his ground. He was not going to be afraid of them. They could no longer hurt him.

His eyes penetrated through his brothers, who were all startled to see him looking so confident. His gaze faltered slightly when met with his father's but Rigby forced himself to maintain eye contact. Buck stepped back slightly in surprise and was met with a rifle barrel in his back.

There were only two cells in the jailhouse, and Vickery was going to split the men up. Carl caught his arm just as he was reaching for the keys.

"I want Rigby in a cell alone," he said quietly but firmly. Vickery and Holding both turned questioning eyes to him, but realizing that he must know something they did not, Vickery obeyed. He opened the door to the other cell and led the men inside.

"Carl, thanks for holding down the fort while we were gone," Holding said.

"This is Ian Porter and Ryan Turner," he introduced. "They were sent to help us get the men back here safely. They'll be returning in the morning. Thanks for all of your help, men." The two nodded and then made their way to the hotel in desperate need of baths and a hot meal. Once they had gone, Holding motioned for Vickery and Carl to follow him into his office.

Holding's office was set just off from the main entrance of the jailhouse and was a small cubbyhole of a room. But it did hold a certain amount of privacy, which was what Holding wanted.

"What's been happening while we were gone, Carl?" Holding came straight to the point. Carl filled them both in on everything, putting special emphasis on Rigby's cooperativeness and the visit from Pastor Tyler and Caleb. Holding and Vickery listened in stunned silence. Carl ended with the scene he witnessed last night and Rigby's salvation.

Holding let out a low whistle.

"Well, if I wasn't convinced before, I sure am now that God works in mysterious ways. And you were absolutely right in keeping Rigby separated from his family." Holding raked a hand through his hair as his mind whirled. The father in him wanted to take Rigby home, adopt him, and teach him. But he knew that was impossible and felt greatly relieved that he was not the judge as well. A judge was being wired to come to town for the trial as soon as the other brother was caught.

"I noticed you only had three men," Carl remarked.

"One got away," Vickery said in disgust. "We came upon them in their camp and had them all surrounded, but one was down by the river with his horse and got away."

"Did they tell you their names?" Carl wanted to know.

"The oldest one is Buck. He's their father. Then there's George and Bob. The one that got away is called Cotton."

"Cotton, huh? Interesting name," Carl said dryly.

"The sheriff in Missouri said they would keep a look out for him, and they've sent more posters to the neighboring towns. Actually"—Holding's voice dropped lower at this point as he leaned closer to the men—"I think Cotton will be here visiting us at some point. The only life and family he knows are right here. My guess is we'll find him around here someday soon."

Carl and Vickery both nodded. Holding was probably right.

"Listen, Tom, why don't I stay on here for a couple more days? You haven't seen your family in over a month," Carl graciously offered. Holding's shoulders slumped in relief. More than anything else, he wanted to embrace his family. The brothers exchanged an understanding look, and it was settled.

"That goes for you too, Vickery. You need some rest as well," Carl added.

"Thanks, but I'll try and be in sometime tomorrow to help out." Vickery did not have a family of his own and did not relish the idea of sitting at home alone wishing that he did.

Just outside of the office door another conversation was taking place.

"You betrayed us," Buck addressed his youngest son in a dark, coarse voice. He leveled Rigby with a look before he continued. "You snuck that girl out, and then you turned us in."

In a burst of courage Rigby said calmly, "Yes, pa, I did. And I ain't never been more proud of anything I done in my whole life." He met his father's eyes and stared straight into them. Buck had never felt so taken aback. Rigby never stood up for himself or anyone else before. His brothers had a few nasty remarks of their own, and Rigby took them all calmly, secure in his newfound faith.

Caleb and Alicia rode slowly into town. There were people loitering outside all of the buildings, which would not have been so unusual if they were chatting and acting normally. Today they stood in huddled groups talking quietly and motioning every now and then to the jailhouse. As soon as Caleb and Alicia rode in, various groups would turn to stare at them and then begin to whisper. Caleb watched them intently, trying to figure out what was going on.

"Caleb, what's wrong with everyone?" Alicia was beginning to feel unnerved. She cautiously watched people turn to her as they rode by. They did not so much as offer a wave as they passed, which was very unusual.

"They keep looking to the jailhouse. Maybe they are surprised that you're going there," Caleb said, doubting his own words.

"They don't know where I'm going," Alicia pointed out.

Caleb was stumped as he stopped the horses in front of the jailhouse and climbed down from the buggy. By now every eye in town was upon them.

"Come on," Caleb said as he took Alicia's elbow and turned her away from the prying eyes.

Holding, Vickery, and Carl were just coming out of the office as Caleb and Alicia entered.

"Oh!" Alicia gasped. Her gaze fell immediately on the three men that Holding and Vickery had just brought in. She clutched Caleb's arm fiercely. Her legs felt as if they would go out from under her. Caleb put a strong arm around her waist and placed a hand on top of the one that was clinging to him.

Caleb's eyes moved to the cell where three men

stood, sneering at Alicia. Their eyes told that they were well pleased with her fearful reaction. Their foul smiles revealed decaying teeth. All of them were filthy, and Caleb was loath to look at them. His first thought was of horror at the idea that these men had kept Alicia for so long. No wonder she had nightmares. Alicia turned eyes filled with terror to Caleb, but before he could usher her outside, Holding grabbed Caleb and motioned them into his office. Once again, everyone stood in the privacy of the little room.

"What are you doing here?" Holding asked Alicia. He didn't attempt to cover his surprise.

"I, well, I just...you see..." Alicia's voice broke and tears began to well in her eyes. She certainly wasn't prepared for this.

"We came to speak with Rigby," Caleb answered. Alicia's grip was still firm on his arm, and her knuckles were going white. He kept a protective arm tightly around her.

"Why?" Vickery asked in disbelief. Why Alicia would want anything to do with Rigby was beyond him.

"Because, well, I just thought that I..." Alicia put her face in her hands and could not stop the rush of tears. She silently cried and fought to pull herself together. She was embarrassed to be crying so harshly in front of all these men. Caleb guided her to a chair, and she sat down and tried to regain some composure.

"Carl told us that you and Pastor Tyler visited Rigby earlier," Holding addressed Caleb. "That was very good of you. Is that why you came, Alicia?" His voice turned soft as he looked at the poor girl.

"Yes." She quietly hiccupped. "And to tell him that I accepted Christ into my life last night."

"That's wonderful, Alicia," Holding said sincerely. "I

think we might be able to arrange for you to speak with him alone if you'd like."

"Oh no," she said as her head flew up. Her tear-stained face broke the hearts of all the men. "Not now, not today. I can't. I just can't." Her eyes searched his for understanding.

"Of course not. You need time to adjust to having them all here. But Alicia, I promise you that you are perfectly safe now."

She nodded and stood. She had her crying under control and walked to the door. Right before she opened the door to leave the office, she turned and addressed Carl.

"Was there ever a ransom demand made for me?"

"No, I can't say as there was."

"They said they were going to hold me for ransom," she said quietly.

She had her face turned from the prisoners as she left the office. Caleb shot a glance their way as they left as if to dare them to speak, and they all wisely kept silent.

Once outside, Caleb assisted Alicia into the buggy. Before he had a chance to climb on himself, Holding took his arm and pulled him aside.

"Caleb," he said in a hushed voice, "We only caught three of the four men. The man they call Cotton is still on the loose and will probably find his way to Darby looking for his family. You need to keep an eye out." Caleb nodded. Everyone outside was still standing exactly as they had when Caleb and Alicia entered. They tried to ignore the stares as they quickly made their way out of town.

"What?" Claire and Mark said in unison at the dinner table that night. Caleb and Alicia had just recounted the events of earlier that afternoon at the jailhouse, and Claire and Mark could barely believe their ears.

"They finally caught them?" Claire asked.

"Well, all but one. Cotton is still on the loose." Caleb informed them.

"Cotton?" Mark laughed in between bites. "What a name. Is it short for something?"

"I don't know," Alicia said. Ever since that afternoon, her mind seemed to be a million miles away. The other three at the table noticed and decided to change the subject. Lighter topics were discussed, and Alicia even ended up laughing at one point. The evening went by quickly, and before anyone was ready, Caleb was hitching the team to the wagon to take Mark home.

At first after the accident, Mark did not like having to depend on other people to get him in and out of town, but he did not seem to mind much anymore. Caleb was his soon to be brother-in-law, and he was at ease with him. Once they were on their way, the women headed upstairs to ready themselves for bed.

Alicia lay in bed for what seemed like hours, waiting for sleep to come. She tossed and her mind replayed the scene in the jail over and over again. She could still see with perfect clarity the satisfied looks on Buck, George, and Bob's faces while they sent her threatening looks and bared nasty teeth. She remembered the look of compassion on Rigby's face as he watched the exchange. Alicia tried to pray and rid her mind of the tormenting thoughts, but she simply could not. She finally threw back the covers and got up. She put on her robe and quietly exited her room.

She began walking down the hall toward the kitchen when she noticed that there was still a light on underneath Claire's door. She lightly tapped on the door and heard a quiet "Come in."

"Hi," Claire greeted her. "Can you not sleep?" She looked to Alicia with compassion.

"Not really."

"Come on." Claire patted the edge of the bed beside her, and Alicia sat down. Claire watched her patiently, waiting for her to speak.

"I can't stop thinking about this afternoon. The whole thing just keeps replaying itself over and over in my mind," she finally said quietly.

"I know. I wish I had been there to help you."

"But Claire, I really do want to speak with Rigby. I just don't know if I can face going there again. Sheriff Holding said he could arrange for us to talk alone, but I don't know if I can even look at the others another time." Tears began to form in her eyes, and Claire searched her mind, desperate for words of comfort to offer her beloved friend.

"Perhaps Caleb can talk to the sheriff, and he can arrange for you to meet somewhere other than the jail," Claire offered, though she was not sure that the sheriff would actually do that.

Alicia was suddenly hit with a realization. In being so fearful of her former captors, she was allowing them to once again control her life. She said as much to Claire, who simply nodded in return. Claire had already thought of that but did not want to mention it because she did not want Alicia to feel even worse.

"No," she said, her voice lined with determination, "I'm going back there to speak with Rigby, and I will not be afraid. I'll look them all in the eye and let them know that they have no more power over me."

Claire's eyes began to dance with merriment.

"Is something funny?" Alicia demanded.

"You are," Claire said as a giggle escaped. "I can just see you walking up to them and staring them down all the while calmly letting them know who the boss is now." Alicia could not help but smile at Claire's description. She was right.

"Well, maybe I'll just show up and quietly go into Sheriff Holding's office, then," she said.

Claire stopped smiling, and her voice turned serious.

"Honestly, though, Alicia, I really think that you would be doing the right thing in going back."

"I think so too. Thanks, Claire." She smiled and quickly changed topics.

"So have you and Mark set another date yet?" They were originally supposed to be married in June, and now the wedding had been postponed indefinitely.

Claire looked away as she thought. She knew Alicia would eventually ask that question; she actually expected her to ask sooner. She and Mark had not set another date as of yet because as long as Alicia was still with them at the ranch, Claire could not leave. But she was not about to tell Alicia that. Now that almost all of the men had been caught, hopefully the two would not have to wait much longer.

"We still have not decided. Probably in the fall," Claire honestly replied. It was early July, and she felt sure that by the fall all would be settled.

"Is it because of me?" They had become so close that it was not unusual for one to read the other, but Claire had hoped that this would not be one of those times.

"I don't want you to postpone your wedding because of me. I will be perfectly fine living in my house by the school. I promise." Alicia suddenly felt very guilty. She honestly had not thought about their reasons before, and now she was horrified to discover that she was slowing them down.

"Alicia," Claire took one of her hands and looked her directly in the eye, "there are a lot of reasons why we need to wait. Now simply is not a good time. Yes, Mark and I do not want you to move back to your house yet, so we want to wait, but it is not the only reason. Mark and I want to see this ordeal with these men over before we begin our new life together. He and I will both have to testify in front of the judge, and there's just no telling when all of this will take place. When we begin our new life, we want it to be fresh and joyous. We do not want an upcoming trial to cloud any of it."

Alicia looked as relieved as she felt. She was certain that she was the only cause, but Claire's explanation made perfect sense. It would be better if the two of them waited.

"Now it's my turn to ask the questions," Claire began with a twinkle in her eye. Alicia raised an eyebrow. "When are you going to realize that you're in love with my big brother?"

"What?" Alicia practically jumped off the bed. "What on earth are you talking about?"

"You can't fool me. I've seen the way you look at him. I know he must be more to you than just a friend."

Alicia stood and began to pace. "I just don't know. My feelings are so jumbled. You know I care a great deal for Caleb, but I don't think I'm in love with him." She wrung her hands, and Claire waited for her to continue.

"Gloria told me that I can't let my past run my future. She said I needed to allow myself to feel and accept love again. But I just can't seem to do that."

"You accepted God's love," Claire pointed out.

"But it's not the same. God isn't going anywhere. When my parents died, I was shattered. I don't know if I can risk going through that again."

"There are no guarantees in this life, Alicia. You can't be afraid to live in the moment and let God take care of the future."

"Claire, I don't even know if I am in love with your brother."

"Well, let's not think about it anymore tonight. You need your rest."

"Thanks, Claire. Good night."

"Good night."

As Alicia silently made her way back to her bedroom, Claire wondered when Alicia would see what everyone else could see—that she was irreversibly in love with Caleb Carter.

The next morning, Caleb and Alicia got an early start to the jail. Caleb questioned Alicia several times to make certain that she was truly up to going. Alicia patiently assured him of all of his questions, and they were finally off. Claire decided to join them as well. She had some shopping to do at the general store, and she wanted to be there in case Alicia needed some moral support. They stopped in front of the jail, and Claire saw what they meant when they said that everyone watched them. She glanced around to find all eyes on them. Everyone who was walking along in town stopped, plus she noticed some people peering out of windows.

"I'm disappointed," Claire said to them quietly. "I thought they all had better things to do than pry into your business." She addressed Alicia, who merely nodded. Her mind was fully focused on going back inside. Claire already decided to meet them when they were through. She did not want Alicia to feel overwhelmed with people when she spoke with Rigby. She made her way down the boardwalk and was careful not to look back for fear that everyone in town would notice her concern.

"Are you sure you want to do this?" Caleb asked just before they went inside.

"Yes," said Alicia with more confidence than she felt as she squared her shoulders and resolutely pushed open the door.

She walked inside, and her nose was assailed with foul scents coming from the prisoners. She forced herself to remain neutral and not crinkle her nose. She bravely eyed all of them who were glaring at her and tossed a slight smile toward Rigby. He grinned back and then looked to his father and brothers in cool satisfaction.

Alicia walked up to the desk where Carl Holding and Paul Vickery were talking.

"Hello, Carl. Hello, Paul," she casually greeted. The men stood. Clearly they were both surprised to see her back so soon, and Vickery looked completely dumbfounded.

"Alicia," Vickery said. "What brings you here?"

"I came to speak with Rigby," she calmly answered. Carl nodded in understanding and motioned toward the office. Alicia and Caleb both walked toward it but were stopped when they heard a string of foul language coming from the other three men. Caleb gently pushed Alicia inside and shut the door.

"Silence!" Carl's voice rang out in anger. "The next man who speaks will find himself sitting in chains." He leveled them all with a look as Vickery unlocked Rigby's cell. Caleb, Carl, Vickery, and Rigby were all furious with the others for exposing Alicia to that kind of language. Caleb looked ready to explode, but knew he had to calm himself for Alicia's sake. Caleb and Rigby quietly walked into the office as Carl and Vickery stood outside the door continuing to send glares toward the prisoners.

"Hello, Rigby," Alicia said. Rigby stared at her. He always thought that she was pretty, but today she seemed radiant. She was no longer dirty or had torn clothes, and her eye was healed except for a barely noticeable scar directly underneath where it had been cut. She was wearing a simple green frock, but it did wonders to her green eyes and auburn hair.

They sat opposite each other with Rigby in a chair by the door, and Alicia's chair in front of Holding's desk. Caleb sat on the edge of the desk and rested his hand on Alicia's shoulder.

"I came by to talk with you, and to thank you for saving my life," she began.

"Don't thank me, Miss Barnes. I shoulda taken you outta there long before then." His eyes were pained and dropped to the floor. Alicia leaned forward slightly in her chair.

"What is your last name, Rigby?"

"Buchanan."

"You have a nice name."

Rigby looked up at her before he mumbled thank you.

"I'm much obliged to ya fer sendin' back my ma's Bible." He kept his eyes on the ground as he spoke. Alicia looked at him and felt her heart turn over.

"You're very welcome, Rigby. I'm so glad that you let me use it while I was being held captive. It really spoke to me and got me thinking again."

"Me too, Miss Barnes." Rigby looked up as his voice began to strengthen with excitement. "The best thing happened to me just the night before my family was brung in. I realized that I needed a Savior, and I gave my life over to Jesus." He grinned wide, and Alicia beamed back at him. Rigby noticed that Caleb had a large smile covering his face as well.

"That's wonderful, Rigby!"

Caleb stood up and moved to shake the young boy's hand.

"I'm proud of you, son," Caleb said. Rigby sat frozen as they shook hands. *I'm proud of you, son.* The words echoed in his mind. No one had ever said those words to him before. Both Caleb and Alicia watched as tears pooled up in his eyes. He impatiently moved the back of his hand across his face. Caleb shook his hand as if he were a man. He said he was proud of him. He called him son. Rigby was so moved that he could not speak.

"Rigby, are you all right?" Alicia questioned gently.

"I'm fine, ma'am," he said after a moment.

"Wait a minute," Alicia said suddenly. "Did you say that it was the night before your father and brothers were brought in?"

"Yes, ma'am."

"What do you know…" she said thoughtfully as she turned to Caleb. He grinned. "Rigby, I came here to talk to you about that very thing. You see, that same night, I realized the void in my own life that only God can fill. I also realized how tired I was of running from God, so I surrendered my life to him that night too."

Rigby stared at her in disbelief.

"It seems as though God used the kidnapping to reach both of us," Alicia remarked with a smile.

———

Vickery walked through the streets of town as dusk began to fall. He had to get out of the office to clear his head. So much had happened lately, and he needed to process things. He had waited twenty-five years to meet someone he could love, and when he thought he had met her it turned out that she didn't care for him. He was amazed at Alicia's courage. She survived the kidnapping, she came to know the Lord, and she had the strength to share that with one of her kidnappers. But she would never be his. Vickery sighed as he turned a corner that brought him around behind the buildings. He started walking back up toward the sheriff's office. Lost in thought, he continued up the back road when he felt a thud against his side.

A little boy ran into him and fell back on the ground.

"Let me help you, little man." He reached out a hand to help him up and looked down the alley where the little boy seemingly appeared out of nowhere.

"Thanks, mister."

Vickery looked down at the boy, who appeared to be no more than eight years old. *A trouble-making age*, Vickery thought with a grin. He squatted down so that he was eye level with the boy.

"What's your name?"

"Travis Atkinson."

"How old are you, Travis?"

"I'm seven and a half," he said proudly.

"Well, what's a big boy like you doing running down this alley?"

"I was playing a game."

"What kind of game?"

"Travis! Travis!" Vickery looked up to see a young woman running down the alley toward them. He slowly stood and kept his hand lightly on the boy's shoulder to keep him from trying to run off again.

"Travis Atkinson, I declare! What on earth were you thinkin,' running away from me like that?" The young woman carried a basketful of supplies from the mercantile. She reached them and took Travis by the hand. Then she looked over at Vickery.

"I'm so sorry about that, sir," she began then noticed his deputy badge. "Oh no! Please tell me he ain't in no trouble. I declare, he'll be the death of me yet."

"No, ma'am. No trouble here." He looked down at the little boy and winked. "He was just telling me about a game he was playing."

"Humph! That was no game. He was tryin' my last nerve, that's what. Well, I'm much obliged to ya for catchin' him for me."

"Wait," Vickery called as she turned to leave. "Are you new in town, Mrs . . . ?"

"Atkinson. Trudy Atkinson."

"Paul Vickery," he responded as he extended his hand. Trudy returned the handshake.

"Nice to meet ya. And no, sir. I just don't get to town much since my husband passed on. He left me with an awful lot of work to do on the farm."

"I'm sorry to hear that, Mrs. Atkinson."

She looked up at him, and Vickery noticed the soft brown color of her eyes.

"Thank ya kindly."

"May I escort you and Travis back to your farm?"

"I don't want to be no bother to ya, Deputy. I got my wagon right out in front of the mercantile."

"It would be my pleasure, Mrs. Atkinson. I'll get my horse and meet you outside the mercantile."

"Well, thank ya."

Vickery walked with a lighter step as he went to get his horse.

⁓

Alicia was thrilled when they got back to the ranch and Caleb suggested a ride on the stallions. Claire opted to work on some sewing, and Caleb and Alicia quickly saddled the horses and flew off across the open land. After riding for a while, they stopped at a pond to let the horses get a drink. Alicia slid easily out of the saddle and walked over to the shade of a nearby tree. After the horses had drunk their fill, Caleb tethered them to a branch and joined Alicia.

"Have I told you how proud I am of you?" Caleb asked. Alicia looked over at him in surprise.

"Why?"

"Because of the way you reached out to Rigby. Even after the rest of his family came to town, you had the courage to face them."

"Thanks, but I couldn't have done it without you."

"Of course you could have."

"I wonder when the trial will be?" Alicia thought aloud. Caleb ran a hand through his hair.

"Sooner rather than later, I hope," he responded. "I'll be glad when this is all over."

"I hope it will be soon too. Then Mark and Claire can finally be married." Alicia and Caleb sat in comfortable silence for a while. Finally Alicia started to stand.

"Well, we should—"

"Alicia," Caleb interrupted as he took her hand. He gently pulled her back down, and she looked at him with questioning eyes.

"You must know how much I care for you," he began.

"Oh Caleb, please don't," Alicia pleaded as she quickly slipped her hand out of his.

"What is it?" he gently prodded.

"I think I know what you're about to say, and I just don't feel that way about you." Alicia knew that was only a half-truth. She was afraid to allow herself to feel too much, but she also knew that she cared a great deal for him. "I can't allow myself to feel anything for you other than the friendship we have now. I know firsthand the risk that comes when you care too much for someone, and I just can't go through that again. I'm sorry." Alicia jumped up, and in a matter of seconds she had mounted Knight.

"Alicia, wait!" Caleb called.

"I'm sorry." She tossed the words over her shoulder as she began to ride off toward the house.

Chapter 24

Light streamed into Alicia's window early Saturday morning. Her eyes fluttered slowly open, and she stretched underneath the covers as she glanced toward the window. It was going to be a beautiful day. She tossed the covers back and sat up. She quickly readied herself then made her way downstairs.

It was still early, but both Caleb and Claire had already been up and were gone. Everyone had his own plans for the day, and it came as rather a relief to Alicia that she would have the entire day all to herself. Rarely did she find solitude anymore, and she found that she missed it just a bit.

Caleb was out somewhere on the ranch taking care of things that had been neglected as of late. Claire was going to be in town with Mark all day. Alicia decided that it was the perfect time for her to go work on her own little house by the school. She wanted to give it a thorough cleaning, plus she wanted to check on her garden. She just began a vegetable garden before she was kidnapped, and she was sure that it was covered in weeds by now. It was time to get things back in order. Life needed to move on. Then there was the school. She knew that it was taken care of because it also served as the church, but she wanted to clean anyway and go over some school supplies that she left.

With all of this in mind, she made short work of breakfast and was swiftly on her way. She hummed a little tune as she walked. The sun was shining down brightly, and everything was so green and fresh. She began to pray and praise God for his goodness and the beautiful day.

Cotton paced back and forth as he took occasional glances toward the small town. He had been perched on the outskirts of town for two days and was growing frantic. He had no idea how to get his father and brothers out of jail, but he knew he at least had to try. If only they had just let Alicia go, they would not be in this mess. The other men would not have tracked them for weeks at a time for only money. It was because they had Alicia Barnes. They knew she would be trouble from the start, but Buck insisted they keep her. *A lot of good keeping her did us,* Cotton thought.

He kneeled down and leaned back on his heels, staring into town. *What should I do?* The thought kept repeating itself in his mind. After about an hour of deep contemplation, he moved to sit under a large tree with a plan finally formulating in his mind.

Alicia opened the door to her house and was greeted by a cloud of dust. The inside was dark, dusty, and had a stale odor. She left the door open and went inside. She pushed back the curtains and proceeded to open all of the windows. She only had three of them—one in the bedroom, and two in the main living area. For having such a small house, she was amazed at the large task she had on her hands. She dusted the entire house, then swept the floors and scrubbed them until they fairly glowed. She took down all of the curtains and her bedspread and sheets and brought them outside, where she cleaned them thoroughly then hung them up on a line outside to dry. Next came the windows. She polished them both inside and out. This continued for hours until late into the afternoon. Her stomach began to rumble, and she realized she had not eaten since breakfast.

She fixed a snack for herself and was rather glad no one was there to see her eating so quickly. When she was done, she washed and dried her dishes and left the kitchen neat and orderly. Satisfied with the house, she then took herself outside to inspect the garden.

It was as she suspected—a mess of weeds. A few of her vegetables were hanging on bravely, but many had died. It was a small garden just off to the right of her house in the back. She planted peas, green beans, okra, carrots, cabbage, and tomatoes. She looked down now at the disarray she called her garden and quickly got to work. Seeing as it was so late in the day, she decided to pull up all of the weeds and then next time work on salvaging her remaining plants.

She stood up after about an hour of work, covered from head to toe in dirt. She went back inside to change and clean herself up. She swept out the house again after tracking in all of the dirt and then headed toward the school. She was already feeling tired from her day's worth of work, but she did so want to inspect things at the school while she was already there. She stepped inside and walked over to the bookcases on the wall in the back. She thoroughly looked over everything that was there and then inspected its condition. She then went up front to her desk and sat down. Dark was swiftly approaching, but she was so consumed in her work that she took absolutely no notice.

She also took no notice of the shadowy figure that went past her window.

Cotton snuck around the outside of the schoolhouse and thought that it was too good to be true. Alicia Barnes was in there all alone. He quietly brought around a large keg of whiskey that he got from the neighboring town. He was not recognized because he shaved and cleaned his clothes before he went. He was proud of himself over his cunning little scheme. Everything was working out beautifully.

As he made his way to the front entrance of the building, he spotted a wooden beam about the size of a baseball bat. He grabbed it and continued on his way. He peeked around the corner of the schoolhouse to make sure no one was around. Satisfied that he was alone, he opened the whiskey and began to pour it all around the front of the building. He then took what was left and moved to the sides. He made sure all of the shrubbery that was next to the building was doused as well.

Alicia finally looked up from her musings. She stood up and rubbed the small of her back. She was beginning to feel tired and sore. She looked outside to see that all was completely dark. It did not even look like the moon was shining this night. Without a thought, she began to gather her things. A sudden noise caught her attention, and she snapped up with a start. Curious, she went to the front to see if there was an animal or a branch that was making noise.

Cotton heard her begin to walk and stood just outside the door, waiting for her in the shadows. She poked her head out of the door and looked out. She turned and gasped as she saw Cotton.

Then all went black.

Cotton threw the piece of wood to the ground and

dragged Alicia inside to the back corner of the schoolhouse. He left her there, away from all of the windows. The side door was on the opposite side of her and farther toward the front. Cotton went out the side door and stealthily made his way back to the front. Feeling a rush of power, Cotton struck a match and dropped it on the ground.

With all of the whiskey, it did not take long for a large fire to begin to engulf the schoolhouse with Alicia lying unconscious inside.

Claire had been back at the ranch for a few hours when Caleb returned. He strode into the house and went to the kitchen, where smells of delicious foods assailed his senses.

"Smells good," he said pleasantly as he walked in.

Claire turned quickly from the stove and looked at him, fully expecting to find Alicia in tow. Her eyes took on a glint of worry, and her hands came together in front of her. Caleb knew the signs. Claire would always wring her hands whenever she was worried, nervous, or upset over something.

"What's wrong?" he asked as his own heart began to pound.

"Is Alicia with you?"

"No. Isn't she here?"

"No. I thought she would be with you. You don't think she stayed at her house, do you?" Claire asked with a tremor in her voice.

"I don't think so. We were adamant when she said she was going back today to clean that she should return here tonight. I don't think she would decide not to come back without even telling us." Caleb was gripped with real fear as he began to get the feeling that something happened to Alicia.

"I'm going into town to check," he said as he ran to the door.

"So am I." Claire was on his heels as they ran out the kitchen door. There was no way she was going to stay at the ranch. They jumped on their horses, Caleb whistled for Rebel, and they quickly rode out of sight.

Chapter 25

Alicia woke up in a confused daze as she slowly opened her eyes. Her head was throbbing, and she moved her hand to her forehead. It was sore to the touch. She looked around, trying to remember where she was. The smell of smoke began to invade her nostrils as she stood and squinted against the blackness of the thick smoke. She felt surrounded by the dense haze, and it became difficult for her to breathe. She coughed as she slowly made her way to the front of the building. She stopped in her tracks when she noticed that flames engulfed the entire front end of the schoolhouse and were swiftly moving toward her. Panic gripped her as she grabbed at her throat in fear. She turned, frantically trying to find a way out. All the doors were blocked. She ran to the back window and found it to be wedged shut.

I don't understand! she thought in terror. *How did the schoolhouse catch fire? What happened?* Suddenly memories rushed back as she remembered hearing a noise outside and going to look. She unconsciously moved her hand to her aching forehead. Someone had hit her with something. *Cotton!* The name hit her like a blow to the stomach. The last thing she remembered was getting a quick glance at Cotton.

She forced herself to concentrate and find a way out. Her heart nearly pounded out of her chest with fear. Every time she took in a breath she had to cough due to the heavy smoke that was infiltrating her lungs. Her eyes stung fiercely as she looked around the schoolhouse. She saw it then. *The bell.* The bell to the schoolhouse was not in the front but to the right side of the building. It was nearly swallowed in flames by the time Alicia got to it, but she finally made it and gripped the rope that was attached to the bell. She grimaced as she felt the rope burn in her hands, but it was her only choice. She bit down hard on her lip and gave the rope a mighty tug. She heard the bell go off and quickly let go of the rope. Smoke was everywhere now, and she could not see anything. She could hear the fire crackling as it moved closer to her. She closed her eyes and, using the wall as guide, went to the far corner of the building, and crumpled to the floor in the corner. She could barely breathe as the smoke covered the entire room.

She was vaguely aware of hearing a crash when she slipped into unconsciousness.

Tom and Carl Holding and Paul Vickery were all gathered at the sheriff's office chatting around a table playing cards. Carl decided to stay on at the sheriff's office until the matter with the Buchanan family was settled. Both Tom and Paul were grateful for his continued assistance. Paul was just about to declare gin when they heard the church bell sound. It was well after dark, and they knew it could only mean one thing—trouble. They jumped out of their seats almost simultaneously as they raced to the door. They stood at the doorway and stared in disbelief at the church building. There were flames coming up a couple hundred feet in the air.

Jailbreak. That was the first word that popped into Tom Holding's mind.

"Vickery, stand guard around the back of the jail!

Carl, stay here," Holding commanded as he ran as fast as his legs could carry him to the building.

Rigby knew something was wrong, but the schoolhouse was facing the other direction from his window. However, he could smell the smoke and instantly had the situation sized up. He knelt by his bed to pray. His brother was up to something. Then a sudden thought flashed through his mind. *Alicia!* But she would not be at the schoolhouse this late at night in the summertime... but then, who rang the bell? He could not allow himself to finish the thought. He continued to pray fervently despite the crude remarks coming from the cell next to him.

Caleb and Claire were riding hard into town as the bell sounded. Terror gripped them both as they looked toward the schoolhouse and church building. Flames loomed in the air. It was enough to light the whole town. Caleb's stomach dropped as he realized that someone had to be in there in order to ring the bell. *Alicia!* Without a thought to his safety, he galloped past Tom Holding and rode up to the building. That night in the barn flashed through his mind. He knew how afraid Alicia was of fire, and now here she was trapped in a burning building. Determination to save her sped him on.

Just steps away from the building, he heard a crack and watched in horror as the beam that supported the very front of the church and the steps leading up to the front door collapsed. His horse reared back, and his front two legs came off the ground. Caleb expertly remained in the saddle as alarm slammed through him. Holding and all the men from the town that had been coming with water buckets froze in their tracks as well. Claire watched through tear-filled eyes and bravely followed her brother.

Caleb made a hissing noise in his horse's ear and spurred him onward. He made a quick circle of the building to size up the situation. Fear clawed at him over the thought of Alicia being trapped in there. There was no way in except for a single window off to the right side. He jumped off of his horse and ran to the window. It was hot to the touch, and it became very clear to him just how little time he had to save the woman he loved.

He pushed up on it with all of his strength, but it would not budge. Frustration coupled with fear and determination gave him an adrenaline rush and a burst of strength he did not know he possessed. He took a few steps back from the window and ran toward it, hurling himself head first into it with all of his might. He put his fists out in front of his head, and glass shattered as he broke through the window.

A heavy stream of smoke began to race out the window. Claire sat frozen on her horse as she prayed with a fervor like never before that both Caleb and Alicia would make it out alive. The men were watering the building as fast as they could, but it was already too late. They would lose the entire thing—it was only a matter of time before the rest of the building would collapse.

Caleb hit the ground with a thud and stood quickly. Smoke was everywhere and so heavy that he could barely breathe. He took his bandana from around his neck and swiftly tied it so that it covered his mouth and nose. He looked around frantically but could see nothing except black smoke. He dropped to his knees and began to crawl toward the back of the building. He tried shouting Alicia's name, but the sound was drowned out by the roar of the fire. His low position gave him very little visibility, but he knew that it was better than nothing. It was still difficult to breathe, but he had to keep on. He used the wall as a guide and made his way around to the back of the building. When he got to the corner, he moved his legs to turn, and they bumped on something soft. He heard a low moan and looked down with squinted eyes. He reached out his hands to feel a body and relief flooded him. He found her, and she was still alive! Now he had to get her out.

He had to think fast. The fire was approaching with every passing second, and he had to get her out. He could not carry her because the smoke was too thick. He stood up and took her with him and in one smooth move draped her across his back. He then knelt to the floor and used the wall to find his way back to the window. He worried briefly about finding the window again, but he could see smoke exiting right above him, and he knew that he had found it. He set Alicia gently on the ground before picking her up again and standing. As delicately as he could he slid her body through the broken window and felt someone from the other side take her. He then reached up and jumped out himself.

As soon as he hit the ground, he felt a bucket of cold water being splashed on him, then a grown man's weight fall upon him with a large blanket covering his entire body. He had no idea that his left side was on fire when he jumped out of the window.

Tom Holding was standing anxiously by the window from the moment he saw Caleb tear into it. He was beyond relieved when he saw Alicia being lifted through it and was there on the other side to catch her. He and Claire stood by her now; neither sure of what should be done. She was breathing, but it was very shallow. Dr. Clarke quickly made his way to the scene and knelt beside her. He then ordered Holding to carry her to his office as quickly as possible.

Claire ran to her brother's side and gasped when she saw him. He was black from smoke—Alicia was even blacker—but Claire noticed burns and cuts on Caleb that were beginning to swell.

"Caleb, what can I do?" she asked anxiously. "Are you all right?" The question sounded foolish to her own ears, but she did not know what else to say.

"Alicia," he gasped. "Where is she?" He continued to take huge gulps of fresh air.

"She's being taken to Dr. Clarke's office. She's still alive." Claire's shoulders sagged in relief.

"I've got to get over there." Caleb winced as he struggled to get up.

"Take it easy, son," Dr. Clarke said. He walked up to them and glanced at Caleb's burns before going to his other side and allowing Caleb to lean on him for support. "You're on your way to my office too. Claire, you come along. I'll need your help."

"Of course," she said as she gathered the reins of hers and Caleb's horses.

They had only taken a few steps toward town when a huge crash resounded in the night. They all turned back to watch as the rest of the church and schoolhouse collapsed in flames.

Chapter 26

Vickery was standing in the shadows behind the jailhouse. Anxiety was tearing him apart. Who had been in the schoolhouse to ring the bell? Was that person safe? Or even alive? He knew the sheriff's hunch about a jailbreak was probably right. He heard the first crash, and then in the span of about three minutes heard many voices either cheering or talking loudly and feverishly. He hoped everyone was safe.

Just before the final fall of the building, he saw a shadowy figure make his way around the back a few feet from where Vickery stood. He watched as a tall, lean man stealthily made his way to the barred window to look in.

Vickery came up quickly behind him and, with his rifle pointed in his back, told him to put his hands up. The man complied, although slower than Vickery would have liked. He took the man's gun from his holster that was resting on his hip and threw it to the side. He then took a pair of handcuffs from his pocket and securely fastened the man's hands behind his back. Vickery led him inside and was not a bit surprised when Buck exclaimed in disgust, "Cotton! You idiot! Could you have made it any more obvious?"

Vickery shoved him into the cell with his father and brothers and left Carl standing guard. He had to get some answers.

⁓

Caleb slowly made his way into the office with Dr. Clarke supporting him on one side and Claire on the other. He began to feel his skin sting and burn slightly. His left side felt tingly. They barely made it through the door when Caleb asked where Alicia was.

"She's here, Caleb. Don't worry," Dr. Clarke assured him as he gently led Caleb into one of the patient's rooms. He helped Caleb situate himself on the bench. Caleb winced slightly as he bent his body to sit down. Dr. Clarke was prompt to leave—they all realized that Alicia's condition was more serious. Claire remained with Caleb and looked at him with a mixture of relief and worry.

His eyes were closed and his shoulders were slumped. Claire desperately wanted to pull him into a tight embrace and tell him that everything would be all right but did not dare touch him. His shirt was torn in places due to the glass from the window, and it was burned nearly through on the left side. However, she could not see any of the burns, so she was unable to gauge how serious they were.

She went to the chair on the opposite wall and sank into it. She closed her eyes, but the instant they were shut, images of the schoolhouse burning flashed viciously in her mind. She shook her head to clear it, but all she saw was the height of the flames blazing through the night. She opened her eyes and watched Caleb, who had not moved since they arrived. With her eyes on him, she began to pray.

An hour later, Claire walked into the waiting room located in the office lobby. Dr. Clarke's entire office was small, so the waiting area seemed especially cozy. Her head was beginning to throb, and her body began to feel the effects of exhaustion. She unconsciously lifted her hand to her temple.

"Claire, honey, are you all right?"

She recognized the voice and immediately lifted her eyes. Mark was sitting by the window in the waiting room. She ran to him and threw her arms around him. The tears that she suppressed now spilled over in a huge rush. He held her tightly as she wept. When her tears were spent, she sat down in a chair next to him and only then realized that they were not alone. Paul Vickery and Tom Holding were also present. She quickly wiped at her eyes with her handkerchief in embarrassment.

"It's all right, honey," Mark quietly assured her as he reached for her hand. She held it tightly and looked over to the sheriff and deputy.

"How is Alicia, Mr. Holding?" Her voice was still a bit wobbly. "Dr. Clarke did not say much when he came into Caleb's room. He was very preoccupied and sent me right out." Claire was unaware of the fact that the three men had been in the waiting room almost since they first arrived, and Holding had already filled both Mark and Vickery in.

"She'll be fine, Claire," Holding said tenderly as he watched her shoulders visibly sag in relief. "She was not really burned, but she inhaled a great deal of smoke and has difficulty breathing. She's a bit cut from going through the window. The only visible damage is on her hands where she grasped the rope to ring the bell. They have pretty bad blisters. I don't know how Dr. Clarke treated her, though, because I had to leave the room."

"How is Caleb?" Mark inquired. They were all anxious to know how the hero was doing.

"He is holding up pretty well," Claire was glad to admit. "It sounds as though his cuts and burns are much worse than Alicia's, but he did not inhale as much smoke.

His left side was on fire when he came out, but I did not see the actual burns. His hands, arms, and face are cut too."

"I'm so thankful everyone's alive," Mark said quietly.

"So am I," Vickery chimed in. "It was hard standing behind the jail wondering what was going on and not being able to help. It was as we suspected, though. Cotton was behind it all. I caught him as he came around the back of the jail to speak with his family. He's now safely behind bars with the rest of them."

Claire leaned against Mark's shoulder and closed her eyes. Finally everyone was caught. She never admitted to her brother or her fiancé before, but she did not sleep well knowing that one was still out there and probably headed to the town. Every muscle in her body ached from tension, and she made an effort to relax and a light sleep came to claim her.

Holding and Vickery remained in the waiting room with Mark and Claire to await the news on Caleb and Alicia.

Dr. Clarke came down the stairs to find four sleeping adults in his waiting room. It was a hard night for all of them, and their fatigue was completely warranted. Knowing that they were waiting for news, he cleared his throat and gently nudged Mark's arm. He began to stir, and his eyes fluttered open. Upon seeing Dr. Clarke, he sat up straight. The movement caused Claire to wake, and she nearly jumped out of her chair when she saw the doctor.

"How is he?" she asked. The others in the room woke up, and Dr. Clarke soon found himself with a full audience.

"He'll be fine in a few days. Fortunately he was not on fire for long and the clothes absorbed the worst of it. I put some ointment on his burns then bandaged them.

He cut himself pretty well, though. His knuckles are cut up, and I had to give him a few stitches. The cuts on his face are not deep." He watched as their faces went from concern to relief. "Caleb is free to go tomorrow if he wishes, but I would like for Alicia to remain here for another day or two. I want to monitor her breathing." Claire nodded. She was still standing, and the doctor motioned for her to sit back down. He himself pulled up a chair in front of the group. The night was beginning to wear on him as well.

"Alicia will be fine physically. The burns on her hands will heal as will her cuts. I also believe that very soon her breathing will be strong and regular again. But she has taken a terrible toll emotionally. She will probably be quite fatigued for a while and possibly suffer from nightmares. She will really need support from her friends."

"She's been through a lot," Vickery noted. Everyone nodded, knowing it to be all too true.

"She sure knows how to beat the odds," Holding added. "Well, I'd best be off. I have to get some sleep. See you all tomorrow."

"Thanks for all of your help, Sheriff." Dr. Clarke extended a hand to the sheriff. Vickery left with him, and Mark announced he had to leave.

"Dr. Clarke, if it's all right with you, I think I'd like to stay here just for tonight. I would feel so much better just to be near them," Claire said.

"Of course you would. There are two beds in Alicia's room. Go take the other one. See you in the morning." With that Dr. Clarke headed toward his own room in the apartment he had in the back of the building. Claire walked upstairs and quietly opened the door. Alicia was sleeping comfortably for the moment. Relieved, Claire quickly slipped under the covers of her own bed and fell asleep.

The next day, Caleb and Claire left the doctor's office. Claire told Alicia that she would bring over some fresh clothes for her and a book to keep her occupied.

"How do you feel?" Claire asked as they were riding home.

"Fine," he answered absentmindedly. Claire looked down at his bandaged hands.

"We'll have to change those bandages later. It's important we keep the wounds clean."

"All right."

"Caleb? Caleb!" Startled, Caleb looked over.

"Are you all right? You don't need to worry about Alicia. Dr. Clarke said she would be just fine."

"I know and I'm glad of that. It could have been so much worse. Every second counted last night."

"At least you're both safe," Claire said. "Now, what else is troubling you?"

"What do you mean?"

"Caleb, I know you well enough to know that there's something else on your mind. Do you want to talk about it?" They rode along for a while before Caleb broke the silence.

"The other day I tried to tell Alicia how I feel about her, and she didn't want to hear it. She said she doesn't feel that way about me."

"I know. She told me about it. But you know what I think?" Caleb turned in the saddle to look at her. "I think it's only a matter of time before she realizes how deeply she cares for you."

"I've tried to convince myself of that, but I don't know anymore. I've almost lost her more than once. I'm willing to take the risk of loving her, but she doesn't seem to be willing to take the same risk."

"Hang in there, big brother," Claire said reassuringly.

Alicia walked out the front door of the doctor's office and was headed for the general store. She was relieved to be able to leave the doctor's office. She felt so confined in her bed, and other than the bandages on her hands, she was fine. On impulse she turned to look where the schoolhouse had been. It was a heap of charred pieces now. The ground was black underneath it. The sight brought tears to her eyes.

She swallowed them down in a determined effort not to cry. *You cried enough lying in bed*, she reasoned with herself. *What's done is done. You cannot go back in time; you can only move forward.* Her speech, however, did little to soothe the pain in her heart. School would be starting in a month, and there was no building to have school in. The children could not go for an entire year without schooling. It also meant there was no place for church. No church building anyway. What would the town do? Once again tears began to clog Alicia's throat. She forced herself to turn away and keep walking.

As she approached the general store, she heard a familiar laugh and looked up to see Caleb leaving the store with a young woman. She ducked around the side of the building so he wouldn't see her. He was carrying the young woman's purchases and then helped her climb in her buggy.

Caleb was his usual kind self, but Alicia noticed that the woman seemed to be enjoying his attention a little too much. She giggled and batted her eyelashes whenever Caleb spoke. Alicia rolled her eyes and felt a strange emotion welling up inside of her. It took a moment for her to pinpoint what it was. Jealously. *What do you have to be jealous of? You turned Caleb down.* She chastised herself. Yet she couldn't dispel the feeling. She found herself feeling possessive of Caleb. *Stop it, Alicia Barnes.* She continued to watch as he waved goodbye, and the woman clicked to the team and headed off. Caleb went back inside the general store but only for a moment before he came back out with his own packages, mounted Midnight, and rode toward the Blue Star.

Alicia watched him go, and when the coast was clear she came out from her hiding place and went inside the general store. She wanted to make some new dresses, so she began to thumb through the material.

"Watch where you're going!" Alicia heard a shrill voice roughly say.

"I'm sorry," a young voice responded.

"Mrs. Thorne, I apologize. My daughter should have been watching where she was going."

"I should say so," the old woman responded.

"Actually I'm glad we ran into you—not literally of course," the other woman amended. "Some of the ladies in town are organizing to take some meals out to the Crawford farm. Mr. Crawford broke his leg, and his poor wife can hardly keep up with all of the farm chores. We thought it might be nice to help her out in this small way."

"Humph," Alicia heard Mrs. Thorne respond. She stopped looking at the fabric and leaned toward the shelf so she could better hear the conversation taking place on the other side.

"I don't think she wants to help us, Mommy."

"Hush, dear. We would love it if you would help us out, Mrs. Thorne."

"I got other things to do. They got children that can help them. I ain't got nobody and I'm in no mood to be takin' dinner to people who are perfectly capable to make it themselves." Alicia heard the woman curtly thank Mrs.

Thorne and walk away. Alicia stood perfectly still. She had no idea how much time had passed before she turned to leave the store, the material completely forgotten.

She walked slowly toward Gloria's house. She needed her wisdom. Hearing Mrs. Thorne frightened Alicia. If she decided never to allow herself to love, would she end up like poor Mrs. Thorne? An old woman, alone and spiteful? The thought sent chills down her spine. She knew that she didn't want to end up like that. She knocked on Gloria's door.

"Well hello, child," Gloria warmly greeted as she ushered Alicia inside. Alicia's eyes were wide, her face pale. "Come sit down, my dear." They sat down in the living room and Gloria patted Alicia's arm. "Now you just tell me what's on your mind."

Alicia recounted the events of the last few days beginning with her ride with Caleb and ending with the conversation she overheard.

"I don't want to end up like that," she cried.

"Of course you don't. Let me ask you something. What would your life be like if you had no one who cared for you and you didn't care about anyone?"

"Awful," Alicia responded without hesitation. "What a lonely, miserable existence."

"Indeed. We don't necessarily lose all of the people we love. And wouldn't you have rather loved your parents and now can cherish the happy memories you shared rather than grow up as an orphan just to be spared the hurt of losing them?"

"Of course." Alicia thought the answer seemed to go without saying.

"Well, then?" Gloria prompted.

"So what you're telling me is to cherish the moments that I have with those I care about."

"Exactly. Because you never know how long you have.

My dear, God put others on this earth so that we wouldn't be alone. If God has put special people in your life to love and care for, you should embrace that."

"And instead I've been running away from it." Understanding was beginning to dawn on Alicia. "I love Claire like a sister. I would be heartbroken if something was to happen to her, but I don't want to stop being her friend because one day something might possibly happen."

"Exactly," Gloria said with satisfaction. "Enjoy what God has given you. Love those God has blessed you with. Remember the Bible says in Job that the Lord gave and the Lord hath taken away; blessed be the name of the Lord."

"I've been so foolish. I don't want my life to be empty of God's blessings because I'm afraid to lose someone."

"Is there a particular someone you have in mind?" Gloria couldn't resist the question. Alicia looked over at her as color began to rise in her cheeks. She nodded shyly.

"I tried to convince myself that I didn't love Caleb. I tried to convince Claire and even Caleb himself. But Claire was right. Caleb is more than just a friend to me, and I do have strong feelings for him."

"It's not too late, Alicia."

But Alicia wasn't so sure. She saw Caleb with that other woman. Had she missed her chance?

After dinner the next night, Alicia decided to go for a walk. She wanted to stretch her legs, and the night was so beautiful.

"I'm going for a walk," she called as she grabbed her shawl from the peg by the door. She stepped out on the porch and took a deep breath. It was glorious out. The crickets buzzed and the sky was cloudless. The setting sun cast hues of orange and red across the prairie land.

As she walked down the steps, she heard the front door open.

"Mind if I come along?" Caleb already looked ready to go, and Alicia knew he would come whether she minded or not.

"Of course not."

He came down the steps and offered his arm. The gesture caused Alicia's pulse to quicken. Alicia finally allowed herself to recognize the strange things that happen around her heart whenever Caleb was near. She was always disappointed whenever he was not close at hand. And after her talk with Gloria yesterday, she realized that his presence was not merely the comfort of a friend to her anymore. It was as important to her as breathing.

They walked along in companionable silence for a while enjoying the clear night. Their walk ended up leading to Alicia's favorite spot by the brook. They sat down on the stone beneath the oak and watched the brook wind its way along. The moon cast silvery hues on the pond and the ripples seemed to dance under the light.

"Caleb," Alicia tentatively began. He looked at her curiously. "I saw you in town yesterday."

"Really? Why didn't you say hi?"

"You were with another woman."

"What other woman?"

"You know what I'm talking about." Alicia was beginning to feel annoyed. Caleb sat concentrating for a while. "You walked her out of the general store."

"Oh yeah, I remember. Wait a minute. Were you spying on me?" he asked playfully.

"Of course not," Alicia said defensively as she jumped

up. "I just happened to be going by and saw you there. She was very pretty," she added after a pause.

Caleb reached for her hand and pulled her back down.

"Alicia Barnes, are you trying to tell me that you're jealous?"

"Of course not," she said as she jerked her hand out of his. "Why should I be?"

"You shouldn't. She asked me if I would help her take her packages to the buggy. That was all there was to it."

"Fine. It makes no difference to me," Alicia retorted.

"Mm-hm," Caleb murmured. He looked calm on the outside, but on the inside his heart was pounding. Alicia was jealous!

Alicia closed her eyes and tilted her head slightly back, fully enjoying the beauty of the evening. She was holding up quite well. Aside from an occasional coughing spell, she was feeling completely normal. Dr. Clarke's prediction about her nightmares was true enough, but she did not suffer the emotional toll that he predicted. She actually felt relieved and safer than she had in a long time. She inhaled a deep breath contentedly and slowly opened her eyes to gaze upon the stars.

Caleb slid closer to Alicia and was rather surprised when he sensed her relax. Earlier that day, after spending hours in prayer, a full peace had stolen over her heart. In just the course of a few months, her life had been threatened many times, bringing her precariously close to death. A woman who rarely cried, she had a full breakdown just that morning.

The full impact of the events of the past few months came crashing down upon her like a tidal wave crashing against the shore. Another nightmare had assailed her the previous night, and she had once again awoken the house with her screams. Claire and Caleb both ran in, and at Claire's light touch to her arm, Alicia sat up with a start bathed in perspiration. Claire stayed with her for close to an hour—long after she had fallen back to sleep. The idea of leaving her after hearing her screams rip through the house was incomprehensible to Claire, who cared so much for this special woman that God had placed in their lives.

Alicia awoke early the next morning and stood by her window staring out at the open country. She loved to hear the birds chirp in the mornings and watch the mist rise over the hills. But this morning, all of the beauty was lost on her as her mind replayed her dream over and over.

She dreamed that Buck found her at the ranch and had his sons surround the house. Holding Rigby at gunpoint, he forced Alicia to leave the house as he roughly threw her on the back of his horse. She turned to catch another glimpse of the house, and it was covered in flames with Caleb and Claire both frantically trying to break a front window to escape.

She stood like a statue in front of the window and wondered when she would ever feel secure again. Her heart felt heavy, and she seemed to literally sag under the burden she felt. She slowly turned from the window and fell facedown on her bed as a single tear made its way down her cheek. The one tear was the beginning of a torrent of tears as Alicia sobbed into her pillows. The tears of anguish over her parent's death, tears of fear from moving to a new town to being kidnapped and caught in a fire, and tears of exhaustion from being in a constant state of uncertainty over what the next day will bring. The tears that had been stored up for months came rushing upon her, and she wept long and hard in her room.

As the tears finally began to abate, she took up her Bible and began to read and pray. For a solid hour she poured her heart out to the Lord and felt the weight on her heart lift as she continued to give over to God all that had been wearying her soul. She ended her time with a passage in Matthew that stilled her heart. It was the last three verses of Matthew 11, which said, "Come unto me, all ye that labour and are heavy laden, and I will give you rest. Take my yoke upon you, and learn of me; for I am meek and lowly in heart: and ye shall find rest unto your souls. For my yoke is easy, and my burden is light."[4]

Caleb gently slipped his arm around Alicia, and she was swiftly brought back to the present. She looked up at him and leaned into his embrace. His heart felt wedged somewhere in his throat, and he looked down at her lovingly. What she didn't know was that Caleb and Claire heard her sobs that morning. They seemed to echo through the house, and Caleb nearly went crazy in trying to know what to do for her. Every sob that came forth felt like a knife shooting through his heart.

More than once Claire had stopped him from going upstairs to her. She recognized the tears for what they were—release. Alicia needed to be alone to pray and seek and give everything up to the Lord. Not knowing what else to do, Caleb went outside to try and keep himself busy, but it was to no avail. He paced through the stables for a long while until he noticed that the horses had sensed his tension and were growing tense and uneasy themselves. He finally went back inside and, much to his relief, the tears had ceased to occasional sniffles.

He paced through the kitchen until Claire shooed him out, and then decided to go back outside. When he returned at lunchtime, everything seemed normal. Alicia was helping Claire in the kitchen, and they were laughing and talking as usual. Aside from the slight puffiness of her eyes, Alicia seemed more radiant than she had in weeks. Caleb then knew that Alicia had surrendered everything to the Lord.

Her chuckle brought him back to the present.

Seemingly startled, he looked down to find her gazing upon him with amused eyes.

"What's so funny?" he demanded in a good-natured voice.

"You are. You were a million miles away, Caleb Carter." Alicia grinned at him.

"I was just thinking about you," he admitted rather hesitantly. He wanted so much to tell Alicia exactly how he felt about her—that he loved her more than he ever thought possible and that the thought of a life without her made it almost impossible for him to breathe.

Alicia's heart began to beat a little faster as his eyes held hers. There was no doubt in her mind anymore that she was head-over-heels in love with Caleb. She continued to look up at him, unable to form any words.

He reached his hand up and ran his fingers gently down her cheek. He loved how soft her skin was. Before he could take his hand away, Alicia brought hers up and covered his with her own.

"I've been such a fool," she said just above a whisper.

"What do you mean?"

"I mean, it is wrong for me to shut out the people who care for me ... and who I care for," she added timidly, never breaking eye contact. "I wasn't being completely honest with you that day I told you that I didn't care about you the way you care about me." Caleb looked at her hopefully. "I care more than I wanted to admit. You're such a big part of my life now, and I don't want that to change." She looked up at him, and the vulnerability in her eyes melted his heart.

"I love you, Alicia," he said softly, his voice thick with emotion.

"Oh, Caleb, I love you too," she said with no hesitation, her voice equally soft. The moonlight created a silvery glow that rested upon the couple.

"I've loved you for so long and always wanted to tell you. There have been so many times when you were almost taken from me." His voice broke slightly, and he took a deep breath before continuing. He took her hand with both of his own. Alicia loved how protected she felt whenever this man was near.

"The thought of losing you is more than I can bear. I would gladly give my life for you, Alicia."

"Oh, Caleb," she whispered as her eyes filled with tears.

"I promise that I will always be here for you. I want to take care of you and protect you forever. I want to treasure you as my very own—as my wife."

Alicia held her breath as her heart began to swell, and then she heard the sweetest words she had ever heard in her life.

"Will you marry me?"

"Yes," she cried without hesitation as she jumped into his arms. He caught her and swung her around, laughing. Never had either of their hearts felt so full. The love that God had given them for each other was so strong that they were ready to burst with their joy. The thought flashed through Alicia's mind over how much she would be missing if she had decided to never accept Caleb's love. She inwardly shuddered and pushed the thought from her mind to focus on the man who was holding her. The man she loved.

Caleb set her down and simply gazed into her eyes. He tenderly cupped her face in his hands and brushed a gentle kiss across her lips. God had brought them so far from that first day when Caleb saw a frightened but determined young woman on his doorstep dressed like a ranch hand.

The stars twinkled brightly overhead as they sat back

down beneath the oak to discuss plans for their new
future together.

Chapter 27

"I knew it!" Claire exclaimed.

Caleb and Alicia wasted no time in sharing their joyous news with Claire. Despite the late hour, they were all seated with steaming mugs of coffee around the kitchen table.

Caleb and Alicia shared a loving glance as Claire continued to carry on in her excited way.

"I knew that one day you would both see what everyone else has known for quite a while—that you were head-over-heels in love with each other. When are you getting married? Have you talked about plans yet? We're both engaged now, Alicia." Claire's questions and comments tumbled out of her mouth faster than Caleb or Alicia could answer. They simply listened contentedly as she continued on.

"I can't wait until I tell Mark! He's going to be so thrilled. He has wanted to see you both get together from the moment he met you, Alicia." Claire finally paused to take a breath as Caleb threw his head back and let out a hearty laugh. One glimpse of Claire's confused face began Alicia's chuckles.

"What's so funny?" she demanded.

Their laughter turned uproarious as Claire began to look more and more flustered and bemused. Finally understanding began to hit her.

"You're laughing at me, aren't you?" A smile tugged at the corners of her mouth as she fought to keep a straight face. Her feigned indignation only served to worsen the laughter, and pretty soon she was bubbling over with laughter as well. The joy of the moment made everything seem wonderful and humorous, and the three friends laughed together into the wee hours of the morning.

The next day was Sunday, and the three housemates at the ranch were up with the sun. There was too much excitement in the air to feel drowsy after a short night's sleep. They were ready for church with plenty of time to spare. Since it was customary for them to pick up Mark on the way, they left a bit early to be able to have plenty of time to tell him the good news.

A very fidgety Claire rode in the back of the buggy as they made their way into town. One of Alicia's favorite characteristics about her best friend was that Claire was so giving of herself to others. Alicia's news thrilled Claire almost as much as it did Alicia. She was touched that Claire would be so happy over news that was not her own.

Caleb reached over and tenderly took Alicia's hand in his own and entwined their fingers. Alicia looked down in wonder at the two hands that seemed to fit so perfectly together. She was amazed at the goodness of a God who loved her so much that he died for her so that she could live forever in eternity with him. But she stood in awe over how his goodness did not end there. He richly blessed her life, and now a man more wonderful than Alicia had ever dreamed loved her and wanted to marry her. Alicia's heart felt lighter than it had in over a year.

The ride to Mark's was short, and soon the buggy pulled up in front of his house. In a very unladylike fashion, Claire jumped from the back of the buggy before Caleb had a chance to help her down. As Caleb watched her charge toward the door at a near run, he thought she would have taken the steps two at a time if it weren't for her dress.

Caleb helped Alicia down from the buggy, and they walked arm in arm toward the front door. Mark was soon there to greet them. Gauging from Claire's apparent excitement, Mark knew that something was going on. However, Claire still had enough presence of mind to realize that Caleb and Alicia would want to tell their own news.

"Come on in." He maneuvered his chair away from the door and motioned with his arm for them to enter. Claire was already inside and had chosen a small chair in the living room to make herself comfortable in. Mark wheeled himself up next to her and gave her a brief kiss. He held her hand in his lap while Caleb and Alicia seated themselves.

He noticed that the couple fairly radiated with happiness and felt that he knew exactly what was going on.

Caleb cleared his throat slightly.

"Alicia has agreed to be my wife." A smile nearly stretched off his face as he looked from his soon-to-be brother-in-law to his soon-to-be wife.

There were few times when Mark really loathed his confinement to a wheelchair, and now was one of those times. He wanted to jump up and embrace his friend at this announcement. As it was, he was forced to settle with a warm handshake, which Caleb gratefully received. There was much chatter, and in no time it was time to leave for church.

⁓

Alicia fought to stay focused on Pastor Tyler's sermon that morning. It seemed that the entire church family guessed the engagement of Caleb Carter and Alicia Barnes.

The church service was held outside in one of the open fields just behind where the old church building once stood. The men in town had set up some chairs, and Alicia, Caleb, Claire and Mark all sat toward the front. At one point Claire glanced back to find Paul Vickery seated next to a woman she didn't recognize and a young boy. He met her stare and waved slightly. Claire turned back around thinking what a wonderful day it was indeed—a wonderful day for everyone.

Pastor Tyler focused on forgiveness this morning—a sermon that reached right to the heart of Alicia. He spoke about the love and forgiveness of Christ. He took them through the life of Jesus pointing out all of the times when he had unselfishly forgiven over and over again. He ended with Christ's ultimate words of forgiveness as he hung dying on a cross—*Father, forgive them.*

Alicia felt her throat begin to burn over the tears that threatened to spill over. Jesus Christ was God's Son who came to earth and, having never committed a sin of his own, was tortured and crucified on a cross. He died an unfathomably cruel death for the sins of the world, and yet his request was for God to forgive them. Tears nearly blinded Alicia as she reached for Caleb's hand. He squeezed it, understanding fully the emotions that were bombarding his fiancée. Claire reached over for Alicia's other hand, and Alicia looked over to see a single tear slip down her cheek. The bond between these friends was so special after all that they had been through together, and as they sat taking to heart all of the pastor's words, they knew that they would have to pray with renewed fervor for forgiving hearts—especially with the impending trial looming before them.

After the service ended, the entire church family was anxious to speak with Caleb and Alicia to extend their congratulations and best wishes. Hugs were passed around, and the couple heard many people remark, "I knew it." Pastor and Gloria Tyler invited the four young people to their house for lunch. They gratefully accepted the offer and made their way to the Tyler home.

The lunch was wonderful. Thick slices of bread and ham, canned peaches, butter, green beans, and fresh asparagus were enjoyed by all. Light banter filled the kitchen as everyone seemed to talk at once. After the lunch, the men went into the living room for a game of cards, while the women remained in the kitchen to clean up.

Each of the men offered to clean up for the women, but one look at their faces made the women quickly shoo them out of the kitchen. They sported looks of little boys anxious to go run around outside and play. With eyes full of love, and much to the relief of the men, the women told them in no uncertain terms to leave the kitchen.

As Gloria, Claire, and Alicia began to clear the table and wash dishes, Gloria spoke something that had been on her mind for a while.

"Girls, please forgive me if I'm intruding into private business, but how is the upcoming trial going to affect your plans for marriage?"

"We'll wait until it's over," Alicia said simply without looking up from the dish she was drying.

"It's something that Mark and I have discussed in great detail, and we feel that it's best to wait until it's over. We want to start our marriage fresh with no dark clouds looming over us." Claire seated herself at the table and continued to talk to the others.

"One of the biggest lessons that the Lord has really shown Mark and myself is that his provision and timing are perfect. He carried us through every step of life and through every part of our relationship and has made us grow closer because of the obstacles. There was a time when I would have been devastated and frustrated over having to wait for so much longer than I originally anticipated to get married, but now I'm able to rest in the Lord's timing." Claire had a serene look of peace on her face. Gloria's hands remained motionless in the suds, and the dish Alicia was drying was held in mid-air for some moments.

"I'm so proud of you and Mark. The witness that you show in your daily lives to the people of this town is inspiring." Gloria was clearly moved, and it showed in the tears that glistened in her eyes. Her hands began to move slowly again, washing the last plate.

"You know," Alicia began, "in all of my preoccupation with everything that has happened, I honestly did not stop to think of what it might be like for you, Claire. By the time that you and Mark are finally married, you will have been engaged for almost a year. Caleb and I won't have to wait that long, and I must admit that right now I don't know how I would bear it if I were forced to wait so long to begin my life with the man I love."

Alicia's honest admission brought nods from both women. There was nothing like being joined with the man you love forever. Gloria and Alicia finished with the dishes and joined Claire at the table.

"So, are you ready for school to start back again?" Gloria asked.

"Oh yes," Alicia replied enthusiastically. "I miss the children so much. But my heart breaks over our new logistical situation." Alicia referred to the old livery, which was now being used as a temporary church building on rainy Sundays and future schoolhouse until another could be built. The new livery was across the street from the old one. It was the only building large enough to house so many people at one time, so after the church burned down the town came together as one on a Saturday to clean out the old livery and prepare it for new uses.

"But we do not have any of the necessary supplies that we need or even tables and chairs, for that matter." Alicia's tone was sad. "But I'm just thankful that we have a place for the children to continue learning until the new schoolhouse is built."

"My husband thinks we will have the new building up before the cold sets in," Gloria added as she took a sip of the coffee she poured for the three of them.

"That would be wonderful. That's much sooner than I anticipated. I was preparing myself to spend an entire year in that old livery."

"Well, my dear, I'm afraid that would be impossible anyway. It's fine for now, but it will not be able to protect you from the weather in a few months' time."

At that moment Alicia's eyes strayed to Claire, who had remained unusually quiet throughout the exchange. The look on her face was pensive, and she appeared as if she were a million miles away.

"Claire, are you all right?" Alicia asked. When Claire appeared to not have heard her, Alicia spoke with more urgency.

"Claire," she said as she reached for her arm, "what's wrong?"

Claire turned sparkling eyes to her as a smile began to stretch across her face.

"I just had the most wonderful idea!" she practically squealed. She turned in her chair and excitedly began to speak.

"Alicia, why don't we have a double wedding?"

"A what?"

"A double wedding! Oh, wouldn't it be fun for us to marry at the same ceremony? We would have the same anniversary as well. Isn't that grand?" Claire's joy was infectious as a smile began to slowly spread on Alicia's face.

"Claire, I cannot believe we didn't think of it sooner. What a delightful idea! It sounds perfect." Alicia beamed at her best friend as they reached to hug one another.

Gloria was silent, but the way that her eyes danced spoke volumes.

"Aren't you forgetting something, girls?" she asked, a smile playing across her lips. They both turned questioning eyes to her. "Shouldn't you ask the boys?"

Everyone erupted in laughter at that point. In all of the excitement, it did not cross either of their minds to get the input of the men. At that moment, as if on cue, they walked through the door. Curiosity over the squeals and laughter took them away from their game to see what all of the fuss was about.

"What's going on in here?" Caleb asked as the men strode through the door. He was only a step behind Mark's wheelchair, and Pastor Tyler brought up the rear. They each went to stand by the woman they loved as they waited for a response.

Claire and Alicia exchanged a mischievous glance that neither Caleb nor Mark missed. Caleb shrugged at Mark and again implored what was going on.

"We were just thinking," Claire began, "that it would be a wonderful idea to have a double wedding." She looked anxiously toward Mark as Alicia turned a shy smile in Caleb's direction.

"Oh Caleb, wouldn't it be wonderful to share our day together? We've been through so much together already. Wouldn't it be fitting for us to begin our new lives together too?" Pastor Tyler squeezed Gloria's shoulder as he watched Caleb and Mark look helplessly at Alicia and Claire and then at each other. Everyone knew that they would not deny this from the girls if it was what they really wanted. Besides, the idea was beginning to grow on them as well.

To Alicia and Claire, the silence seemed to last much longer than the minute it really was.

"I think that's a great idea," Caleb said enthusiastically.

"So do I," Mark chimed in, his eyes never leaving Claire's.

Pastor Tyler looked at his own wife as they remembered fondly what it was like to be young and on the brink of a new beginning in life. The game of cards was soon forgotten as the rest of the afternoon was spent making preparations for the upcoming double ceremony.

Chapter 28

The quiet little town of Darby was up and running unusually early on this mid-August Saturday. Today was the highly anticipated day of the trial. The small and typically peaceful town was filled with curiosity and interest as the small courtroom began to fill.

The courthouse itself sat back a few yards behind the sheriff's office. There were only small civil cases held there that the mayor always handled, and the town meetings were convened there as well. Never had there been a large trial of any kind before in Darby.

Caleb, Alicia, Mark, and Claire all rode together in silence as they made their way toward the courthouse. The ride was strained as everyone felt anxious and tense. Alicia barely got any sleep the night before as she was assailed with nightmares. Claire spent most of the night up with her, and they eventually decided to move into the kitchen to drink some coffee and read from the Bible.

All were dreading the event, but none more than Alicia. She was aware that she would have to testify and speak of her horrible ordeal in front of the entire town. Her nerves were raw as they drove on. Caleb reached for her hand and squeezed it tightly when he felt her trembling. He was determined to be strong for her today, but in truth he was a bit tense himself. He wanted to see these men brought to justice, and he wanted Alicia to finally be able to feel safe again.

Mark and Claire remained stoic as they continued on.

Mark would have to testify over the bank robbery and shooting, and Claire was fearful of the whole trial.

Alicia gasped as they gained sight of the courthouse. It seemed as if the entire town showed up for the big event. People spilled out of the building. Caleb squeezed her hand in reassurance as he brought the horses to a stop.

The foursome quickly maneuvered past all of the townspeople and made their way toward the front of the room. They all took seats in the front row and waited. After only a few minutes, Sheriff Holding, his brother, and Deputy Vickery escorted all five prisoners into the courthouse. The room, which had been buzzing with whispers, suddenly became eerily silent upon their entrance. They were instructed to sit at a table in front on the other side of Alicia. She was aware of their entrance, but her gaze remained fixed in front of her.

Claire, who had only seen them during the bank robbery, chanced a look in their direction and felt a wave of nausea overcome her. They were filthy and disgusting. They sported smug looks and flashed toothless smiles. Mark shook his head slightly, signaling that it would be best for Claire to not look in their direction. She quickly turned her head back up front but was unable to get the image from her mind.

After only a few minutes of waiting that felt like decades, the judge made a grand entrance into the room. All were instructed to stand, and then after he sat down, the rest of the room sat as well.

"I want it known," Judge Hughes began, "that this is a trial whose sole purpose is to gather evidence. These men will be escorted to the capital city for the rest of their prosecution and sentencing. There will be order in this courtroom at all times, or I will order it emptied." The judge had a commanding presence about him that was accentuated by his deep voice and unwavering eye contact. The judge had dark hair that was graying at the temples, which, to Alicia, gave the impression of a man of great knowledge. The courtroom sat in awed silence as they waited for him to continue.

"Mark Brewer, please come to the stand." The judge wasted no time in beginning and watched as Mark wheeled his way over. He was instructed to lay his right hand on the Bible. The judge then asked him to describe what took place on the day of the bank robbery. Mark did so with clarity and accuracy, his words reminding the town of his position as a businessman.

"He then pulled his gun and fired on me. I was shot in the side, and the bullet went through and damaged my spinal column. I no longer have the use of my legs as a result," Mark concluded. The judge nodded and told him that he could take his seat again. Relieved that it was over, Mark wheeled back to his place. And so the proceedings continued with testimonies from various townspeople, including the sheriff and deputy. Alicia was only able to hear bits and pieces of it as it became closer for her testimony.

"Alicia Barnes." On legs that would barely carry her, she made her way to the front and took her oath. She sat down and turned large, fear-filled eyes to the judge.

"Are you the schoolteacher in this town?" was his first question to her.

"Yes, sir."

"Were you kidnapped by these five men?"

"Yes, sir."

"Tell us what happened." The judge leaned back in his chair, but his eyes remained intent on Alicia. She fumbled with the handkerchief that was in her hand as she tried to decide exactly how much he wanted to know and where to begin.

"Miss Barnes?" he quietly prompted.

Alicia turned frightened eyes to Caleb, and he smiled a small, gentle smile, willing her strength to continue. She raised her chin and in a quiet but firm voice began.

"Well, I saw Mark get shot, and after that things happened so quickly, that they seem like a blur to me. I remember being grabbed by the arm and yanked. It caused me to fall, and then I was being scooped up and carried out. I was thrown on a horse with one of the men, and they rode out of town. As soon as I could collect myself, I began to drop my jewelry along the way as clues in the hope that someone would be able to find me.

"We spent two weeks running. At every stopping point, I would tear off a piece of my petticoat and leave it behind. We crossed over into Missouri, and the men began to hunt out small towns to rob again. They left Rigby in charge while they were away. The others would often come back drunk and would hit and curse at Rigby and myself. The day that Rigby led my escape was the day that I was hit the worst." Alicia knew that most of her story was news to the rest of the townspeople and heard slight gasps from the women and watched the men tense up in their seats. She was gaining strength the longer she was up there. In the midst of the pause, she looked to Caleb, who nodded encouragingly at her.

"Miss Barnes, are you saying that one of your captors actually planned and led your escape?" the judge asked.

"Yes, sir. Rigby Buchanan did." She quickly glanced at him and smiled. "You see, sir, he's only a sixteen-year-old boy. He was forced into a life of crime by his family almost at infancy and was unable to do anything about it. Many days before my rescue, he confessed to me that he wanted to leave that kind of life but did not know how. He was the only one who was helpful and not rough with me. He knew his father and brothers were starving me, and he brought me food. He knew that I was leaving clues, and he never breathed a word. He's only a boy, Your Honor."

"I object!" Buck's loud voice resounded throughout the courthouse as he flew to his feet. Alicia nearly jumped out of her chair in fright. "My youngest boy ain't no better than my other ones, and he don't deserve no better than we do!" Buck's face was an angry red, and his eyes flashed. Sheriff Holding thrust him back down into his chair as Judge Hughes's gavel came crashing down.

"I'll have no more outbursts like that again, Mr. Buchanan. Is that clear?" The judge's voice was loud and authoritative. Buck mumbled something but remained seated.

"Your Honor," Alicia turned to the judge, "may I say something on Rigby's behalf?"

The look on Judge Hughes's face clearly reflected his surprise, but he nodded anyway.

"Your Honor, as this court is gathering evidence against these men, I realize that their crimes go far beyond what happened here in Darby, Kentucky. They have wreaked havoc on the entire Midwest. They are responsible for the deaths of my father and Caleb and Claire Carter's parents during the train robbery of 1867." The judge's eyes widened a bit in surprise at that piece of information.

"But I would ask you to please remember that Rigby is a boy who had his choices taken away from him. He was forced into this life, and I've watched him try to change and better himself. I have every confidence that if given the chance, he would prove himself to be a fine, upstanding citizen as he grows into a man."

The crowd, which had been silent up to this point, began to whisper at Alicia's defense of one of her kidnappers. The look she gave the crowd was lined with determination, and then she turned her eyes back to the judge. He watched her closely for a moment and simply said, "Thank you, Miss Barnes." The questioning proceeded at that point, and Alicia was asked about the night of the fire. She respectfully answered every question, all the while wondering if the judge would really consider anything she said about Rigby.

After what seemed like an eternity to Alicia, she was finally asked to step down. Relief washed over her as she realized it was over.

Buck was fully enraged at this point and, as a man not known for suppressing any feelings of anger or malice, jumped up and hurled himself toward the woman who had given the judge all he needed to see them hang.

Vickery, whose reflexes were quicker than Buck's hasty decision, threw himself in front of Alicia, taking the full impact of Buck's weight. Buck knocked him to the ground, and Caleb pulled Alicia out of harm's way. The entire town gasped and came to their feet to watch. Claire grabbed Alicia, and they held each other in horror. The Holding brothers successfully stopped Buck's sons, save for Rigby who remained seated and still the entire time, from running to their father's aid. The judge's gavel could be heard resounding through the courtroom several times as Caleb and Vickery were finally able to pin Buck down. All of the men were bound by the wrists and quickly moved back to the jailhouse.

The townspeople were swift to exit and milled about on the street, talking in excited whispers over all they had just heard and witnessed. Alicia, not feeling the least bit of excitement over this, wanted nothing more than to return to the comfort and safety of the ranch. Leading her gently by the arm, Caleb helped her mount the buggy, and the four headed back for the Blue Star.

The next day Alicia, escorted by Caleb, went back to

the jailhouse. Alicia wanted one final visit with Rigby. They opened the door and went inside. Alicia quickly slipped into the side office while Caleb told Holding that Alicia wanted to see Rigby. Alicia looked up when she heard the door open and watched as Caleb, Rigby, and Holding walked into the office. Holding shut the door behind them. Rigby stood uncertainly.

"Please have a seat," Alicia said gently. She motioned to a chair across from her. Rigby sat down with drooped shoulders. He was wringing his hands and shuffling his feet back and forth. Caleb put a hand on his shoulder.

"Don't worry, son. Whatever the outcome, you know that God is with you now." Rigby looked up at him gratefully.

"Rigby, I did everything I could at the trial to try and spare your life. I truly believe that you deserve another chance. Caleb and I just want you to know that if you are given a second chance, you are always welcome to come back to Darby. We'll do whatever we can to help you get a fresh start." She reached over and squeezed his hand. Rigby felt tears spring to his eyes, and he impatiently wiped the back of his hand across them. Never in his entire life that he could remember had anyone ever shown him compassion.

"Much obliged," was all he was able to say.

Chapter 29

Alicia found it next to impossible to leave the ranch for the next week. The people milling around town outside of establishments speaking in hushed tones and turning her way every time she passed proved to be too much for her.

Relieved that it was all over and that she could now move on with her life, she spent the next week relaxing at the ranch. She spent a great deal of time riding with Caleb through the open fields on the stallions, enjoying his company and the beautiful late summer weather.

She and Claire began in earnest to plan and prepare for the upcoming double wedding. It was only five weeks away, and the women were soon coming to realize just how much work they had ahead of them. After an entire week at the ranch, Alicia decided it was time to venture into town with Claire to do some wedding shopping.

"What do you think of this material?" Claire asked Alicia and Gloria as they stood in the general store. Claire's dress had been made for months, and now it was time to get Alicia's material and sew her dress.

"It's nice."

"You barely glanced at it." Claire looked over to find her soon to be sister-in-law eyeing one of the loveliest pieces of fabric she had ever seen.

"Oh, Alicia," Claire breathed. "This one is simply gorgeous."

Alicia fingered the beautiful white silk and smiled.

"My dear, we could make this into one of the finest dresses this town has ever seen." Gloria beamed as she watched the young girls' enthusiasm and remembered what it was like to be young herself.

"Look at this lace," Alicia gushed as she moved over to another aisle. "It is perfect for the material." The girls continued their shopping and left excited over their purchases. As they left the general store, Gloria said her good-byes and headed home to help her husband with some Sunday preparations.

"You know, Claire…" Alicia stopped and turned to face Claire. The streets were busy with buggies passing by and people bustling along. It was a beautiful day. "I've been thinking. Now that the Buchanans have left town, perhaps I should move back into my little house until the wedding." Claire looked as if she were about to protest, and Alicia raised her hand up to stop her. "Just listen for a minute. With them gone, I know that I will be safe. Caleb and I will be married in only a few weeks' time." Alicia paused for a minute and smiled, loving the way that sounded. "And," she continued, "then I'll be living permanently at the ranch. I think that for now it would be better, and look better, if I moved back to the little house until the wedding."

Claire opened her mouth and then closed it again. Alicia was right, of course.

"You're right. I really had not thought about it, but you're right. It would be better for you to live here until you are married. Well, I'll tell you one thing, I don't know who will be more disappointed—me or Caleb."

When the girls told Caleb their plan for Alicia to move home, he agreed, though he was disappointed. In fact,

Julie Bell

the idea had already run through Caleb's mind that it might be the best thing. Caleb helped Claire and Alicia move her things back into the small house.

"Don't get too comfortable here," he told Alicia. He looked longingly into her eyes, and she returned the gaze. In her mind, their wedding could not come fast enough.

"Don't worry. I'll be packed with my suitcase by the door," she responded coyly, and he smiled.

"Good. Well, I'll leave you to get settled. I have to check on some things back at the ranch," Caleb told her. "But," he added with an intensity in his voice, "if you ever feel unsafe, come straight back."

"Thanks. I'm sure that everything will be fine. Five weeks will fly by. You'll see." After he walked out, she shut the door and leaned against it. *Will five weeks really fly by?* At the moment, she felt like these would be the longest weeks of her life.

———

Claire came by Alicia's house every day in between visits to Mark. They spent hours pouring over all of the details. They decided to have an early afternoon wedding with a large reception to follow. It seemed as if the whole town wanted to be a part of the celebration. And rightfully so. The journey that the two young couples had been on was known and admired by all. Everyone in town wanted to share in the joy that these four young people so rightfully deserved.

"Claire, who is making the cake?" Alicia asked her fiftieth question of the day to Claire, who had a notepad in front of her with all of the wedding details laid out on it.

"Believe it or not, Mrs. Thorne!" Claire responded with a grin.

254

"Are you kidding? She doesn't seem the type who would make wedding cakes for people," Alicia said, surprised.

"I know. She is always so short and curt with me, you know. I have such a hard time dealing with her, but she's actually not so bad underneath that tough skin. She used to make it so hard for me to keep a civil tongue sometimes, but lately I'll catch her with just a bit of a smile." Claire chuckled. The rest of the reception would be a huge potluck with all of the families bringing food to share.

"Okay, and Gloria's handling the flowers, right?" Alicia asked. Claire looked up from her notepad with a grin.

"What?"

"You've already asked me that," Claire said in mock exasperation. She reached over to pat Alicia's arm. "Everything is under control. We've been over the details many times now, and everything is taken care of."

"You forget, Claire Carter, that I haven't had nearly as much time as you to plan and prepare, and I just keep feeling like something's missing." Alicia sighed and took the notepad from Claire and began to silently run down the list again.

"Is your dress ready?" Claire asked.

"Oh my." Alicia smiled a real smile for the first time that day. "My dress is absolutely perfect. I can't wait for the wedding day." Alicia's eyes took on a dreamy look, and Claire knew Alicia was a million miles away. Well, maybe only more like three or four—at the Blue Star Ranch with Caleb Carter.

"All right." Alicia pulled herself from her reverie. "I'll try to calm down. I'm just so nervous, and I want everything to be perfect."

"It will be," Claire assured her. "Everything is set. Try

to just relax and enjoy it." Alicia knew Claire was right. She did not want a moment of this time of excitement and preparation wasted on unfounded worries. All the details were in place, and soon she would be Mrs. Caleb Carter.

Chapter 30

The days sped by as the preparations continued. Before anyone knew it, the day before the wedding was upon them, and the couples spent the day setting up. Since there was no church building to hold the ceremony, they decided to have the wedding outdoors by the brook at the Blue Star Ranch. Pastor Tyler and Gloria were on hand to help, and soon the whole outdoors area for the wedding was a bower of white flowers and lace. They lined the rows of chairs that were set up and created a beautiful white path that the women would very soon sweep up to join their lives with the men they loved.

They parted company with the Tylers and went back inside the ranch house. They were sitting comfortably in the living room, each occupied with their own tasks, when they heard a horse ride up. Caleb and Mark both looked up from the papers they were reading. They heard footsteps come up the steps onto the porch, and then there was a knock at the door.

When Caleb answered the door, he found Sheriff Holding.

"Is something wrong, Sheriff?" Alicia asked tentatively as she came up behind Caleb. She held her breath waiting for a response, afraid that something would happen to spoil their wedding.

"No, not really."

Alicia looked down and exhaled. Caleb sensed her

anxiety and squeezed her hand. She looked up again and focused her attention back on the sheriff.

"I would like to speak with all of you for a moment, if that's all right," he said.

"Of course," Caleb responded as he made a motion with his hand, indicating for the sheriff to enter. Claire and Alicia exchanged a glance. What could this be about? Alicia had a sinking feeling as she watched Sheriff Holding make himself comfortable in a chair.

The ladies returned to their seats, and Caleb stood by Mark's chair, all waiting to hear the news. After Holding was seated, he pulled a letter out of an envelope.

"This letter just arrived from the capital today," he began. "The Buchanans have all been tried and sentenced. In this letter are the results."

Alicia felt her breath catch in her throat as she leaned forward. Caleb's hand rested on her shoulder, and Claire instinctively reached for Mark's hand. Alicia's heart was pounding. This was it. They were about to learn if the men who caused so much terror, destruction, and death would see justice. It was as if they were collectively holding their breath as they listened. Time seemed to stand still. Alicia closed her eyes for a moment to collect herself.

"Buck, Cotton, George, and Bob are to be hung in a week's time. They are being held at the state prison until the appointed time. Rigby is to spend the next ten years in prison and will probably spend most of that time doing hard labor. Most likely they'll send him out to help the railway companies lay tracks." He stopped and looked at his attentive audience.

Alicia's hand flew over her mouth as tears sprang in her eyes. She was filled with relief. She was finally free from the Buchanans, and Rigby was going to be given another chance at life.

"Thank you for letting us know, Sheriff," Caleb said.

"It sure is a relief for us to know that we will all be safe now."

"I just thought you should hear it from me. The story will be released in tomorrow's paper, and after that everyone in the territory will know."

"Thank you so much for your consideration, Sheriff," Mark added, his voice full of the gratefulness that he felt. "We'll see you tomorrow, right?"

"I wouldn't miss it," Holding said as he came out of his chair and extended his hand first to Caleb then to Mark. "I speak for the entire town when I tell you that everyone is overjoyed about tomorrow's celebration."

"Where's Alicia?" Claire asked as she walked into the living room. Dinner was over, and Mark and Caleb were sitting down to a game of checkers.

"I'm not sure. Why?" Caleb responded as he waited for Mark to make a move.

"I just wanted to go over a couple of last-minute details with her."

"I'll go look for her," Caleb said as he rose from his seat. He was no longer beginning to feel the strong wave of panic that always seemed to overcome him when he thought something might have happened to her.

He approached her favorite oak tree, where the ceremony would take place the next day, and watched as Alicia stood staring out over the brook. Clearing his throat slightly so as not to catch her completely off guard, he walked over slowly to his bride-to-be. She turned and smiled as she watched him come closer.

"I thought I might find you here."

"I needed to walk around for a while and clear my head a bit."

Caleb sat down on the stone beneath the oak tree and motioned for her to sit by him. She responded without hesitation and sat down.

"Second thoughts?" he teased.

"Not on your life!" She giggled as she gave him a slight push.

"So what are you thinking about?" he asked gently. He watched her look out over the brook, the moon casting a brilliant glow on her face. His heart swelled with love as he waited for her to respond.

"I'm just happy, Caleb. A year ago, I thought my life had ended. Both of my parents were dead, and I had no one to turn to. But God gave me another chance and brought me here—to you." She turned to look him fully in the face. "He also brought me to himself. God never gave up on me, and he's been so faithful. I stand in awe of his goodness and mercy. He put the pieces of my broken heart and life back together again and now look where he's brought me. It's more than I ever dreamed of. And now I'm finally free from the almost paralyzing fear of being kidnapped again by the men who killed our parents." She let out a contented sigh and leaned against the arm Caleb brought around her.

"I couldn't have said it better myself, sweetheart. God is so good." The two sat for a while longer and stared over the brook, enjoying the peace of the evening and being in each other's company. Eventually they made their way back to the house, and a short time later Caleb hitched up the wagon to take Mark and Alicia back to town. The couples parted, knowing that after tonight they would never have to say good night and head back to separate homes again.

Chapter 31

"Alicia, hurry up! What's keeping you?" Gloria Tyler called up from the bottom of the staircase. "Honestly, that girl will be late for her own wedding!"

Gloria's carrying on did nothing for Claire's own nerves. Already downstairs with Gloria waiting to head outside, she was pacing like a caged animal around the living room.

"Claire, honey, stop pacing around," Gloria gently chided as she came over and took Claire's trembling hands in her own.

"I can't seem to make myself stop. Is it even possible for a person to feel so many emotions all at one time? This is the day that I have dreamed of my entire life, and now that it is finally here, I'm scared to death. But I'm so excited that I can barely contain myself. I'm nervous and anxious, but I have never felt so happy in my entire life. Does any of that make sense?"

"Of course it does, dear. It is how I felt, and I will bet you anything that it is how Alicia feels right now too. But it's only natural, my dear. You are a woman in love who is about to start a new chapter of her life with the man she adores. From now on, everything in your life will be different. Not every situation or every day will be sunshine and flowers, but you'll have each other to cling to through the good and the bad." Gloria's soothing words helped calm Claire's nerves. Claire always loved hearing the advice of this wise woman.

"You look beautiful," Gloria added.

"Thank you," she responded with a beaming smile.

A shuffling sound turned both of their eyes upward to see Alicia standing at the top of the stairs. The fact that she was nervous and a bit fearful did not escape Claire's observant eye, but she was radiant. Her glow lit up the room as she fairly floated down the stairs with her long train trailing behind her.

The girls embraced at the bottom of the stairs.

"You look beautiful," they said in unison, then broke into giggles.

"I can't believe this day is finally here," Alicia said as she clung to Claire's arm. "We're getting married!" She squealed in delight, and Claire joined her. Gloria stood silently and watched with a prayer of joy and thanks in her heart that she could witness this moment.

"And you know something else…" Claire said when the squealing died down. "In a matter of minutes now we'll be sisters!"

Once again the girls hugged then announced to Gloria that they were ready to go. The three headed out of the house and toward the brook where they knew that their grooms were waiting.

Sheriff Holding stood waiting by the closed door to escort the girls down the aisle.

"You both look so beautiful," he said as each girl took an arm. "It is a true honor for me to have the pleasure of escorting you both down the aisle. I know that both of your fathers would have been proud. You have been through so much and survived remarkably. And," he added with a hint of deep emotion threatening to choke off his words, "I'm proud of you both too."

The girls beamed at him and both reached up to kiss his cheek. Holding grinned as the processional began.

The girls stepped off the porch and walked around to where the ceremony would be held by the brook.

The moment the girls rounded the corner and started walking up the aisle covered in flowers and lace, Alicia and Claire sought the eyes of their waiting grooms. Radiance covered their faces as they began to sweep up the aisle. Caleb's breath left him in a rush as he saw his bride-to-be coming up the aisle toward him. Never had she looked so beautiful. His eyes never left hers as she was given to him.

"I've dreamed of this moment for so long," he whispered in her ear as soon as he had her hand. "I love you."

"I love you too," she whispered back as the ceremony began.

The ceremony went by in a blur, and before they knew it, Pastor Tyler was presenting to the guests the new Mr. and Mrs. Caleb Carter and Mr. and Mrs. Mark Brewer. The guests were on their feet in a flash with thunderous applause and a hint of tears. The young couples joyfully made their way down the aisle, and soon everyone joined them for the tremendous celebration at the reception.

The reception was everything Alicia and Claire hoped for and more. There was a bounty of food, and Mrs. Thorne outdid herself on the cake and very pleasantly manned the cake table and served. Several guests pulled out their fiddles and banjos, and people laughed and danced for hours. Alicia stood back for a moment and watched Caleb laughing with some well-wishers and her friends all dancing to the music and knew that life doesn't get much sweeter. There was no fear or pain in this moment, only joy. Alicia looked around trying to memorize every detail of the day. Her heart felt so full, she thought it might burst. She looked heavenward and, with an overflowing heart, sent a prayer of thanks to God, who brought her to this place of abundance.

⁓

Dear Reader:

Thank you so much for taking this journey with me! When I started writing this book, I was at a crossroads in my life. I didn't know what God had planned for me or where life would take me. I just knew that I had to trust God's will and his timing. Between the first draft of this novel and publishing, God has taken me down many paths—some of which have been the hardest roads of my life. But God is faithful, and he walks with me down every road, both good and challenging. His plan and provision are more than enough.

The main character of this story, Alicia, learns that she can trust God even when life seems so bleak that it is all one can do to make it to the next day. There have been times in my life when things seemed so bleak it was all I could do to make it through each day. But please know that God is faithful. Oftentimes God uses trials to strengthen his children. If you are in the midst of a trial, know that God is in control. He can see the bigger picture, and we have to trust in him. There will always be trials, but he will bring you through them one step at a time. I titled the book A Place of Abundance with Psalm 66:10–12 in mind. It says, "For you, O God, tested us; you refined us like silver. You brought us into prison and laid burdens on our backs. You let men ride over our heads; we went through fire and water, but you brought us to a place of abundance."[5] Every trial that I have faced God has brought me through to a place of abundance.

I pray that you will find and know the same peace

and comfort that I have in my life through my Lord and Savior, Jesus Christ. If you do not have a church home, please find a Bible-believing church where you can go and learn more about the amazing love of God. You will be blessed beyond belief!

God bless you all.
Until next time,

Julie Bell

Endnotes

1   1 Corinthians 13:4–8, 13 (KJV)

2   Psalm 66:10–12 (KJV)

3   Romans 10:9–10 (KJV)

4   Matthew 11:28–30 (KJV)

5   Psalm 66:10–12 (NIV)